Inheritance

By
P.M. May

Eternal Press
A division of Damnation Books, LLC.
P.O. Box 3931
Santa Rosa, CA 95402-9998
www.eternalpress.biz

Inheritance
by P.M. May

Digital ISBN: 978-1-61572-193-1
Print ISBN: 978-1-61572-194-8

Cover art by: Dawné Dominique
Edited by: Ellen Tevault
Copyedited by: Rose Vera Stepney

Copyright 2010 P.M. May

Printed in the United States of America
Worldwide Electronic & Digital Rights
1st North American and UK Print Rights

For Jan

TO KABEY
LOTS OF
VAMP & SEX
YOU'LL LOVE IT
Pete
x

Chapter One

Planes, Trains and Automobiles

Jennifer Chong sat down in her favorite reading chair in her New York apartment, in utter shock and disbelief. She shouldn't really have been that surprised, this had been the year to end all years for shocks and surprises.

She held two pieces of a letter in her trembling hands and kept re-reading and flicking from the covering lawyer's letter to the more detailed will stapled behind it.

Her Great Aunt Gwen had recently passed away back in her grandfather's home town of Oxsteaden in England. Her grandfather John had long since died and both her English-American born father and her Korean-American mother had perished in the 9/11 attacks on the twin towers.

She, Jennifer Elizabeth Chong (formally Adams) sat in her divorce settlement apartment with only a reading light on. Outside, the hustle and bustle of the Big Apple continued on without her for a while.

"What the blazes am I going to do with a British country home?" She asked herself, finally putting the letters down on her hexagonal mahogany table, where she always put the book she was currently reading.

Then a beautiful smile played across the attractive lips of the six month gone divorcee. "I forgot I can do anything I freaking like."

She had thrown herself into her writing and had finished not one, but two books on Chinese/American and Korean/American fusion food for release next year. She was one book up on the writing side and had no man baggage to hold her back. A whole new adventurous world lay out there for her and now it was her chance to grab with both oven mittens.

"Jennifer Chong, no, fuck George, Jennifer Adams is heading back to the land of her forefathers, to kick back in her British house and maybe get laid by some Colin Firth, Mister Darcy lookalike." She then proceeded to dance about her apartment, from room to room, shedding clothes as she sang 'God Save the Queen,' at the top of her voice.

* * * *

"You so got to go, girlfriend. This is your big chance to reboot your life."

Jennifer held the documents from her great aunt's lawyers in England and looked from them to Valerie. "It's a big step."

Valerie took a big gulp of wine as they stood on the balcony of Jennifer's plush apartment. "Ditching that no good son-of-a-bitch husband was a big step. This is your step, your first step into a wider world, full of hard-cocked men, waiting to fulfill you to the core."

"Jesus Val, is that all you think of?"

They giggled at her agent's words. Jen took a long sip of cold wine now.

"No, I think this could be a great business opportunity for you and my bank balance. We get the BBC on board for a cookery show and a new Brit-fusion book going on to accompany the series. There is more?"

"More?"

"You go to England and find yourself some fine bit of English man-muffin, and I get to babysit your apartment for you. Nobody loses."

Jennifer chinked her glass against her friend's drained one and shook her head smiling. "So, you and your man-eating pussy get to make the beast with two backs all over my lovely and very expensive apartment, while I have to go to England and work."

"That's the plan, sister. Who knows, you might even get a pity-fuck yourself while you're there."

"Okay I'll do it." Jen raised her glass in a toast. "Here's to new beginnings, new countries and pity-fucks."

"To pity-fucks." Valerie cheered and handed her glass over to Jennifer. "Now, go get me some more wine outta my new kitchen."

Jen raised her top-left lip and sneered as she left Valerie doing a funky happy-dance on her balcony.

* * * *

Two weeks later, she was on a plane over the North Atlantic on her way to Heathrow airport, with her friend Valerie happily ensconced in her apartment. She touched down just after midday and felt pleasantly surprised to find Britain caught in the sweaty palmed grip of an Indian summer.

Jennifer had watched far too many BBC costume dramas and expected the September weather to be wet and windy with piles of brown leaves everywhere. She pleasantly discovered that the weather was 75 degrees with only a sparse amount of white cotton wool clouds in a blue English sky.

She grabbed a trolley through customs, offloaded her coat and brown cardigan on top of her bag and laptop case that rested upon her two suitcases, and headed for the exit.

Once outside the doors, she suddenly had a momentary loss of confidence in her new kick-ass divorced self. Here she was, a five foot two woman in her early thirties, all alone in a new country, without a friend or guidance.

"Fuck it, Jen. Get with the program." She hissed at herself, causing two t-shirted young men walking past to stare at her and laugh.

Seeing no knights in shining armor, only concrete and cars, she knew she could only help herself. So, she did the only thing she possibly could do in such a situation. Steeling herself, she approached a man of Chinese descent waiting by a set of luggage with two whining kids under the age of five running around his legs.

"Excuse me. Could you tell me where I could get a cab?" Jennifer smiled with her perfect white teeth and hoped for the best. She felt very glad Valerie wasn't here to see her go ask a man out.

"If you wanna taxi, love, dthere down dthere." The man pointed to a neon yellow sign with a taxi cab picture on it, sounding more like Ringo Starr than she had expected.

"Thanks," Jennifer said over the noise of his two children before she bustled her suitcases toward the queue for taxis.

* * * *

Once inside, she gave the man sitting in the right hand driver's seat, behind a glass partition, the address of her late great aunt's London lawyers.

"On 'oliday, are we?" The bearded taxi driver with the fattest arms she had ever seen on a human asked her after a while.

"Yes. No. Well kinda." Jennifer's words trailed away into

murmurs.

"Don't'cha know, love?" The driver guffawed then beeped his horn and swore like a trooper out of his open driver's side window.

"My great aunt died and left me a house, so there might be, you know business to sort out."

"Sorry to hear about your aunt." His response sounded to Jennifer like 'aren't' not 'ant', the way she pronounced it.

The journey lapsed into silence for a couple of minutes, but 'Ballsy Jen Adams' replaced Jennifer 'Meek & Mild.'

"Great weather you're having this fall?" She tried again, because she was going to stay awhile in England and better start interacting with the natives.

"Who's had a fall?" The driver swerved past a V-signing cyclist, not hearing Jennifer's sentence properly.

"The fall weather, it's so sunny and warm." Jennifer half-repeated, feeling like George Chong's quiet little wife once more.

"Ohh." The driver replied as the taxi cab entered the streets of Central London . "Autumn, you mean; yeah it's been right barmy hot, love."

"Autumn, right." Jennifer smiled and relaxed back into her seat. This new independent life in another country, divided by the same language was going to be a rough transition, she could tell.

Jennifer watched the people walking along on the sidewalk (mental slap, pavements) and wondered, not for the first time, if she was doing the right thing jumping in at the deep end. *Maybe she should have started with an all-inclusive cruise around the Caribbean first?*

She was jolted out of her daydreams ten minutes later, when the black taxi pulled up in front of a street full of three or four story Georgian town houses.

"'Ear we are. That'll be twenty-four pounds." The driver climbed out of his door and helped her get her suitcases up to the front gates of the house. Probably the most exercise the man would get all day.

Jennifer gave the driver a twenty pound note and a ten, then looked up at the black door up some stone steps before her.

'The British League of Conformists' read a brass square plaque, next to the huge door.

"Hey, come back!" Jennifer tried to hurdle her luggage and nearly fell as the taxi drove off at high speed.

Jennifer put her hand on the black railings to steady herself and extradited her right leg from between her two cases, glad that she wore slacks, not a skirt.

Then, she noticed a dirty wooden plaque by her hand and a set of stone steps leading down to a basement set of windows and a peeling blue door.

'Rardin and Keene Solicitors,' it read. With a struggle and a real chance of falling on her ass, Jennifer somehow carried her luggage, handbag and laptop in its carrying case down the seven steep steps.

To her left and under the shadows of the above steps to the upper house stood the blue wooden door. It had no knocker or buzzer, but only at its side a black ring attached to a long black flaky piece of old ironmongery. She pulled it hard and inside muffled by the door and the traffic above came the distant peels of bells.

Jennifer sucked her teeth and waited, then waited some more. She was just reaching up to the doorbell contraption once again, when the door was pulled quickly inwards. A tall ginger-headed man in a charcoal gray suit looked down his long, freckled nose at her.

"Can I help you?" he asked very briskly with an Irish lilt, sounding like help was the last thing he wanted to give.

"I'm Jennifer Chong. Well, Adams now, I suppose." She grinned, then regretted it by the look on the tall man's face. "I'm Gwen Adams's great-niece; I have a letter here someplace."

"Follow me." The tall man turned and strode off down a long, thin shadowy corridor with flock wallpaper and ancient looking oil paintings. He left Jennifer to struggle with her suitcases inside the building to place them against the wall, before she could shut the lawyer's front door.

"Shall I leave my bags here?" she asked the back of the retreating man's head.

"Please hurry, we been waiting your arrival for some time." The man passed a square reception area that looked very Dickensian and continued up the corridor passed several doors on each side.

Jennifer left her suitcases, but took her handbag and laptop, before she hurried after the rude man, wishing for a bit of old-fashioned U.S. customer service.

The pale looking man opened a teak door at the end of the long corridor marked Rardin and ushered her in. "This way."

Jennifer was only just inside the office beyond, when the door was closed quickly and loudly behind her, missing her butt by only the width of a cigarette.

"Ah, Missus Chong, a pleasure to meet you at long last."

Jennifer looked up to see a young handsome man in his early thirties rise from behind an ancient looking mahogany desk.

"I prefer Miss Adams now, or Jennifer." She forced the words boldly from her lips, before she had time to think and chicken out with a wimpy reply.

The out of place man in his sharp new business suit reached out a hand and Jennifer grabbed at it and politely shook it.

"Please take a seat." He led her to an antique looking chair sitting before his desk. "Would you like some tea?"

"Yes please." She beamed. *Now he was more like it*, her adventurous side thought. She watched him move to a corner of the room. He busied himself with a packet of Earl Grey and boiled a small kettle sitting next to a small pile of cups and saucers.

"So, are you, Mister Rardin or Mister Keene?" she asked, putting her laptop and handbag down to the side of the chair; as the kettle boiled.

"Gladly neither." He replied, without looking back at her, "Milk and sugar?"

"Erm, milk and one sugar, please." She mumbled, the Mrs. Chong side rising from within again. "Why are you glad not to be them?"

"Because Jennifer, I may call you, Jennifer?" he asked turning with two cups of tea on saucers in his hands.

"Sure." She smiled and inwardly blushed at a lewd thought. *You can call me bitch if you strip off and make love to me over your desk*, her new surely Valerie aided mindset chirped as he approached.

"Because, they have both been dead for one hundred and twenty-nine years." He finally answered with a wink of his left eye and handed over her cup and saucer.

"Well, I'm glad you're not them then." She sat the saucer on her lap, as the solicitor walked back around his desk and deposited his tea on his ink blotter

"I suppose I better introduce myself then." He smiled, with a sly sexy confident air that made Jennifer want to cross her legs.

"I was wondering?" She grinned and stuck her neck out, then hoped she didn't resemble a mad goose.

"I am Mister Vaine and I am in-charge of your late great aunts estate, which as you know, she left mainly to your good self."

"Mainly, I thought I was her only living relative?" Jennifer asked intrigued, hoping that she had a distant cousin stashed somewhere.

"You are Jennifer." Mr. Vaine paused to lift and blow on the surface of his tea, then placed it back onto his blotter. "Your great aunt left a few parts of the estate to certain people and charities."

"Oh, which ones?" Jennifer sat on the board for A.S.A.D.A, the charity based in New York that helped with people like herself who suffered with Seasonal Affective Disorder.

"Mainly sums of monies to her maid, nurse, her cook and her grounds man, plus half a million pounds to the hemophilia charity she long championed."

"Oh, I see." Good old Great Aunt Gwen, a champion of small charities like me.

"Right, what I need now is to get you to sign a few papers and deeds in triplicate. Then I can get Mister Candlestick, our clerk to order you a taxi to the train station.

"Oh, do I have to go there right away? I was hoping to sight-see in London for a couple-a-days."

"Your great aunt's will is quite precise I am afraid, Miss Adams." Mr. Vaine took some paperwork from a buff folder and put it on her side of the desk with the late addition of a gold fountain pen. "Once in England you must take up immediate residency within twelve hours and live there for at least a month or forfeit the entire estate, which has net assets of forty millions pounds."

"Oh." Jennifer put her tea on the edge of his desk. "Is it far and how do I get there?" she replied, but a neon flashing sign pulsed in her brain £40 million pounds.

"As I said, our clerk will order you a taxi to Paddington station. We've taken the liberty of booking you a ticket on a train that leaves in forty minutes time. You will be met at the other end by a Henry Greenwood, your great aunt's and now your grounds man. He will drive you to your new home, Adams House." Vaine smiled smugly at her. "Once there, London will seem a million miles away, I promise."

"Okay." Jennifer frowned and looked down to sign the papers, not liking the fact of having a man boss her around again.

"Splendid." Vaine clapped his hands together in glee as she signed and then sat back and sipped at his cooled tea.

"Done." She exhaled and handed the pen and papers back to the waiting solicitor.

"There is one more thing before you leave." Mr. Vaine opened a drawer and pulled an off white envelope from it and passed it to Jennifer.

"What's this?" She waved the heavy envelope in the air and

noticed it had one of those red wax seals on it, like from Olde England.

"A letter from your Great Aunt Gwen not to be opened until you are inside Adams House itself."

"Why?"

Mr. Vaine shrugged his shoulders. "We are just the Adams' family servants. Ours is not to reason why?"

Jennifer clicked the fingers of her right hand twice and pointed at Vaine and giggled. "Loving the Adams family joke."

"I don't understand, Miss Adams. We here at Rardin and Keene take our service to your family very seriously. We've been your family's lawyers for over three hundred years now." Mr. Vaine's handsome face creased in several serious places as he spoke.

"Don't worry about it." She shook her head and wrinkled her nose in embarrassment. *Jeez-Louise, don't these Brits watch films or television?*

"I think your taxi is here, now." Vaine stood, walked around his desk to the office door and opened it. "Please ring us any hour of the night or day, if you have any trouble of a legal variety. We are your humble servants." Vaine bowed, then pointed out the open office door.

"Oh, right." Jennifer stood, hastily gathered her things and saw Mr. Candlestick waiting at the open front door to the solicitor's office with one of her suitcases in each hand.

"Safe journey, Miss Adams."

Jennifer walked out of the office. The sound of Mr. Vaine's office door slamming shut behind her drowned out her 'goodbye.'

"So much for handsome English gentlemen," she muttered under her breath as she followed the tall Mr. Candlestick up the outside steps to her waiting black taxi cab.

* * * *

An hour later and in a better mood, because she was already ten minutes into her train journey, she decided train travel was her thing. She had been royally pissed at her Limey lawyers at first and then the blame slowly shifted back to her as usual.

She was a very rich, single, successful, single, attractive, nicely-racked, single female and author of not one, but two best selling cookbooks. *So, why the hell had she turned to Jello at the hands of her very odd lawyers, whom she now employed.* Jennifer made a mental note to dispense with their services as-soon-as-possible;

once ensconced in her new home, and really become the kick-ass bitch Valerie told her she could be.

Once the train had left the outskirts of Greater London behind, her anger ebbed away and the sunny countryside made her eyes half-close in lazy pleasure.

Fields of yellow, green and brown replaced concrete and high-rises. Sometimes cows and sheep whizzed past on banked meadows, through the train windows. With every mile away from the big smoke, she rewrote her encounter with Messer's Vaine and Candlestick to just a case of Anglo-American confusion.

She pulled a half-read Tasha Alexander book from her handbag and read twenty or so pages before the long hours of travel drifted her to sleep.

Chapter Two

Adams House

Luckily for her a large female ticket inspector woke her to punch her ticket, ten minutes before she was due to reach her stop. Jennifer couldn't help but notice the poor woman had a few dark hairs under her nose and the stains of perspiration under her pits. Men sweat and ladies perspire, her father use to tell her and about 101 other things on personal etiquette.

Jennifer stretched, put her book away and readied her things to disembark the train. It only took her about thirty seconds and she mentally chided herself for preparing too early. That was fine in cooking, but in life it was a little anal. At least she knew her faults, unlike George.

The train finally pulled into a small station after ages of waiting and watching hedges fly past. The journey had flown by, but the last five minutes sitting in readiness to stand and not forget all her things seemed to go on for eons.

It was much like this morning, having to wake at four to catch her flight from JFK. Because she had an early alarm set to wake her, she actually woke at one, two, three, three-thirty and then three fifty-six in the morning.

She struggled out with her cases, bags and suitcases, with still no sign of her Mr. Darcy to come to her luggage aid. In fact only four other people exited at the quaint old train station and none of them were from her carriage. She adjusted her bags, pulled out the handles of her cases and dragged them behind her. She followed the other passengers the way out, with baskets of multi-colored Petunias to line her route to the station exit.

There were no automated ticket gates or even a man in uniform to check her ticket; just an open gated exit to a small square car park. Jennifer watched one male fellow passenger jump in a local minicab and drive off while the other three, made their way to their respective cars parked nearby.

A road ran across the parking lot leading to a bridge over the railway tracks. Apart from tall poplar trees and high hedges, she could see nothing of Oxsteaden, which must be a little ways away from the train station.

Jennifer watched until all her fellow passengers had driven off into the sunset so to speak and stood alone by her cases, wondering whether to put on her ninety-five dollar sunglasses.

Once again she felt like Mrs. Jennifer Chong, George's meek and mild wife, alone and without a thought of what to do next. She felt every inch the alien tourist, a stranger in a very strange land indeed.

She pulled her cell phone from her bag and toyed with the idea of calling her creepy lawyers, to make sure: a) she was at the right station and b) her new gardener would pick her up.

Then she noticed an old man sitting in a green beat-up Land Rover, eyeing her from where he was parked at the far end of the car park.

She stared at him and he stared back at her. He looked like he might be an outdoorsy grounds man type, wearing some strange crumpled excuse of a folded green hat.

"Jen Adams, come on girl I need you." She said aloud, grabbing her bags and cases. She dragged them and herself over the hot tarmac to the Land Rover.

The window was rolled down and the Irish lilt of some disk-jockey could be heard enthusing over some obscure record, like soft porn.

"Hi there?" Jennifer smiled and hoped for the best once more today. "You wouldn't know the way to Adams House, by any chance?"

The hoary, red-cheeked man leaned forward and stretched at his back, while a black and white hunting dog sat in the passenger seat disinterested.

"You her then?" he asked gruffly, his right eye nearest Jennifer half-closed compared to its left companion.

"I'm Jennifer Adams, how do you do?" Jennifer continued to smile even if it'd surely soon give her lockjaw and reached out her right hand.

"You look more foreign than I expected," his only response.

Jennifer had to shuffle back quickly as he suddenly opened his driver's side door. "You're Henry Greenwood I presume?" Her smile faltered, at the strange vibes she was picking up from this old guy.

"You get in next to Purdy. I'll put ya cases in the back." The old man nodded into the car to the seat where the dog lay sprawled.

"Oh, okay." Jennifer took her laptop case and handbag around the hood of the car, as the man, who must already be claiming his pension, easily lifted the two suitcases and took them to the canvas back of the Land Rover.

"Hi, girl." Jennifer patted the dog as she squeezed herself in next to the hound, which both wined and farted at the same instant. Jennifer wrinkled up her petite nose and pulled her seatbelt across her bosom, as the old man loaded her cases in the back.

It felt odd sitting in the left hand side of the car and having no steering wheel or pedals in front of her.

"You have your grandfather's chin," the old gardener stated as he climbed into the driver's seat.

"That's nice of you to say." Jen smiled without showing any teeth, this time.

"Is it?" He muttered and started the engine, "I'm Henry Greenwood, your gardener and grounds man and odd-job man, miss."

"You can call me Jen," she replied, trying to remain perky and, what did the English say in those many Walt Disney movies, 'stay chipper.'

"Thank you, miss." Henry drove out of the parking lot at breakneck speed and into the road ahead without bothering to signal.

* * * *

The road led after a short while through a small village with chocolate box cottages. They had small stonewalled front gardens with bountiful blooms of purple Verbena and sun-colored Red Hot Pokers and roses of every shape and hue.

Jennifer noted two pubs, a garage, a village shop and post office, a bank, a garage, an old church and not much else. They drove through the quaint village and further on where the roads looked dangerously thin for one car, let alone two. She doubted half of her friends Fords or Chevys could've even driven down such roads without their wheels going into a ditch or hedge.

Jen felt tired and had enough of being pointed and prodded onto various forms of transportation for one day. She and not men, was supposed to be in-charge now. Still for the sake of politeness, she tried once again with conversation.

"So, have you worked at Adams House for long?"

Henry laughed gruffly at first. "Man and boy, miss."

"Look out!" Jennifer cried out, but even before she had wailed her second word, the front suspension skipped a little. She knew they had run something small-n-furry over.

Henry Greenwood continued driving along the country lane, a slight correction on the steering wheel, the only indication that anything had happened.

"I think we hit something?" Jennifer turned to look at the weathered, lived-in face of the old grounds man, but he didn't take his eyes off the road ahead.

"Be just a piece of cony road-kill now, miss. Off to bunny heaven."

Still the he wouldn't look at her, so she slumped back in her seat and tried to breathe shallowly. All this travel and flattening of animals had made her feel a little sick to her stomach. Purdy looked up her, whined and then fell back to sleep.

Luckily their journey was nearing its end, as they drove through a vast wood, with a high stone wall on the driver's side of the vehicle. The woods then opened up on Jennifer's side to reveal a fenced, sallow field. On the right the wall curved inwards to a large black set of gates, which stood over twenty feet tall.

Henry drove up to the metal gates and stopped only a couple of feet short of hitting them with the Land Rover's animal grill. Without a word, the sprightly old man jumped out of his car, pulled out a wad of keys and proceeded to unlock a padlocked chain that held the tall imposing gates shut. Jennifer felt glad for the breeze that came through the open driver's door and breathed in the fresh country air.

Henry pulled the chain free, rattling through the gates and one-after-the-other pushed the black-painted gates inwards, with a grating wail of old protesting hinges. He jumped back into the idling Land Rover and drove forward about twenty feet inside the grounds of Jennifer's new home.

"I think you better read that letter your lawyers fellows gave ya now, miss." Henry made eye contact with her, then jumped out of the vehicle again.

"How did you know?" she asked his retreating back. Then she realized just inside the gate, a strange looking white-washed house set back from the road. It looked like a community of blind architects and cake makers designed it.

A blank white wall, with a sky blue alcove faced her adorned with a white stone vase or huge ornamental pot. This lead back to form an L-shape that connected to another small L-shape that formed to her eyes a huge capital letter G of a hodgepodge building.

Windows only showed on the inner parts of the two story 'white house.' A courtyard of flowers led up to a sky blue door and all the windows had matching shutters like a house from a Greek island.

Jen reached into her bag, pulled the letter from it and tore open the seal, which seemed such a shame to spoil the red wax. Meanwhile Henry closed and locked the gates again and checked a huge, black mailbox welded to the right gate for any new mail.

She unfolded the letter and Jen read the few lines of ornate calligraphy, surely scribed with a fountain pen.

My dearest Great Niece,

Welcome home, Jennifer. For I hope you will stay at Adams House and come to cherish it, as I have during my long years here.

My faithful Henry Greenwood has the key to your new home and much more. Trust him with your life, as I did.

Yours faithfully,

Gwyneth Elizabeth Jennifer Adams

Jen looked up from the yellow paper of the brief letter to see Henry Greenwood disappear through the open blue door of the white house.

She hastily exited the passenger seat with her handbag and laptop case and headed down the path to the courtyard of the strange abode. She was nearly at the sky blue front door, when Henry Greenwood reappeared clutching another sealed letter in his hand, much like the one she had just read.

"What are you doing?" he asked with angry suspicion.

"Der, looking at my new house," she retorted, getting a little pissed because of all the haughty and rude Englishmen she had encountered so far today.

"This is my bloody house, and you can keep your thieving foreign hands off it. Miss Adams' left me White Lodge in her will and no bloody yank or her poofy lawyers are going to get their hands on it." Henry's sun-kissed skin wrinkled up in red rage at the thought of losing his home.

"This isn't Adams House?"

"This," Henry jerked a thumb backwards, "is White Lodge and my house, miss."

At last their eyes met, and Henry saw a spark in Jennifer's pupils that reminded him of his late employer. The laughter burst forth from their lips in near unison, except Henry's had more woodbines spittle to his.

"You better have this." He handed over another letter, which Jennifer took, still grinning like a loon.

Inheritance

"Another letter?"

"This is the real deal, miss. The key to the house Miss Gwen called it. She entrusted it to me to give to you because those lawyers of hers are true to their profession and are not to be trusted." Henry led the way back to the idling open-doored Land Rover, as Jen opened the new letter.

Henry stopped her and Jen looked up into his face.

"No, not here, miss. Wait until you're inside the house. You're to read it as soon as that front door is closed behind you. They were my instructions."

Jen nodded, then clambered back into the Land Rover and closed the doors. Jen wondered, as they set off again if every real estate deal in the UK was so God-damn convoluted.

The road led on through the overhanging tress of her private woods, twisting this way and that.

Suddenly the trees shot by and the road curved around a lake that appeared in a landscaped roll of gentle hillocks.

"Adams House," Henry stated as the road snaked around the lake and then curved back to zigzag twice up to the house of her forefathers.

Jennifer (Chong) Adams gasped aloud in shock, all air propelled from her lungs in one instant. On top of a slope above the grounds and framed in the background by a single line of beech trees stood Adams House.

House being the inadequate understatement of the year, as it looked like Darcy's home in Pride and Prejudice and could easily have housed a hundred people in its hay-day. It was huge, the size of her ten story apartment block, if Superman had come along and laid it on its side and added chimneys, buttresses and gargoyles to it.

"No fucking way," Jen swore as the house grew in size and stature as they pulled up at the front steps.

"You're great aunt mainly kept to the West wing to catch the most of the setting sun. The East wing is a bit ropey on the second floor, with the odd bit of damp in the winter." Henry smiled, then looked at his wrist watch and patted the steering wheel.

"It's so awesomely big for just one person," she said still in shock at the sheer scale of her inheritance.

"Let's get you and your bags inside and settle you in before dark, eh." Henry climbed out and went to get Jennifer's suitcases.

She staggered out and approached the three steps to the wide front door. It made her feel like a child approaching the gates for her first day at kindergarten.

Henry, strong and agile for his advanced years, caught her up on the last step and placed her suitcases beside the wide imposing black front door.

"Oh, you might be needing these," Henry said, fishing a ring of five keys upon it and placed them in her waiting palm.

"What do these open?" she asked in a daze, wondering how many hundreds of doors and rooms lay beyond her new front door.

"Just to ease you in, miss; gates, garage, front door, back kitchen door and your bedroom key for starters."

Henry stood up straight now at attention, his old military stance coming back easily as he waited for further instructions.

"This one?"

Jennifer held one key up from the ring which fit with the lock before her. The door to her new single life, as lady of the house, miles from anywhere, God, she hoped Aunt Gwen had cable.

"Good choice, Miss Jennifer." Henry nodded and watched her tentatively poke the key into the lock of her new front door.

Taking a deep breath, she turned the key in the lock and pushed the heavy wooden door inwards to gaze for the first time into her new domain. She crossed the threshold, onto a parquet floor entrance hall of enormous proportions.

A vast staircase swept upwards to the next floor with carpets fixed with brass rods, with gaps of polished wood on either side. She half expected to see Vivien Leigh flounce down it in a big dress into the arms of Clark Gable.

Doors assaulted her eyes from every wall and archways, one left and one right and one ahead set back behind the grand staircase, which led off to wings, kitchens, parlors and rooms that had names with no meanings to New York Jenny-from-the –block.

She spun around trying to take in the enormity of the wood-paneled walls and twenty foot high full scale portraits. Henry put her suitcases down on the polished floor and only then she noticed the mosaic in the wood floor. Silver birch had been used to form the sign of a cross just behind the doorstep of the front entrance. Below the four by three foot cross, were words, also in the same wood, but written in Latin.

"What does it say?"

"God bless and protect this house," Henry replied.

"It's all too awesome to take in." Jen patted her hands together, feeling like a lowly serving girl, coming to the palace to be its new fairytale princess.

"And it takes a Sheik's fortune to heat in the winter time." Henry gazed around the giddy heights of the hallway, his eyes seeing cobwebs, not grandeur.

"I don't know where to start?"

"Then I'll take you to the drawing room, so you can read your letter in peace. Then I'll make us a drink. I bought some coffee yesterday in the village if you would like it?"

"I'm in England now, so I think I will have tea." Jen smiled and walked over to the ornate banister of her fairytale staircase, which looked wide enough for five people to climb at once. "Do you have Earl Grey or Lady Grey or Assam?"

"PG Tips, miss."

"Are those good then?"

"Like heaven in a cup." Henry smiled. "Drawing room is through that door miss."

Jennifer headed to the door his finger pointed to in the left hand wall.

"Thank you, Henry."

"I'll put the kettle on and afterwards take your suitcases up to your room."

"Cool."

Jen smiled widely, showing off her perfect small white teeth and headed for the drawing room door, her shoes making loud tip-tap noises across the entrance hall.

Henry passed her and headed down an archway toward the kitchens as Jen opened the door to a magical new life. She peeked around the door like a burglar, rather than the lady of the manor and saw before her a room of Georgian splendor that no costume drama could hope to match.

She entered the room, not daring to touch a sideboard or a chair, as it wasn't really sinking in that this all belonged to her. She hesitantly sat on a green upholstered settee and pulled the new letter that Henry had given her from her handbag. She tore it open and managed to tear her gaze away from the opulent room to read it.

My dearest Jennifer,

I am sorry we never had the chance to meet in person and now that I am dying, I know we never will. Please excuse the cloak and dagger espionage with the letters. Rardin and Keene have been our family's lawyers for centuries, but they are not to be trusted, but with the simplest of tasks.

Henry has my entire trust and I have faith, even though I have made him a rich man in my will, that he will serve you as well as me.

Now down to business. I am afraid the house pretty much looks after itself. Henry will do any small repairs, but there is a five million pound fund which will cover any major repairs. Mr. Jordan who runs the bank in the village will help you with this.

Now to the most important and expeditious matter I must impart to you, my Great Niece. I hope my words will be sufficient to warn you and you do not think they are the ramblings of an insane and lonely old spinster.

Once night falls, you must never leave the house. The grounds hold many nocturnal animals that only come out of the woods at night to drink at the lake.

Always keep your doors locked and the shutters at your windows closed during the hours of darkness. We have a colony of bats that flock to any light source, and they often slam themselves against the windows.

An almanac of when dusk and dawn occur sits on the desk in the library. A place as a cookery author you will mentally devour and relish. We have many out of print and ancient English cookbooks in the library. I hope they will be of interest to you, as your cookbooks were to me.

I am most serious and insistent that you must never open the doors and windows after dark. If someone knocks upon the front door, just ignore it.

If a pallid handsome, yet thin-cheeked man comes to call upon you after dusk and before dawn, do not talk to him or give him permission to cross the threshold of the house. You are the new mistress of this house and he will heed your words. Yet, he is sly and cunning as a serpent. His name is Silas Cromity.

This sad inheritance comes with the house I am afraid and no power on earth can end that. He is a revenant of Adams House's long bloody past and only has evil intent in his cold, black heart.

Remember he can only enter the house if you give him permission. That is his only weakness and your only power over him. Societies and King's Paladin have tried to rid this vile creature from our lives and all have failed.

Trust not his words or actions, speak to him not, drown him out with loud music, light and laughter.

I am sorry you now bear this burden. It was one your grandfather, my brother, refused to shoulder, but I lay no blame at his door. Yet there is a great life here and when the sun rises and its glorious rays shine down upon this house. There is no finer place to be in England. The herb garden, the orchard beyond is a sight to behold in the summer. I hope you enjoy your lifetime here; I did and never once felt lonely.

Fear the dark, trust the light.

Yours forever,

Gwen Adams

P.S. Even if you think me insane, do not go out after dark. Please follow this dying woman's last wish.

Jennifer stared at the words on the page in shock. She might have expected the odd eccentric request, but not the words written in front of her.

Just then the door opened and Henry came in balancing a tea tray on one strong arm.

"Henry." She paused in thought trying to find words to put her question. "Have I inherited a ghost?"

"I think the correct term is vampire-revenant, miss," he replied matter-of-factly, setting the tea things down on the table in front of the settee.

"A what?"

Jen's eyes were wide showing a lot of white eyeball. *Had this house made it out of the Middle Ages yet*, her mind pondered.

"Cromity." Henry exhaled, sitting down next to Jennifer. "He's like an echo that won't stop resonating. A ghost by day and cold bones and flesh by night and a real pain-in-the-arse in the winter months."

"Is this like joining a fraternity, like hazing the new guy? You're joking, right? This letter is a cruel joke because my father and grandfather never came back to visit mad, old Gwen?" Jennifer started out at a simmer and finished her rant at a boiling point.

"Gwyneth Adams wasn't mad. She was the strongest person I've ever known." Henry stood, his turn to be angry. "And no bloody Yank who happens to share a quart of her blood has the right to question her sanity, not in my presence."

"Well, maybe you," she pointed at his chest, "should leave *my house then!*"

"With pleasure," Henry barked back and slipped a folded piece of paper into her hand. "The directions to your room from the hall."

Then he left, stomping his boots out of the room, across the parquet floor and out of the front door.

"Go fuck yourself, mister, 'cause all Englishmen are queer, in-breed, buck-toothed weirdoes!" She shouted and then lowered her voice to add, "Except my grandfather and father."

Jennifer Adams ran in a fiery rage across the hall to bolt the front door shut.

"Jes-us Christ, what have you got yourself into Jenny Adams." She headed down the archway that Henry had earlier vanish down in search of the comfort of the kitchen and to brew herself a pot of coffee.

* * * *

A box of fresh fruit and vegetables stood on one of the many kitchen counters. The cupboards were well stocked with soups, pasta and other stranger oddities like Marmite and Mushy Peas. The fridge had milk, eggs and cheese and nothing else, but she did find an old coffee pot hidden in the back of a cupboard. A jar of instant coffee sat next to the kettle, mentioned earlier by Henry. She suddenly felt the urge to cook, to ease her agitated state and fill the rumbling void in her stomach.

She quickly made herself coffee to sip as she gathered ingredients. She soon whipped up a zucchini and scallion (spring onion) frittata and wolfed it down.

"See, I don't need a man," she said to herself, still simmering from her altercation with Henry. "I found the kitchen and now, I'm bitching."

Taking her coffee remains with her, she retraced her steps to the hall and started opening doors for fun and she found a small lavatory first. Then a billiard room, another room with a green crush velvet card table and stacks of booze, decantered into priceless crystal. A large walk-in cloakroom, like you might find at a club or theatre on Broadway.

She glanced at her watch and felt surprised to find it was six past six already. Jen put her empty coffee cup next to a vase of fake flowers and stared at her suitcase, willing them to teleport upstairs to her bedroom.

"Piss off the staff after they take your bags up to your room next time, Jenny," she scolded herself.

She then took her bag and laptop case and using the map hand-drawn by Henry, Jen headed up the wide sweeping staircase for the very first time, to try and locate her bedroom.

A wide square landing went around the first floor (second floor to Jennifer) and a huge, high window dominated the back wall. Jen was far too small to see what the view would be and headed down the arched corridor of the west wing.

She passed a daunting array of her ancestor's portraits, all of which had a haughty air that the well-to-do and arrogant rich shared. Through this darkening maze of mahogany she walked feeling like a small child again, when her parents took her to Disneyland at six.

At last she turned a corner and the rough map indicated the room on the left as hers. A window at the far end of the corridor showed the sun wasn't far from setting.

So tired, annoyed, with her brain travel-frazzled and feeling rather sweaty in the crotch and under-bra areas, she reached out for the doorknob to her bedroom.

She felt surprised to find it was locked. With an audible sigh she fumbled in her handbag for the keys Henry the groundskeeper had given her.

Finally unlocked, she turned the knob and pushed the tall wide door inwards with the help of her right shoe. The bedroom looked thick with darkness, since the shutters were pulled across the windows. Fondling the wallpaper to her left, her hand came across cold brass and a thin knobby switch. Jennifer flicked the switch on and a mini crystal candelabrum shone twinkling light across her new bedroom.

She gasped in shock, a gasp of explicit joy and delight, as one of her childhood princess dreams suddenly came true. Her new bed was a monstrous construction of a four poster Queen Anne bed, with a wooden pelmets and canopy covered with sashes of lilac silk, hanging slightly down.

Jennifer put down her bag and laptop on a dressing table, kicked off her shoes and rushed over to the bed of her dreams.

"Come to mamma."

She cried as she dove onto the small double four poster bed, rolled onto her back and giggled. She forgot all the strange events of the day now and spread her arms and legs like she was making a snow angel in her sheets. "Now this is more like it."

She lay on the cool sheets and stared up at the canopy. A little feeling of guilt passed through her mind because she'd live alone in a house that could house ten or more families.

"No guilt trips today, Jenny Adams," she reprimanded herself.

She sat up quick, before the urge to sleep over-took her urge to explore. Then another thought tumbled into her tired mind, a more ghoulish unwanted thought.

"Jeez, I hope Great Aunt Gwen didn't die in this bed?"

Jen hopped off the bed after a couple of pushes of her palms behind her and headed for a door half-hidden by a changing screen, on the other side of the dressing table.

She pulled it open to reveal a large walk-in wardrobe area with a pull cord light, full length mirror and acres of space for her tiny collection of clothes.

She left the closet, exited her new bedroom and headed down the corridor to the last room on the left, next to hers. The door was thankfully unlocked and the shutters pulled aside to reveal two large windows in the corner end of the west wing, bathed in the orange glow of the setting sun.

From her great aunt's second letter Jen reckoned this must be the bedroom she had mentioned and the feel of the sunlight through the windows warmed Jennifer's heart. If she was going to die of old age, this would be her place of choice. The tall trees caused the dusk light to shine through their boughs and leaves like ribbons of yellow and gold streamers. A gap had been made in the line of trees by the look of the stumps to make sure the last rays of light made it through the north facing window, while the view through the west window showed the line of trees. Jen squinted at the ball of fire as it sank beneath the view.

She moved closer to the window and soaked up the last rays of the day, wash over her tired face. Opening her eyes she saw far away on the edge the grounds a row of tree stumps where more trees had been cut down in a direct line to the north window where the sun would set in the misty distance.

She wanted to stay and watch the sunset, but knew she needed to get the rest of her suitcases upstairs. She needed both, because she had no idea where she had packed her PJ's.

Leaving her great aunt's room with a skip in her step she headed along the long corridors toward the first floor landing, darkening quickly now. She trotted bare-footed across the parquet flooring of the hall and switched on a bank of light-switches that sent illumination around the hall, the corridors beyond and the staircase above.

"This place could do with an elevator," she grumbled, trundling her suitcase across the hall up to the first step. Pushing down the handles she grabbed the fixed ones and one-by-one, step-by-step she lifted her suitcases up the very grand staircase. She decided if or when she left, she'd set them at the top step and just push them to slide down to the bottom and hope for the best.

She was three quarters of the way up when there came a shrill ringing of a telephone from somewhere in the hall below. The shock nearly sent the suitcase in her right hand back down the stairs, in some awful parody of a Laurel and Hardy film. She pushed both her suitcases into a secure position on the wide steps and ran down to answer the echoing phone.

Holding her chest as she hurried, she found the ringing phone, from some black and white movie era, behind a great vase on a little desk with a cushioned red seat.

"Hello?" She answered a little out of breath, not sure whether to say her name or something posh like Adams House, the lady of the house speaking.

"Ah, Miss Adams, I'm so glad to have found you at home. This is Mister Vaine speaking, your lawyers." The cool, yet sly voice oozed like oil down the phone line into her ear.

"Yeah, here I am, safe and sound," she replied, then put her hand over the mouthpiece and exhaled loud and hard.

"Long may you remain that way. I hope you find Adams House to your liking?"

"Well, I sure have a lot to explore and do, so if you will excuse me," Jen bravely said, tiredness and her dislike of the man, added to her new found bravado.

"Of course, I was just checking that you had complied with the stipulations in your great aunt's will. Have a good night's sleep Jennifer and don't let the bed bugs bite," Mr. Vaine said with insincere jollity.

"I will. Thank you," she replied, then hastily replaced the receiver on its black base, with a proper numbered dial on it. "Asswipe," she spat at the phone, "can't believe I wasted my naughty thoughts on you."

Then with weary shoulders she trudged up the stairs once more and huffed and puffed her suitcases to the top, glad that her bedroom wasn't on the floor above this one.

"Jesus, I need to pee." She dragged the cases behind her on their wheels, back to her new bedroom, hoping that she wouldn't have to pee in a Ming vase before she found a bathroom.

Leaving her suitcases outside her open bedroom door, she guessed that old people had weak bladders and figured the toilet must be somewhere close-by. She tried the door across the hall from her late great aunt's bedroom, doing a pee-pressure jig from one foot to the next.

She opened the door and turned on a modern light switch and once more the room before her shocked her. A modern styled walk-in shower area, a new bath with a disability side door, stood in a white and blue mosaic walled and floored bathroom.

"Oh, come on."

She whined crossing her legs a little, because it was just a bathroom, with no toilet. She left it and tried the next door along, which at last to her bladders relief she found a toilet. Jen pulled a light switch on a cord, wriggled down her trousers and panties and hopped over to the toilet to relieve herself.

With the toilet, bathroom, kitchen and bedroom found, she had finished exploring for day one of her stay, all the rest would be a bonus. She felt happy to have all the basic rooms covered for now and wondered how many other types of room there could be in a house this size.

By the time she had washed her hands and face and left the toilet with her panties on and her trousers over her arm, the sun had set. Back in her new bedroom she laid her slacks over the back of a chair by her dresser and sat on her princess bed and texted her friend and agent Valerie back home in New York. She'd have phoned, but wasn't entirely sure what time of the day or night it was back on the east coast of America.

She put on Katy Perry via her cell phone to break up the silence and laid her suitcases on the bed to unpack them. Her small amount of clothes was soon lost in the large walk-in wardrobe. Soon she sang along, while putting her blouses on hangers and underwear in drawers.

Jen felt hot already and the walking back and forth had made her sticky in some most uncomfortable places. Her Mrs. Chong side made her lock the bedroom door from the inside, while her Miss Adams side saw her peel off her remaining clothes to the rhythm of the music.

Jen unhooked and slid off her bra with a hiss of discomfort. Letting the bra drop to the carpet she approached the full length mirror, with trepidation like most women over the age of thirty. She lifted her breasts with her palms, to see red heat rashes underneath and the red lines her bra wire had made across her skin. Jogging, half-dancing back to her suitcases, she found her toiletries bag and pulled out a tube of skin cream to rub onto her tender under-boobs.

"Now, if I could get my Mister Darcy to do this for me, that would be progress," she said to her reflection in the mirror as she applied the cream. "Right, gotta find one first."

Putting her hands on her hips, she turned sideward's eyeing her slim yet curvy, short figure in the mirror.

"Come on, this body has to get some English lord in a lather."

Then with a dimpled smile she pulled down her panties, over one buttock with a hooked thumb.

"Take me, Mister Darcy. I'm most definitely yours."

Jen with a shoulder rising yawn turned and walked over to the dressing table. There she collected her half bottle of water and Tasha Alexander novel she had read half of on the plane and train. She climbed into the cool bed and fluffed the two pillows behind her up to read. The water bottle went on a bedside table with her watch and rings, next to her cell phone.

She only read ten pages in when she found, she had re-read the same paragraph three times because of her nodding head and eyes. Giving up, she turned on the bedside lamp, put her book next to it and hopped out of bed to turn off the main light switch. Light from the corridor beyond crept under the doorway, as the shadows settled across her new bedroom.

"You forgot the hall lights, Jen," she said, looking down at her naked torso and frowned. A trip in bare feet and topless back to the hall didn't appeal to her sleepy head.

"Fuck it. They can bill me and I can afford it."

Jen headed back to her bed, lay down, pulled up the sheets and sneaked out a hand to click off the bedside light.

Darkness, total and uncompromising gave her eyes nothing to see and she fell asleep within forty seconds of her dark locks hitting her cotton pillow case.

Any outside noises or knockings she just slept through. In fact a bomb could have gone off on the drive and she probably would've slept through it.

Chapter Three

Exploring

With Jennifer's travel weariness, she slept for twelve hours and her body only woke her up after nine am, still in comparative darkness with a pressing need to relieve her aching bladder again.

She rushed from her bed, across the carpet of her shuttered bedroom, then unlocked and pulled open her door to find a sunny September day had dawned. The lights remained on making her sleepy eyes wince from the brightness. Jen crashed through the lavatory door and spun, sat on the open toilet and peed with a long whistle of relief.

Jen yawned and rubbed at her bleary, wet eyes, loaded with the Sandman's finest work. She exhaled and looked around the bare looking room, wondering if she had brushed her teeth last night. She shivered a little since the floor felt cold beneath her bare feet, and the temperature outside was probably warmer than inside her new lavatory.

She slowly padded back to her bedroom after a pad, wipe and hand wash and noted again that the hall lights remained on, even though it was morning. She easily subdued her green side, pushing it over to the not quite awake side of her brain.

Once inside she had to turn on the light to see sufficiently to figure out how to open the tall shutters at her one large window. In the end she had to cast off her clothes of the previous day from the ornate chair she had dumped them on last night and move it near the window, to reach up to unhook the latch.

With a self-praising cry of her self-help ingenuity she pulled the shutters back, which folded over painted hinges so they retracted back into the window frames.

Sunlight chased the night's shadows from the bedroom and Jen looked down from her lofty castle like room to see Henry Greenwood and dog companion looking up at her from the west lawn.

It took a microsecond after seeing the shocked look on the old gardener's face that Jennifer realized she was standing on a chair,

totally naked in full view at her bedroom window. With a too em-
barrassed-to-be-embarrassed wave, she covered her assets with
her left arm and jumped off the chair out of sight.

* * * *

Outside Henry Greenwood felt glad to see the feisty new
Adams lady of the house was in such rude health this fine morning and headed off to the orchard, with a rare smile on his lips.

* * * *

Jen wiped at her eyes again, then put her left palm over her
wrinkled forehead and sat down on the seat of the chair she had
just jumped off.

"Way-da-go, Jen. You've just flashed your boobs at an old guy
who hates your guts."

Jennifer rubbed at her top lip and picked up her watch which
showed the time to be twenty-six minutes past nine.

Jen used the lovely, modern walk-in shower room and wore
her dressing gown both to and from the bedroom.

Feeling more like the new woman she tried hard to be, she left
the safety of her bedroom in jeans and comfortable top, with a
jacket over her left arm, which held her cell phone, a square block
pad of differing colored post-it notes and a marker pen. In her
back pocket she put the map Henry had given her and the set of
keys.

Switching off the upstairs lights as she went, Jen headed back
to the base-camp safety of the hall and switched off the lights
there also. Her first quest was obvious. She headed to the immense kitchen to rustle up a scrambled egg on toast breakfast and
a coffee to kick-start her day.

Jen realized she'd have to stock up on food soon or her eggs
diet would have the bed smelling of Satan's sulphurs pit. Good
thing she didn't have any male company of the take-to-bed variety
at the moment.

Jennifer ate at one of the work surfaces sitting on a stool, while
gazing out at the herb garden and vegetable plot directly outside
the kitchen windows. She read a long antsy text from Valerie about
a boxer she had picked up, whose muscle definition was great, but
the muscle that counted wasn't in any way, shape or form in the
same league. Smiling at the fact that life did go on without her in

NY, she took a deep breath, jumped off her stool and decided to explore her new life. She left her plates and pan in the Belfast sink to soak, after a fruitless search for a dishwasher.

Then began her quest of exploration of her new abode in earnest and headed back to the entrance hall of her palatial new house.

She wrote on the top post-it note, went over to the drawing room and stuck it on the door, giving it the obvious title of Drawing Room.

Then struck with a dose of Mrs. Chong self-doubt, opened, peeked and shut the drawing room door with a self-deprivating shake of her head.

"Now, where to start?"

Jen pursed her lips, her hands on her hips holding post-it notes and pen, looking around at the daunting task it would be. She mentally shrugged and urged herself past the west wing archway to a door in the same wall as the drawing room.

She pushed it open to reveal a bright dining area, with a table that sat eight, cupboards, food tables and another door that led into the west wing passage. She stepped out, closed the door behind her and put a Dining Room post-it on the door.

Then with a glance back to the hall, she headed down the west wing ground floor corridor, or first floor to her American mind.

She put Dining Room Door 2 on the next door. Then she approached the door after that on the same side, a set of double doors which opened inwards to reveal another even longer rectangular shaped room, with another vastly longer table in it that could seat thirty or so diners easily.

"Jeez, how many places to eat do I need?"

Then an idea popped into her head from the novel she was reading. Jen retraced her steps and took down the last two post-its and scribbled two new replacements marked, Breakfast Room.

Then back to the longer doubled-doored sunny room and put Dining Room on the right hand door of the pair.

Jen then crossed the passage and entered the next room opposite to find a windowless oblong room, mainly occupied with a huge billiard table, with large long-low hanging hooded lights and sets of cues fixed to brackets in the flock wallpapered walls. She frowned a little. Surely she had been in this room briefly last night. *Wasn't it nearer the hall?*

"I probably got two of these babies."

Pool Room went on the door and then she bustled off to see

what the next room held.

Sitting Room followed on the sunny corner, then a Sewing Room because of the works of lace framed on the wall, with pictures of long dead relatives and an old wheel cranked sewing machine in the corner.

Then she discovered a room that simply took her breath away and made her instantly fall in love with her old, new home, the library. It was cathedral in size and beech shelved grandeur. The place stood two stories high and square in shape and larger than the sitting room, drawing room and pool room, pushed together.

She walked across the well trod Indian made red carpet with gold and green patterns in Hindu and just twirled in awestruck reverence.

"Awesome," she whispered, like she was in a church. It reminded her of frequent visits to the New York Library.

She sang a few lines of a Paul Simon song as she spun herself slowly around, as she gazed upon wood and plaster angel, gargoyles and cherubs. The high ceiling was carved and painted upon with pictures of gothic Christian scenes from the Bible and the artistry just blew her socks off. The books, thousands of leather bound volumes and tomes, mixed with more modern paperbacks, hardbacks and soft covers.

Then she saw something and raced up to a twelve foot high bookcase, with its twin opposite, bisecting the room and adding to its cathedral appearance.

Third shelf up on an empty part of the wide bookcase sat her first two cook books. Jennifer touched the very familiar spines, resting in such auspicious company. She felt humbled that her books had been read by her unknown great aunt. They stood in line, with such great works of learning, philosophy and fiction.

A desk, small and unassuming sat in the far dark corner of the library, a winding staircase sat opposite leading to an upper walkway that rounded the upper echelons of the library. On the desk as promised in her great aunt's letter was 'Warbeck's Almanac,' which had the sunrises and sunsets of every day of the year.

She flicked it open to today's date and then noticed two of the highest curtains she had ever seen outside a Broadway theatre. At one side, a scarlet rope was fixed to a pulling system. With a squeal of protest, she pulled it; the curtains drew apart. They revealed a huge stain glass window that must be at least twenty-five feet tall.

In pieces of glass of differing hues smoked a great dragon of green glass, standing before the worm with a sword pointed at its belly, was a knight in black armor. On his other 2D arm was a red shield with a golden heart shape in its center and three gold crosses around it in a downwards triangle positions.

"Unreal."

Jennifer exhaled and hoped she didn't have to get the Windex to it and clean it herself. She resisted the urge to climb the winding staircase and with a heavy heart left the library, vowing to return soon and continued the exploration of her inheritance.

On the corner roughly beneath her bedroom was a study, with mahogany shelves, a large dresser with a worn red leather inlaid top. There were no computers in this old house's study, but the room at least had a modern phone jack for the telephone. Jen made a mental note to get the phone company out to install a wireless internet connection as-soon-as-possible.

With post-its reading Study and Library in place, she retraced her steps back to the entrance hallway, took a deep breath and headed down the east wing corridor. The first room she encountered seemed to be a clone of the west wing sitting room, so Jennifer put Sitting Room 2 (East). Confirming the fact she had more rooms than she could ever use.

The next room had dust sheets over shapes of furniture and a rough smell emanating from the dark brown swirled pattern carpet. After a quick look at the yellowed ceiling, Jen designated this room as the Smoking Room.

The following room had the same covers over settees, cupboard and sideboards, so instead of writing Sitting Room 3, she chose to write Living Room, for a change.

The next rooms were the oddest she had encountered and made little sense until later on in her exploration of the east wing.

She put Gentlemen on one door and Ladies on the next. Inside the ladies she saw a lavatory comparable in size to ones she had visited in clubs and restaurants.

"I have a four cubicle girl's toilet, in-my-house?"

Then feeling the urge suddenly, probably because she was in there, Jen tried out the facilities. She flushed and washed her hands, but resisted a long inspection of the men's room, for the time being at least.

Turning around, she saw before her two huge double doors that nearly rose to the ceiling of the east wing corridor. Above it on a wooden plaque, just above the upper door frame were the words, The Reclamation Room.

Having, not a clue what that meant, she turned both door handles at once and pushed the heavy doors open and once again felt stunned at what her eyes befell.

Had she been paying attention she'd have noticed the lack of doors on the left hand side of the east wing L-shaped corridor. It might have given her a clue, but nothing could prepare her eyes for the opulence of the Reclamation Room Ballroom.

It looked immense in size. She had thought the library big, but this was over double its size and just as tall.

Jen found a red backed chair up against the wall by the doors and had to sit down. She saw a mass of gold, carvings, friezes, mezzotints, portraits and general splendor that her home country couldn't match. It made her eyes weep with a wondrous overpowering joy.

"First toilets, now I have an aircraft hanger sized freaking ballroom in my house."

Jen reckoned she could easily get a pro basketball court and stands in this place that only an NBA team could fill. She expected to see waltzing ladies in crinoline rush past her at any second, dancing in rows with haughty chinned gentlemen, in tails and high boots.

At the far end of the ballroom, a raised bandstand stood with an old big gramophone that the dog used to look into on that record label of her youth.

Giggling with joy she left the ballroom and found a Smoking Room 2 and a vast conservatory full of exotic plants and trees. This led around to a wide stone balcony outside for cocktail parties and ballroom overspill. At this point her brain couldn't process any more grand rooms, so she broke for lunch.

Jennifer walked back to the safety of the kitchen, a room that held no fears and found a new box of vegetables on the side, next to a bottle of wine. Jennifer found no note, so took it as an apology from Henry Greenwood.

She made herself a cheese and tomato sandwich and put the white wine in her still near-empty refrigerator. On a post-it she wrote as she ate:

1). Phone company, internet
2). Talk to Henry- make peace
3). Get a lift to village, get supplies, need candy bars.
4). Explore upstairs tomorrow
5) Ring Valerie
6) Work out time in NYC? (Make this 4.5)

7)

Number seven stayed blank for a while as she ate. Then she added:

7) Explore grounds.

Jen drank a glass of milk after her lunch and then ate an apple, one of many Henry had left her. After the fruit she added a number eight to her list, small and squeezed in at the bottom of the post-it:

8). Visit bank!

Having enough of the inside of her new home, she unlocked the back kitchen door and stepped out into the warm midday sun and her walled herb garden.

"Now this is home."

The large plot made her window box of herbs back in her New York apartment look puny. As the sun moved over Adams House, Jen moved among the herbs, picking the odd leaf to bring to her nose to sniff. She wished she had started in the gardens first, as she wandered from section to section feeling calm and at home for the very first time since arriving here.

Chapter Four

Rollers and Shakers

When Jen had washed and dried her lunch plate and knives, she wandered back to the hall to find Henry Greenwood kneeling on the floor before a strange looking radiator.

"Hi there," Jen said with her arms crossed, because nothing more eloquent or profound came to mind.

"Afternoon, Miss Adams," he replied gruffly, as he pulled a Phillips screwdriver from the toolbox beside him and began unscrewing the front of the radiator thing.

"So, whatcha doing there, Henry?" she asked tentatively, edging forward. She hoped she came across as interested and not some dumbass broad.

"This storage heater is playing up," he spoke as he worked, "I can fix it now, but I'll have to pop back late tonight to test if it works. If that is okay with you, miss?"

"That's fine." Jen leaned one arm out against the wall. "So, why can't you test that it works now?"

"It's an economy storage heater. It only goes on at night. It heats up the bricks inside and then sends out the heat the next day. You don't need it at the moment with this weather, but you will soon."

"Look, I'm sorry about our little spat yesterday. I was bushed and this place kinda blew me away, you know?" Jennifer stated, hoping she sounded like a reasonable, mature woman of the world and not some foreign chick calling the shots.

"I apologize too, miss. This house can take a lot of getting used to." Henry looked up at her and winked, his blue eyes shining and still attractive though the years had ravaged his face. He had promised to look after her, for Gwen's sake and the family and on reflection he probably would have reacted the same way if he had been her.

"Cool, 'cause really I need some help?"

"What with miss?"

"It's Jennifer, okay." She smiled down at him warmly. "I need to contact the phone company to sort out an internet connection, visit the village to get some groceries in, oh, and visit my new bank manager."

"Well, the bank pays all the bills from a special trust fund, so you can ask him, Mister Jordan, the bank manager about phones and the like."

Henry had finished his repairs of the storage heater and began to replace the front cover.

"Erm, could you perhaps give me a lift?" she asked in a stranded by the freeway, change my tire mister feminine whiles way.

"Banks' closed now for today, half day Wednesday closing Miss Jennifer, but if you can drive I can show you something far better than getting a lift in my smelly old Land Rover?"

"Hey, I'm an American. We are taught to drive and fire automatic weapons in high school," she teased with a relieved giggle.

"Then Jennifer Adams of New York City, I think I have a treat in store for you."

* * * *

Five minutes later they stood before a huge triple, two story garage that stood alone away from the east wing of the house, with its own little road that backed onto the edge of the woods.

The garage was some later Baroque addition to the other outbuildings nearest the house. It had been built in the 1920's when garages replaced stables across the country.

Henry un-padlocked all three metal garage doors and then lifted them up manually one-by-one to reveal the prized automobiles kept inside. Then he entered and switched on the interior lights even though the sun beat down on their necks. He pulled the covers off three very different and magnificent angels of the road.

"This Jennifer was your grandfather's car. It's a nineteen thirty-three Wolseley Hornet." Henry smiled as Jennifer approached and touched the large headlights of her late grandfather's classic sports car.

"It's so old, but still shiny," she enthused, "bet that's your doing, Henry?

Jen tried to picture her grandfather, looking young and driving such a car along the tight bends of Oxsteaden.

"Guilty as charged, miss." Henry smiled, he was proud of the fact he kept these cars in such prime working condition.

"Wow, what's this?" Jennifer moved to the next car with its British Racing Green sleek bodywork and ran her palm up over the hood.

"Believe it or not, your great aunt used to tear up the country lanes in this back in the sixties. She was quite a lady."

"I can see, is it a Jag?" Jennifer asked. She didn't know a whole lot about classic British cars, but she did know a thing of beauty when she saw it.

"Better than a Jag, miss. It's an Aston Martin Dee-Bee four Zagoto. They don't make them like this anymore." Of the three cars, the Aston Martin was his favorite and he'd driven it around the grounds on many occasions.

"Now even I know that's a Rolls-Royce." Jennifer walked the short distance to a golden looking Rolls.

"Yep, she's a Rolls-Royce Silver Shadow Mark One; what your great aunt was chauffeured around in her twilight years. So, do you want to take one out for a spin around the grounds?"

"The Aston Henry!" Jen enjoyed this moment of pure ballsy new Miss Adams; this was the person she wanted to be and what a car to show off her new self in.

"I'll get the keys then, miss." Henry smiled and walked over to a locked key cabinet, on the wall over a workbench.

* * * *

Jennifer twirled the keys of the Aston Martin on her ever growing set of keys, for the garage, the house and the front gates, on her forefinger as she headed upstairs to her bedroom. Tomorrow she'd explore the village of Oxsteaden, sort out some vital supplies (like chocolate) and visit the bank manager.

The drive around the grounds with Henry had been both a challenge and a thrill. Sitting in the wrong seat to drive felt weird, but at least she had no other traffic to contend with on the estate. It also helped break the ice a little with Henry and no mention of spooky ghosts, passed either of their lips.

She entered her bedroom and changed out of her hot clothes into a baggy Dido tour T-shirt and sweatpants for comfort. She looked in her full length mirror and smiled at her reflection. She loved the shade of her skin, from her Korean mother's side and the strong American-English heritage of her bone structure of her face. This in school hadn't always been the case, where her teeth had always seemed too big for her small face and mouth. Now just over thirty, where others with Asian features started to look old before their time, her features now came into their own.

Henry had informed her that the West Wing Sitting Room had a television in a cabinet, but only the five terrestrial channels. He had cable or what he called Sky, so he could watch boxing and cricket. So she needed that sorted out. She'd die if she didn't get to see *Grey's Anatomy* or *CNN* soon.

Time had flown past once again, on her second hot fall, correction autumn's day in England, so she trooped down to the kitchen to rustle up a pasta using herbs from the garden and fresh garlic and tomatoes supplied by Henry. The pasta was the dried variety, found just-in-date on a shelf in the pantry.

She swallowed her hot meal with a glass of wine and watched the low autumn sun as it descended toward the line of trees behind the house. The sunlight streamed through onto her face and bare arms, and she felt a peace she had never felt before during her life in New York and her college days in Washington.

"Washing," she suddenly stated, knowing that her small supply of fresh clothes would need a washing machine sometime soon. She made a new note on a post-it, to remind her to ask Henry the next day and stuck it to the front of the fridge.

* * * *

As the sun set over the hill, Jennifer settled down in front of the cabinet hid television, with a second glass of wine resting on the arm of the sofa.

Her choice of viewing consisted of two news programs, one quiz program with peanuts for prizes. Plus, she could watch an Australian soap where people kissed and shouted at each other or an English rural version which they did much the same only with the same sex.

"I kissed a girl..." Jen sang and toasted the lipstick lesbians on her TV screen, two hours before the watershed.

Jen wondered what to do next when her cell phone chirped to tell her she had a new message. She smiled, as she read it came from Valerie, joking she had the Giants football team to stay at Jen's apartment last night. She now knew what a Tight-End was. The message ended with a smiley face and three xxx.

Jen typed something cruel and crude in reply and then relaxed back in her comfy sofa to see what else British Television would throw at her.

Her cell chirped again. Putting down her wine on an occasional table, she picked up her phone from where it had been resting in her lap, Jen pulled her head back and made a face at the small screen of her phone; the text wasn't from Valerie this time, but sender unknown. She opened it and frowned with her lips and forehead.

"*End the curse. Invite him into your heart and soul tonight.*"

"What-the-fuck?" Jen hissed and checked from what phone it had been sent, but it just read number withheld.

She then tried to reply to the text, thinking it had been misdirected, but was unable to. She just pressed delete and then drained her glass of wine.

A welcome delight of a Jane Austin drama came on next on the third channel along. So wrapped up in it, she quickly forgot about the erroneous text. The program finished at ten, so she decided to have a quick read then turn in for the night. She left the hall light on again and trudged upstairs to her bedroom, not before a lavatorial pit-stop.

Jen realized as she sat on the toilet, that she still had the rest of the floor her bedroom was on, plus the story above to explore and any attics and basements also.

"I may need some more post-it notes," she said aloud to herself, resting the back of her calves on the cold porcelain because of the heat. Feeling happy at how the day had panned out and excited about exploring the local village, she stripped down to her panties ready for bed.

She only read a few pages of her book before the wine took a drowsy effect. She closed it on her bookmark, switched off her bedside light and fell asleep in her princess four-poster bed.

Her bladder aching for attention woke her at five to twelve, and she switched on only her bedside lamp and padded off across the hall to the toilet.

With hands still damp from the post pee wash in the basin, she started to cross the dark corridor to her bedroom and warm inviting bed. When, she heard a faint knocking echoing from down the west wing corridor. Jennifer rushed into her room in her bare feet and pulled her Dido tour t-shirt over her head to cover her modesty. As it had once been George's it covered her butt like an A-line dress.

Jennifer crept down the passage that turned to the left before turning right onto the landing of the staircase.

She felt sure she heard the front door open and a voice speak.

Then she remembered Henry was going to check the heater thing downstairs in the hall tonight.

She reached the end of the wall and peeked around over the banisters, to just make sure her assumptions had been correct.

She saw Henry standing at the open front door, but from her vantage point, over the top of the door she could only see the dark arm of a coated figure of someone else standing outside.

"Be off with you, dead man. My mistress Gwen is in her grave now, so leave this house in peace," Henry said to the mystery person standing on her dark doorstep at night.

Jennifer then heard the person outside speak, but just couldn't make out any of the words spoken, from where she stood.

"Mrs. Chong owns the place now. Chong, not Adams. Now, sling-yer-hook back to hell," Henry retorted with an overture of malice in his country accent.

Again the person outside spoke with manly tones, but with words that just escaped her hearing capacity

."I'm not afraid of a bag of bones like you. I'm not an Adams, so I don't fear you. Nor do I live here, so be gone back to your cold tomb." With that Henry shut and bolted the front door.

Jen turned away, hidden behind the walls of the west wing corridor. She didn't want Henry to notice her and needed time to cogitate on what she had just witnessed.

Jen crept back to her bedroom and locked the door behind her, putting the key on the bedside cabinet, next to the lamp. Then, she stopped, hurried back to the dressing table, took the chair and hooked that under the doorknob, like they did in thriller movies.

She returned, scrambled into bed and reached out to turn off the bedside lamp. Then withdrew her hand, no, she'd sleep with the light on for a while. Jen kept her t-shirt on, feeling cold for some reason. Even though it felt warm inside and out, she snuggled down under her covers once more.

"I'll ask him tomorrow." She promised herself to talk to Henry about the nocturnal visitor to Adams House, in the morning. She fell into a fitful sleep thirty minutes later and dreamed of men in frilly hats chasing her through the woods by the house.

* * * *

Outside in the all encompassing dark, something looked up at the corner windows of the bedroom that had once been Gwen Adams's room and hissed with ancient pent-up frustration.

Chapter Five

Village & Visitor

Jen, being an early bird, was showered, dressed and scrambled egg fed by half-past eight. She stuffed her every expanding ring of keys, cell phone and purse into her handbag and headed out the front door, toward the garage.

The day was mild and sunny, with an autumnal nip in the air. She zipped up her jacket and looked around the grounds for Henry as she walked. Her staff-of-one had already opened the garage door and had left a local map of the area, marked with post-it note instructions detailing the route to the village and beyond.

She popped upstairs to the apartment above the garage, but it was empty. She saw only the few remaining bits of furniture covered with dust sheets.

"Note to self, buy shares in a dust-sheet company," she said as she walked back downstairs to the garage.

Jen really wanted to quiz Henry about last night's late visitor. She half-decided to visit White Lodge, since she'd have to drive past it to leave her estate. She hoped her Mrs. Chong side hadn't talked her out of it by then.

The Aston Martin purred like an adult lion, as she started the classic car up. It had its original AM radio, but this only picked up static and whistles. So, she put on some loud Duffy on her cell phone and wedged it a little way in the crease of the passenger seat.

Jen wondered if the stick shift flicked up to reveal a James Bond red button for an ejector seat, but sadly it didn't. Humming along to Duffy, she swung the car out of the garage and bombed it down her private road toward White Lodge.

Jennifer knocked on Henry's front door, but received no answer, not even a dog bark. She headed then to un-padlock the gates while sucking her teeth in thought. She'd catch up with Henry later she promised herself.

* * * *

She only passed two cars and a tractor on the way to the village, which Jen was most grateful for. She parked in the nearest pub's parking lot, climbed out and had to remember to manually lock the doors of the vehicle.

The sun had risen slightly warming the mid-September morning and Jen took a good look around the village and smirked. It reminded her of the country soap opera she had watched last night and she wondered where all the lipstick lesbians lived.

Jen walked under the sign for the pub fixed to a roadside gray stone wall, named the King's Head. The garage stood next to it and across the two lane road was the Post Office and Village Shop, a butchers', a café, the bank and then a gap to another pub called the Cromwell Arms.

"Arms, heads? What a violent little place," she muttered. With a few hellos to older bemused villagers, she headed for the bank first. Only to find it closed, she glanced at her watch to find it was still only ten to nine and the sign stuck to the window stated it opened at nine today.

So Jen headed into the half-full tea room café, walked up to the counter and ordered a cup of tea and a bacon sandwich, because her stomach craved meat. She hadn't eaten any since she had arrived in England, and more importantly it smelled intoxicating.

"You visiting then, dear?" the plump, middle-aged woman behind the counter, with a frizzy brown perm asked.

"No, I guess I kinda live here now." Jen smiled back and paid for her food with some money she had exchanged at Heathrow airport.

"Do you?" The cafe owner with a real need of a hair straightener asked incredulously. "Where?"

"Up at Adams House, I'm Gwen Adam's great niece," Jen replied, her accent beamed out foreign stranger, in this quaint English village.

"Sit down, and I'll bring yer food over," the woman said tartly and turned to grill the bacon.

A little taken aback, Jen turned to find a free table, only to find all the customers in the cafe staring at her like she was an alien from Mars with three heads.

Jen walked with an uncomfortable feeling running down from her neck to her lower spine, toward the front of the cafe to find a free table with only two seats that looked out onto the street. Her tea and sandwich followed five minutes later. She felt sure the back of her head would catch fire from all the eyes boring into it from behind.

"Thanks," she said to the cafe owner as she put down the plate before her and a mug of tea to her left, dropping a spoon and white packets of sugar next to it without any pleasantries.

Jen breathed in, ignored the rudeness of frizzy hair and dove into her bacon sandwich with gusto. Her late grandfather used to make her these in secret after her parents had left for work. She played with her healthy cereal until they had left. Then grandpa would cook them both bacon sarnies as he called them. Then he'd walk her to school, having retired from the firm he built in his late fifties. Her grandfather let Jen's parents take over the import/export business he had started up, when he and Nana had emigrated to America just after the Second World War

"Have you met him yet?" A voice of a greasy looking young man in unkempt clothes asked, shocking her from her fond memories, as he sat down opposite her.

"Sorry, what, who?" Jennifer asked, confused and pissed at the unwanted intrusion.

"Old Cromwellian Cromity, lady." The greasy, full-bearded man, with a young face underneath asked with wild blue eyes.

"Saul, leave the poor woman alone," frizzy hair from behind the counter said.

"Look, I'm not really sure what you want, but I need to visit the bank now, okay?" Jennifer pushed back her wooden chair with a squeal of protest, when Saul flashed a hand across the table and grabbed hold of her jacket sleeve, knocking her half-drunk tea onto the floor in the process.

"I've met him, out in the woods at night. Told me stuff he did, all about you bloody high and mighty Adams," the obviously deranged or high on something young man snarled.

"Please, let go of my arm!"

Jennifer stood, but Saul stood with her, twisting his grip on her sleeve.

"Saul, let the young lady go." A voice next to them said in a mild but firm voice. The man grabbed Saul's arm and pulled if off Jennifer's arm. "I think you better go back to your Nan's house now and have a lie down."

Both Jennifer and Saul turned to see a tall, blonde man in his mid-thirties suited and booted, holding tightly onto the young man's forearm. Saul sneered, shrugged off the taller man's grip and fled from the cafe.

"You okay?" the handsome man who had just rescued her

asked.

"I think so." She smiled. "That was a little intense for so early in the morning."

"Indeed." He smiled back at her. "I'm Paul Jordan by the way and by your lovely accent, you must be Miss Adams of Adams House."

Jordan's smiled widened to reveal perfect white teeth and Jennifer couldn't help feel an instant twinge of attraction.

"News travels fast around here." Jennifer reached out a hand and then shook hands. She remembered to add, "Thanks."

"It's a small village and Henry also called me to give me the heads-up. I'm your friendly local bank manager by the way."

"Ah, pleased to meet you. I was just about to pay you a visit."

Now, this was more like the English male she wanted to get attention from, not scruffy vagrants or weirdo lawyers.

"Shall we retire to my office in the bank then? The service here leaves a lot to be desired sometimes." He smiled, not bothering to lower his voice as he insulted the cafe.

"I heard that," frizzy hair from behind her counter barked.

"Maggie, the only hope this place has of getting a Michelin star is if someone throws a burning tire through the window," Paul Jordon said back before he led Jennifer out of the cafe toward the bank, both with wicked grins on their faces.

* * * *

"I would say they get better with age, but I would be lying," Paul Jordan said. He sat in a low, comfy chair, he had for touchy-feely staff appraisals, opposite Jennifer, as they chatted about the local villagers.

"That's good to know." She smiled back which wasn't much of a task with the bank manager's handsome features. "So, have you lived here long then?"

"Five years and still I'm very much the outsider from the Big City."

"London?"

"No, Swindon." He chuckled. "A town with more people than animals is a city to most of the cave-dwellers of Oxsteaden."

"Why are you here then?" she asked, tugging off her jacket, her subconscious mind doing flirtatious things behind her back. Jen gazed at Paul's blue eyes, appraising him from head-to-toe, licked her lips and pouted without realizing she did.

"I needed a change. My wife died of cervical cancer six years ago and this came up. It seemed a perfect chance to leave some bad memories behind." Paul folded his arms and stared at the table between them.

"I'm so sorry to hear that."

"It's fine really. Time heals all they say, which is bollocks really." He looked into her eyes and Jen sensed a vulnerable side behind his strong, manly exterior.

"Bollocks, eh. That's a new one for my vocabulary. Is it used in polite society conversations?" She half-grinned trying to change the tone of their chat.

"Probably best not to." He laughed and then clapped his hands on his knees. "So, what can we do for you today, Jennifer?"

"Henry says you pay all the house's bills from a special fund held here. I was counting on you to give me the details of the phone company, maybe an old bill so I can get wireless internet connection for the study, maybe even satellite TV?"

"Well, I can arrange all that for you if you give me the details. " He picked up a pad and pen from the table.

"Really? That would be awesome if you could because once I can get on the web I can order other stuff online." Jen's head bobbed up and down like a happy puppy.

"Would be my pleasure."

"Banks back in the U.S. don't normally do this type of service for their clients, so why is this bank different?"

Jen found herself leaning forward and slapped herself mentally, because it gave Paul an eyeful of her cleavage in the deep cut V-neck top she wore.

"Banks here normally don't offer this kind of service either, but we are paid a retainer of the interest of the Adams House maintenance fund to run it. That and it sounds more fun than my usual days work here. Just think of it as a welcoming present to make up for the unpleasantness at the cafe and..." His voice trailed off into a mumble and his eyes flicked down to his polished leather shoes.

"And what?"

"And it gives me an excuse to come visit you at, erm your lovely house one day soon, you know." He cleared his throat as his voice raised an octave. "The hands on approach."

"We better get started then, Mister Jordan." Jen gave her cutest smile, knowing she had this strong sweet man eating out the palm of her hand.

* * * *

"The post office come shop sells the basics, but if you want Oreos and such other American fare. There is a Tesco's not far along the Royalist Road, half-a-mile past the train station." Paul advised from the open doorway of the bank, as he ushered Jennifer out the door.

"So, you're an expert on North American food also. Well, you have such hidden depths for a bank manager?" she teased. *Teased? She was in full loose woman mode.*

"Yes, hot dogs, chili dogs, Twinkies, cotton candy and the afore-mentioned Oreos. I am a U.S. culinary king."

"I can see you are," she replied stepping away from him, before his aftershave made her do something really silly like ask him out on a date.

"Good luck with the food shopping." He raised his fist and gave it a shake of good luck toward her, putting on a fake serious voice and look.

"I'll wait for your call." She smiled back retreating to the edge of the curb and then added, "About the internet etcetera."

"Yes, and if you need any more help, just ring. We could discuss it over a pub lunch one day?" He ventured, making nervous wrinkles in his forehead.

"Maybe. One day; rain check, okay?"

He nodded like a dashboard dog ornament, and she gave a small lustful smile to keep him keen before turning and crossing the road.

* * * *

"Rain check, now is that good or bad?" Paul Jordan wondered as he wandered back into the bank.

* * * *

Across the road Jen's cheeks hurt from the smile fixed like some botched plastic surgery on her face. Then she realized she had crossed the road for no reason at all and crossed back a little further along to the post office and shop. With a spring in her step, like she wore winged boots of the gods, she gathered up two metal baskets full of food and women's products in the small, but well-stocked shop.

* * * *

Jennifer saved the trip to the larger supermarket for another day and drove back to her new home, with the windows open and Bon Jovi playing loud from her cell phone.

Henry still wasn't at home, so she drove back up, parked the Aston right outside the front door and took her plastic bags bulging with ladies products, food and UK's Cosmo into the kitchen. She found herself whistling show tunes as she put the food into the cupboard and meat from the butchers into the fridge and freezer compartments.

She opened a packet of chips she had bought and headed to the first floor bathroom to drop off the other non-food supplies. Then she headed back downstairs to the study, munching on the flavorful crisps to grab post-its and a marker to explore the first floor (or second floor to her).

"Taste and look like chips to me," she stated, looking at the back of the packet of Salt 'n Vinegar crisps.

* * * *

Jennifer spent the afternoon exploring the rooms upstairs and found out she could easily sleep in a different bed each night for over a fortnight.

"I wonder if Paul could keep up with me." She teased herself by speaking the naughty thoughts that raced through her single, available mind.

In the last room on the second floor of the east wing, she found a door with a staircase behind it leading up. Most of the second floor rooms she had skipped past for another look on another day. The cobwebbed stairs led up to the hugest attic she had ever seen, cluttered and divided into junk filled rooms, not by walls but the old furniture and old castoff bits of people lives, now long deceased.

It looked like no one had been up there in years and Jen followed a path made in the piles of moldy curtains; tea chest, sea chest, army trunks, wardrobes and old pictures stacked everywhere.

Halfway across the attic she found a pile of swords, just lying on a blanket, waiting for a long forgotten war to break out. Near a supporting wall and behind a First World War officer's uniform on a mannequin, almost hidden from view stood a door.

"Sorry, general," she said, putting her arms around the mannequin's waist as she picked it up and deposited it elsewhere, upsetting a colony of woodlice.

The door looked almost the color of the dirty brickwork and had a black latch and padlock on it to keep it barred from the curious.

Feeling thirsty, dusty and hot, she decided to curtail her explorations for the afternoon and head back to the kitchen. She was once again shocked to find it was nearly six o'clock and set about fixing herself a large plate of Spaghetti Bolognaise. In fact she prepared enough for two more meals.

Once it cooled, and after she had gobbled up her portion with gusto, she put them in Tupperware in the freezer for another day. She could never get used to cooking for one. Being a chef she had always made meals for four like in her cookbooks.

She poured another glass of Burgundy and headed off to the sitting room to watch some TV and catch that soap, she was secretly now getting into.

Only cop shows and reality rubbish followed. Finding her second glass of red wine empty, she headed back to the kitchen to have a third.

She made it back from the kitchen as far as the main hall, before on a whim she skipped down the east wing corridor, patting her cell phone in her pocket. She hurried to the ballroom and flung both doors open wide, sipping at her wine, as not to spill it.

She wandered like a giddy schoolgirl to the raised area at the end, where the bands and musicians must have played. Then she spotted the large gramophone in the corner at the back of the stage. Jen clicked her fingers, pointed to it and with another sip of the intoxicating wine, made a B-line for it. She lifted the lid to find an old 78 record sitting on the turntable.

"The Vienna Waltz," she said and frowned. Classical music wasn't her thing at all; she loved pop and girly singers.

She put the needle on the outside smooth edge of the record and cranked the handle twenty or so times as she drained her third glass of wine. Then clicked a switch that set the record turning and an acoustic peel of dusty crackles came from the large tuba shaped speaker.

Then the music started, and she recognized the tune from a few old TV commercials. Quickly she put down her empty glass on the stage area and jumped onto the polished wood floor, to dance.

The creaky sounding music soon grew to fill the ballroom, as Jen spun this way and that, holding out an imaginary frock like she was some American Civil War Southern Belle. She laughed and pranced, smiled and sadly drooled a little as the old music swept her away. She could almost see the dancers of the past twirling and swaying beside her, until the record ran slower and slower to a stop. She stopped with it and once more felt alone in this great house, her forebears had constructed.

With a sad, little smile, she headed back to the sitting room and dozed off in front of some cooking show.

Jennifer came to at about half past ten, her bleary eyes staring at a naked man's butt going for it big-time on top of a very willing woman. She watched the late night film for a while and was rewarded for her effort of will to stay awake, by more butt scenes from the dishy lead actor.

The film finished at half past eleven. With a pit stop at the kitchen to collect a small cold bottle of mineral water from the fridge, she headed for her bed.

She managed to brush her teeth, but any other moisturizing chores flew out of the window, as she hopped into bed naked and turned off the light. Yet, she didn't sleep, the raunchy film and images of Paul, her personal banker kept springing to mind.

Jen's hand, palm against her skin, slowly moved down from her chest over her taught tummy and down through her trimmed pubic hair to her already moist opening. Images of Paul on top of her, confused with the six-pack, great assed actor from the film, made her fingers delve, stop, rub and circle in time with her elevated breathing.

She swallowed hard and played slowly, something George never got the hang of and built up the passion and pace. She used both hands now and the pressure of sexual release neared its peak.

Her left hand traveled up her perspiring body and lightly pulled at her erect nipples, as she arched her back and readied herself for the final crescendo. Her right hand was working at blurry speed beneath the sheets, until a strangled cry and long exhaling gasp, cum cry signaled the waves of orgasm that wracked her spasmening body.

She lay with her eyes closed panting for at least five minutes, her blankets pushed down to her belly button, as the darkness caressed her naked torso and neck.

She was about to reach for her water and end her self-love-making-session, when she heard the faint raps of the door knocker onto the brass plate on the front door. She stiffened to strain to listen as the continuing knocks beat steadily on the front entrance to Adams House.

A sudden post-masturbatory guilt hit Jen. She climbed out of bed and switched on her bedside lamp. She dressed quickly into her old clothes and put on a baggy jumper to cover the fact she wore no bra.

Still the knocker beat upon her front door and with isolated trepidation Jennifer rushed along the first floor west wing corridor to the balcony landing over the entrance hall. As usual the hall still had its lights on and she stopped at the top of the stairs. Her knees trembled from her recent orgasm or just fear.

The door was strong, about four inches thick and had three set of bolts across it. She inched down the stairs by the wall holding onto the banister for support as she descended. Her bare feet walked down on the wood part of the steps as the pounding on the knocker continued to grow louder without rest or loss of beat.

Jennifer took a long breath and reminded herself of the time she had kicked that Central Park purse snatcher in the family jewels and continued across the cold wooden floor to the front door.

As soon as she reached the cross inlaid in the parquet floor, the rapping of the door knocker ceased its chilling persistent peel.

She stopped and waited, the house waited and outside on the doorstep someone else waited. Then chastising her irrational fear, she moved over the cross and peered through the peep hole on tip-toes. She blinked a watery eye and looked out onto the well-lit entrance porch beyond.

She pulled her eye back immediately in shock, because standing before the front door was a man in a black circular hat, showing only his tall frame and handsome thin protruding cheeks, with wet dark eyes that danced like wildfire.

Jen ran back to her bedroom, locked the door behind her, dove into bed and pulled the bedcovers over her head. Still dressed, she gasped for air because of her nocturnal run through the large house and spoke only one word aloud, before sleep finally took her two hours later.

"Cromity."

Chapter Six

This Old House

"So, who was that at the door the other night?" Jennifer asked the back of Henry's head as she walked up behind him carrying a brown paper bag in her left hand.

Henry Greenwood stabbed his spade into the summer bed he was clearing of faded blooms and turned to face the new mistress of Adams House. "Depends?" He replied, taking an old, red hanky from the pocket of his cords and mopped his large brow.

"Depends on what?" Jennifer asked, then waved the bag at him."Oh, this is for you, a homemade cheese and apple chutney sandwich."

"My answer depends on what you're willing to hear, Miss Jennifer." He reached out and took the offering with a nod. "Thank you."

"Let's say I'm more open now, to other explanations," she replied, picking her words tactfully.

"Seen the bugger, have ya?" Henry frowned and snarled. "Didn't talk to the swine, did you?"

"I peeked through the peep hole in the front door. He gave me the shivers." Jennifer put her right hand on her hip and tilted her head to that side. It was time for some proper answers.

"I bet he did, that old Roundhead rascal."

"So, he's the resident ghost here then?"

"He's a ghost by day and some sort of revenant vampire at night. That's why nobody has ever got rid of him. If you refuse him permission to enter the house, you are safe, 'cause once he gets inside, you're a goner." Henry peeked inside the sandwich bag, a little embarrassed by the words he just had to utter.

"But who is he, and why is he haunting Adams House?" Jen couldn't quite believe the conversation she was having. She had wanted a new life and new beginning, but this was a bit extreme.

"He dates back to the original house that stood here. He was of Cromwell's top Roundhead captains during the English Civil War. He burnt down the old house it's said, killing two of Sir Walter

Adams's daughters in the process. Cromity was caught and buried alive in one of his ancestor's tombs. Took him a month to die they say. Each day Walter and his sons took turns at his resting place listening to his screams of bloody revenge." Henry paused to blow his nose and then put his hanky away.

"So, how did he come back from the dead?" Jen asked, wondering if this really was the new life she had hankered for. It was not, as-they-say, as advertised in the brochure.

"Nobody knows, Miss Jennifer. After the month was up, no sounds came from the tomb, so they broke the led seals on it and opened it up to find no body inside."

"Where'd he go, did someone rescue him?"

"No. I said they found no body inside, but what they did find was a shadow. A man shaped silhouette on the bottom of the tomb and it wasn't even a sunny day. No torch or candle could cast it off and no scrubbing could rub it off. So, they put a cross inside and buried the tomb under a hill of soil and planted holly bushes on top to keep his evil inside."

"Did that help?"

"For sixty years no one saw sight of him again; until at last a great-grand-daughter to the late Sir Walter was born in the new house built on the cinders and foundations of the old one. When she turned sixteen, old Cromity appeared at her window each night or knocked upon the front door, begging to be let in. In the end the silly girl charmed by his words and looks let him in, because no one had spoken of him since his bloody death. They found her dead one morning in bed, drained of blood and on the wall written in her blood was written 'Cromity wants his house back', or words to that effect."

"So, he only bothers ladies of the house then. Why is that?"

"Nobody knows or cares much to ask him. Every Adams female in the house over the centuries has been targeted by him. That's why when your grandparents found out they had a baby due after the war, they moved to America just in case it was a girl to be born."

"But it was a boy, my father, so why not move back?"

"Dunno, they had a new life among the living I suppose. This place here is old and steeped in blood, Jennifer. If you're gonna stay here, you gotta promise me not to talk to Cromity?"

Henry moved closer and took one of her hands in his.

"Well, you have no fear of that Henry, talking to a dead guy isn't on my top ten list of things to do."

"Good to hear it, miss." He smiled, as Jennifer's cell phone began to ring.

"Excuse me." She opened the phone and apologized to her gardener.

"Not at all, got things to do myself." Henry's smile faded to a frown. He turned and walked off to find Purdy chasing hares in the back field.

"Hello?"

"It's Paul from the bank here. I got some good news for you. The engineers are coming to you on Monday to sort your internet needs and add extra phone lines."

"Thanks, awesome news, Paul, thanks."

"I'll be there too, just in case things go tits-up, which I'm sure they won't," he added quickly, not quite believing he put tits into a conversation with a valued customer.

"Great job, Paul. What time?"

"About tenish?"

"Cool, then I can do you." She coughed over her Freudian slip. "Some lunch," Jennifer added in a squeaky, embarrassed voice.

"It's a date then." He paused. "Well, not a date as such, a business lunch."

"Sounds fun either way," she teased, "thanks again, Paul."

"It does, see you next Monday then, okay?"

Jen said her goodbyes and closed her phone and took a long deep breath before she turned and skipped back to the backdoor of the house.

* * * *

Jennifer spoke to her friend and agent, Valerie in the afternoon. She imparted tales of wild sexual conquests and more importantly a possible BBC cooking series in the future, since she was already in the UK.

With a contented smile and thoughts of Cromity pushed to the back of her mind, she explored the upper reaches of the library and found an original Mrs. Beaton and some unfathomable tome about Tudor cooking.

Jen took them and a few other cookbooks down to the library reading desk and found about a hundred and one recipes for turbot, turnips and Lark's tongues.

She found a pad of paper in the bottom drawer and a silver and gold-plated pen as well as a golden key, some old copper pennies and a rubber band ball.

Jen sat bolt upright on the chair and cried, "Aha!"

As an idea for a new cookbook suddenly hit her like a bolt of muse enthused lightening. On the top of the page over her scribbled notes she wrote:

Pop goes Tudor, 21st Century Asian Fusion re-workings of classic English dishes of the Tudor Age by Jennifer Adams (Not fucking Chong)

Note: All old cookbooks, revised with new covers with Jenny Adams as Author....!!!!!

Jen spent the rest of the afternoon looking through the various cookbooks she had found, noting on the pad, pages of recipes that she could update and modernize. She tittered, wondering if there was anywhere in Upstate New York that could get Lark's tongues or Ginny Fowl?

She worked on until half past five, when her stomach protested. She gathered up the cook books and notes and took them to the study. She put them next to her laptop, with a promise to type up a book proposal for Valerie sometime next week.

Saturday, if the weather held, she'd get up earlish, make a packed lunch and spend the day exploring the grounds of Adams House.

Feeling lazy, she took some chicken from the fridge and cooked up a quick lemon chicken stir-fry for dinner, which she ate in her immense, lonely dining room. Then she headed back to the sitting room to watch the rustic farm folk of her new favorite TV show. Maybe she could reclassify this as the Television or audio visual room. Once she had the internet up, she'd order one of those immense fuck-off-and-die wall TV's the size of a small cinema.

After that, she couldn't find much on to watch, but kept the TV on for background noise, as she read more of the book she had started in the States.

By nine she had enough of reading and didn't want any wine, so she went around the empty house closing the odd curtain or window shutter. She also had a mental note to a get a DVD player and mega-sound system or two for the place.

Jen found herself in the huge conservatory or arboretum or whatever it was called and wandered around the exotic tender plants and flowers. The blackness of night pressed against the glass frames of the plant festooned place, as she wondered at the different smells, hues and leaves of the vegetation.

From the roof of the house, through the glass ceiling of the conservatory, dead eyes watched her progress through the exotics.

* * * *

The knocking at twelve midnight, that woke her from her dreamless sleep, seemed to her half-awake ears much closer this time. Jen shivered and sat up in her four-poster-bed, which in its confines, she felt safe because of its enclosing design.

Knock, knock.

The rapping of a fist on wood came, yet not as distant as her front door. No, it was coming from her adjacent great-aunt's room. Jennifer pulled back her covers and climbed out of bed. Instantly she felt the cold of the September night on her bare skin, spine and nipples.

She turned on her bedside lamp and pulled on a long butt covering cardigan and wrapped the belt around her to keep out the chill. She moved on bare soles across the carpet to her bedroom door and listened; her right ear pressed as close to the wood as possible, without actually touching the grainy panels.

Knock, knock came the rapping again.

With a deep breath, she unlocked and opened her bedroom door. She groaned inwardly as it suddenly released a loud long hinge squeal. It took all of her re-found Adams courage to venture into the dark hallway.

The window at the end of the west wing corridor revealed nothing but the night, so she made her reluctant feet move forward. Soon she stood in front of her late Great Aunt Gwen's bedroom.

She turned the handle in unison to the next set of knocks, entered the un-shuttered bedroom and turned on the light. Icy cold assaulted her feet at once and spread rapidly up her bare legs and thighs. A thin layer of frost coated the outside windows of the bedroom, yet there was no frost on the corridor window just outside. As she moved further in past her beneficiary's death bed, the freezing cold flew up her thighs and deep into the openings in her panties.

On shivering legs and with the arctic rape of her lower abdomen, she spotted some words written in the outside frost that clung to each window pane.

She staggered closer, her feet numb blocks of ice upon her involuntary shaking pins, as the cold air reached up her spine to grasp it in a Jack Frost crushing embrace.

Truth whilst come out was written on one pane. *Weft wood*

I layeth, read another, *open thee the locked highest room*. The last sentence chilled Jen's already frozen body to the core. *Let me come infïde.*

Jennifer turned on frozen legs and ran from the room. Her peripheral vision caught a face staring at her from the other window of the bedroom. Once outside, she slammed her great aunt's bedroom door shut and turned to look at the end corridor window.

The icy touch departed her, yet from her lips issued a scream, the like of which she hadn't wailed since pre-pubescence. The thin-cheeked revenant, known as Silas Cromity, floated at the corridor window.

"What do you want?" Jennifer screamed at the ghastly apparition at the window.

"Only to tell thee my tale, then I will leave you in peace," the oddly rich voice from outside the window said.

The sound of his voice was too much for Jennifer. She rushed back into her bedroom and locked it. Then ran over and jumped into her bed. Pulled the covers over her head and shivered until near dawn.

* * * *

Jennifer sat bolt upright in bed the covers falling off her naked torso; the light of Saturday morning pawed at the edges of her bedroom shutters, to be let in.

She looked at her naked chest, puzzled. On the chair across the semi-gloom of her bedroom laid her cardigan. Though she had no recollection of taking it off after her ghostly visitation, or turning off her bedside lamp.

She gingerly climbed out of bed, her legs warm from the heavy covers and opened the shutters to let the early morning light enter her room. Her face screwed up from the brightness; the frown lines on her forehead were also lines of confusion.

Had the talk of Cromity with Henry just brought about the vivid nightmares or had the events of last night been real. Ignoring the cardigan for some untrusting reason, she pulled on a sweatshirt, sweatpants and slippers and headed to the next bedroom to check it.

Inside the corner bedroom it was light and very warm, No sign of frost or writing remained on the window panes. On closer inspections, not even any smudges of the writing remained on the outside of the glass, nor any other finger marks.

The frost written words remained fresh in her mind, so she hurried next door to write them down on the envelope her plane tickets had been sent in. Thinking and biting her thumbnail, she went and took a long, hot shower to try to clear away the cobwebs of the night before.

While in the shower, she decided the attic would be on the agenda after breakfast. That was the only locked room she had found in the house so far. Then a trip out into the woods and the rest of the grounds to see what secrets this place held for her.

She had a quick coffee and plain toast. With her keys she headed for the garage to find something to bash the padlock in the attic open with. She could of course ask Henry for the key, but she wanted to keep everything under-the-radar for the time being.

After George had cheated on her, she vowed never to trust any man more than 90% again.

She found no hammers in the garage, but on a work bench sat a hand held hatchet. Its rear flat end could be used as a makeshift hammer. She saw no sign of Henry or his dog on her trip to and from the garage and absently wondered if the old guy got the weekends off or not.

By the time she had reached the locked door in the attic, she already felt hot and out of breath from climbing so many steps.

"Who needs a gym with the steps in his house," she stated to the army-dressed mannequin, as she took off the hatchet's blade cover.

Jen turned the little one-handed axe, so the blade faced toward her, contravening at least five health and safety guidelines. She aimed and swung at the padlock. She missed it entirely and nearly bashed her right kneecap in the process.

Changing her gait to a legs apart stance, Jennifer swung the hatchet again, connecting with the top of the padlock with a hand-jarring whack. The bottom of the padlock fell into a box of plates and the U-shaped part spun twice and fell off also.

"Fuck you, George," she muttered. Laying down the hatchet on an old sideboard, Jennifer pulled the hidden door open to reveal a small room containing only picture canvases.

A naked bulb above her head shone light in the dusty dirty room as she moved toward it. Swatting away at the cobwebs, she entered the musty smelling attic room. Leaning against one wall covered with a sackcloth stood the backs of some picture canvases.

Jen bent down on her haunches, leaned back the first one and pulled the rotten covering to find an ancient looking portrait of two young ladies in white Venetian type shifts, aged in their mid-teen years. Both looked angelic and pink-cheeked and beautiful for their age. Jennifer carefully put it against the other wall and picked up the next portrait that revealed to her a familiar-faced handsome man in the uniform of a Parliamentarian Officer from the English Civil War. This was unmistakably Silas Cromity as he looked in life.

The last portrait had suffered from dampness and insects, but still showed a family scene of love. Cromity stood with a beautiful wife at his side and his two daughters, faces green from wear, stood before them.

Cromity had been a loving family man before his fall unto death and the creature he became. Jen wondered *why the revenant had wanted her to see him in his former existence?*

Jen scratched an itch behind her right ear, then left the locked room and pulled the dummy across the closed door like nothing had happened. She headed back downstairs to the study and found a sketch pad in a desk drawer and two pencils in the top one. With a detour to the kitchen to grab a small bottle of water, she was going to pad back to the front door to leave the house.

She immediately slapped her forehead, unlocked the back door and left that way instead. She made her way through the herb and then the vegetable gardens, through the large formal gardens and headed around the house toward the west woods.

Her mouth felt dry from the dusty air, so she broke the seal, popped the lid of the water and drank as she headed across the grass. Then down the hot-summer yellowed lawn that sloped away from the house. She took a deep breath and entered the woods (her woods) for the first time.

She felt glad of the late September sunshine, which cast dappled light through the leaves above her. They were turning red now, some brown, but some were still of varying hues of green.

She walked twenty feet in and then sat on an old fallen log to sketch a rough map of the area she had explored. She added the house, garage, lake, road, gate and finally White Lodge to the map. Satisfied with the scale of the rough drawing, Jen then added an arrow from the back of the house to her current position.

She hopped off her log and brushed off her behind. Then she wandered straight as the tree trunks would allow, through the west woods.

After ten minutes the house had been lost from view and after another five minutes she came to a small clearing.

At the dead epicenter was a risen mound, not quite a hill, with wild holly growing around its top like a crown of thorns. Jennifer gazed at the earthly resting place of Silas Cromity, mortal and immortal enemy of the Adams line.

"So, here you rest, or not in your case," she said quietly to the grassy mound, meted with holly.

Above her the sun was lost behind a long cloud and the atmosphere emanating from the woods felt so different suddenly, not cold, but like an electric storm was on the way.

A crashing in the undergrowth and ferns caused her to spin around to locate the incoming sound. Something headed her way from the confines of the woods, something unseen.

A bush shook not more than ten feet away, causing her to involuntary step backwards. A barbed holly leaf pricked her left hand in the palm as she reached out behind her.

"Son-of-a-bitch." She whipped her hand back to suck on her pricked skin as something ran from the ferns right toward her.

"Purdy, come back here you, daft, old bitch," the gruff call of Henry Greenwood said, not far behind.

Purdy stood before Jennifer, all four paws firmly planted growling deep from within her throat at the new American mistress of Adams House.

"Come away," Henry called, entering the clearing from behind a large sycamore tree. Jen went to move and then saw Purdy rush over to circle around Henry's legs. "What the bloody hell are you doing here?" Now, Henry shouted at her. His face didn't look like he was in the greatest of moods.

"Like, I own the place." Jen heard herself reply, regretting it immediately. She needed Mrs. Chong's almost silent tact and diplomacy, not the ball-breaking Miss Adams.

"You got hundreds of acres of land on the estate. How come you turned up here, where that old beggar lies?" Henry's voice had toned down from shocked shouts, to just stern simmering displeasure.

"Look, Henry. I don't have to justify where I walk on my land. You ain't family. You're just the old, cranky fellow that came with the house. Get off my back, okay? When I want your help, I'll ask for it." Jen's accent dipped to street level New York, but out of respect for her Adam's family ancestors didn't resort to cussing yet.

"Sorry, Miss Adams. I overstepped the mark, but it was just concern for your safety. This is his resting place, or would be if he didn't go wandering around after dark. Your great aunt told me to look after ye, and that's what I intend to do, even though it may get on your nerves at times."

Jen looked at him. He stared back into her eyes, until she cracked a grown, as her grand pap used to call it. A grown, was the look when your frown cracked and a grin started to show; he could always snap her out of her teenage sulks.

"I appreciate the concern, Henry. I really do, but this has gone far enough. I don't want to hear his name mentioned again. It's over. Finished. 'A new broom sweeps clear', as my old dad used to say. Enough of the ghosts from Adams's House past no more, okay? I came here to start afresh after my shitty divorce. I don't need this kinda crap."

Jen put her hands on her hips and stared at Henry, anger raging inside her now. No man was going to stop her from doing what she wanted ever again. The frosty panes the other night must have been a dream and the man at the door, was just a man.

"I understand and I will drop the subject, Miss Jennifer. But even though I don't talk about it and you don't want to listen: he won't forget." Henry pointed toward the mound, turned and ushered Purdy away with him.

Jen watched Henry go, turning this way and that in agitation, like she had red ants in her sneakers; her gaze finally settled on the mound topped with holly.

"You handled that situation superbly, Jen. Congratulations. I'm sure a seat on the UN is waiting for you." Jennifer picked up a fallen branch and threw it as hard as she could into the holly bushes that circled the top of the mound, before she stormed off northwards through the woods.

An hour later, after getting hot, bothered and a bit sniffy from the flora, she exited the woods and headed back to the house. Green-crap from the bark of the old trees covered her jeans, and her heels hurt like she had a blister or two coming on.

She went straight upstairs, drew herself a hot, steaming bubble bath and played tunes from her phone as her aching limbs relaxed in the tub. She stayed in until the water became too cold and her fingers looked like they had been melted in prune juice. She quickly towel-dried her hair, then twirled it into a pigtail, as she had no visitors to worry about and dressed into new fresh clothes, which she was rapidly running out of.

Heading back downstairs, she fried up an eggy-bread, bacon and grated cheese sandwich and washed it down with two glasses of white wine from the fridge. Not in the mood for exploring, inside or outside, she headed to the TV room, channel-hopped the few stations she had, before she found an old black and white Hayley Mills film and curled up on the couch to watch it.

By the end of the film and her third glass of wine, she dismissed the gaunt man at the door as probably a friend of that strange, scruffy lad she had met in the café. She figured the constant mentioning of ghouls and vampires had sparked her subconscious fears into overdrive. *Shit, her therapist would have a field day with her over this.* With a promise of rational thought, hard evidence and the odd image in her head of Paul Jordan naked, she drew a line in the mental sand.

Only sports and news followed the old film, so she wandered into the pool room to play and try to make the time hasten along until Monday, when she'd get the internet up and running and see the handsome, widowed bank manager again. She found no pool balls so she played reds against colors with the snooker ones, taking turns against herself. As an only child she had grown used to her own company and finding things to do alone.

Darts followed for a few throws after four long games of pool on the immense table, but half of her throws hit the wall. For the safety of her listed building, she stopped.

A call from Valerie in the States lasting for over an hour wasted some more free time. She felt good to hear a friendly voice again and told her all about Paul, but nothing about Cromity.

"Well, I better let you go, Val. I'm thinking of your phone bill now."

"Don't sweat it, sweetie-pie. I'm calling from your apartment, so it's your bill, babes," Valerie informed her, with a riotous laugh that ended up sounding like a kicked mule.

"Bitch!"

"Bank guy's ho!"

"Laters, honey."

"Laters, unless bank guy has a brother, then I'm on the next plane over there, sister."

"I'll ask. Bye," Jen stated with the phone cutting off.

"'Better?" Valerie asked, and the call from America ended.

With a rueful smile and pouting lips, Jennifer stared at the screen of her phone and tutted. Leaving the Pool Room she headed around to the kitchen to rustle up something naughty for her evening meal.

That night she drank some more and vegged out in front of the TV until she couldn't keep her eyes open anymore. She took a bottle of water up to bed, locked herself in and crashed on top of her covers in her underwear. She didn't wake up until nine the next morning, with a cracking headache and a bottom of the bird-cage for a mouth.

It took a long, hot shower, several cups of sweet tea, and banana sandwiches to get her into any kinda shape to face the day. By then it was already noon and she ate on her concrete balcony, sipping coffee, with her sunglasses on, letting the autumn breeze cool the skin the sun made hot.

On days like this, she felt glad she lived alone and had no one to impress enough to get dressed, so she had a sweatpants day. Her only major achievement was finding the washing machine, by accident, because the front was covered with a fake drawer front to blend in with the other cupboards in the utility room. She put in a few washes and found also a dryer, spare fridge and freezers, which she had just dismissed as cupboards before. The windowless room felt rather cool. By dinner time, she felt like herself again, whoever that was.

She ate her supper of deli meat and salad, followed by a fruit salad and then yogurt to counter the imbalance of her last few fatty meals, and she stayed off the vino. She pampered herself after that and drew another hot bath and dressed in her robe, before she stared at the face in her bathroom cabinet mirror.

"P-P-P." She grinned as memories of her roommate at college washed down over her. Louisa Li had been the ideal girl to bring her out of her quiet bookish inner-self. She too was half-white American, half-Asian in background and the most beautiful woman inside and out Jen had ever met.

Lo had brought out the inner Adams in her, taught her make-up, how to dress hot, not trashy and even how to kiss properly. Jen could feel herself blush as other memories, hidden ones resurfaced.

Louisa Li would have loved the woman she was trying so hard to recapture as much as she'd have loathed the Mrs. Chong she dutifully became. Louisa Li never got old, never saw what Jen became and never left college. A week before graduation, a man walked onto campus with a Heckler & Koch Universal Self-Loading Pistol taped to his back under his shirt. He walked over to the outside tables by the campus cafeteria and shot every non-white face he saw until he ran out of rounds. He shot Louisa Li in the face, as she tried to pull another injured student to safety, killing her instantly.

Jennifer, who had been in the library across campus, hadn't even heard a shot fired. She was already dating the young exciting George at the time. When he proposed six months later, she said, 'yes' and clung to him for over eleven years before she reclaimed inch-by-inch the person she should have been.

"Still works, Lo." Jen smiled, even though tears of sadness for her lost friend rolled down her cheeks and into the sink below. "Pits, pussy and pins."

The first rule of dating was PPP. Louisa had taught her, shaving all three before a date, made you feel in the mood and gave the guy an easier target to aim at downstairs.

Jen let her robe drop and went over to put her left leg on the side of the hot bubbly bath to start the PPP shaving routine. After putting her things in the bathroom cabinet, she found a box of earplugs, grabbed them and padded back to her bedroom. The sun through the end corridor window had set and only purple and lighter smudges of blue remained on the horizon. She put on shorts and a sleeveless nightwear top and tutted again as she looked in the mirror of her walk-in wardrobe.

"Gotta buy some more eye-popping stuff if I'm ever gonna get me a man," Jen stated, pulling down her top and pulling up a shoulder fallen strap.

She headed downstairs, brewed herself a lemon tea and curled up to watch some TV for a while. Feeling both tired and excited about tomorrow Jen headed off to bed at ten and read for half-n-hour. She picked up the earplugs, then put the box on the bed-cover, opened it and then put it down again.

Jen shook her head from side-to-side for a minute, thinking, then took two ear plugs out of the box and shoved them deep into each ear. Then she lay down, reached out and let the night do its worst.

The knocking at her front door came at the stroke of midnight, but she didn't hear it. The cold came to Great Aunt Gwen's room, but with the bedcovers over her neck she didn't feel the creeping cold. She slept well until seven the next morning, snoring loudly for no one to hear.

Chapter Seven

Two Suitors

Jennifer rushed around the large, old house like a whirling-dervish, from bedroom to bathroom, to kitchen for a hasty breakfast, back to the bathroom to brush her teeth again and then into the bedroom to change her outfit for the second time that morning.

Once happy with her breath, armpit and other odors, she walked downstairs to wait for Paul and the phone people, at only ten to nine. She had plenty of time to spare, but didn't want to stray too far from the hall, in case she didn't hear the doorbell.

So she popped into the study quickly and collected some of the old recipe books to scan through while she waited. She went to the breakfast room and put the three weighty cookbooks on the table, while she headed to the net curtain to peer out and check that no one was at her front door yet.

"Must calm down," she muttered, returning to the breakfast table. "I am not a love struck teenager."

Then to prove herself wrong, she went to the closed door that led to the hall and opened it as wide as possible, just to make sure she could hear even an infant tapping on the front door.

Jen played with her long hair and forced herself to sit down and start skimming through the tomes of recipes long out of fashion. Then she stood up, because she had to pee, so she rushed off to the small hall lavatory.

Paul Jordan finally arrived for Jen's nervous bladder's sake ten minutes early. The ringing at the front door pull nearly gave her a seizure. She jumped up from her chair, nearly sending it falling over backwards, ran into the hall before she eased herself into a walk and forced her mind and body to slow down.

Jen reached the closed door, took a deep breath in and out, straightened her clothes with both hands and touched her hair on her forehead at least three times, before she opened the front door. She cast her serenest smile across her pretty small featured face.

"Hi." Paul raised his hand in an awkward, dippy looking way and brought it down quickly. All the witty lines he had rehearsed in the car on the drive up had vanished when he had seen the vision of loveliness of Jennifer Adams standing before him.

"Hi, welcome to Adams House. Come on in."

Even though her heart fluttered in her chest, she could see that he looked even more nervous than her. This made her feel more at ease. He was here now. Now, they only had to wait for the phone engineers to turn up. Yet with Paul here, the internet didn't seem so interesting.

"I got a call from the engineers; they are running ten minutes late," he said, walking past her into the vast entrance hall. He wondered if he should add a compliment about her looks.

"Time for a cup of tea, then?" She smiled and closed the door behind him.

"I would kill for a coffee really." He smirked, noticing the enticing smile that had briefly played across her lips a moment ago.

"Trying to make me feel at home, how sweet of you." She said and slowly headed to the back of the hall and Paul followed, easily keeping up next to her with his long strides.

"No need, this place is palatial and you look at home in it, Jennifer." He winked at her.

She smiled back and led him to the kitchen.

* * * *

The phone engineers' ten minutes later equated into double that, but neither Jennifer nor Paul minded too much. They spent three hours fixing phone lines in her bedroom, library and TV room and testing the connections. They said her broadband should be up and running in the next 48 hours, with wireless routers and new phone sockets in the rooms she wanted.

Paul dealt with the engineers, while Jen cooked them all both savory, sweet muffins to nibble on and copious amounts of industrial strength tea. If fact they probably would have finished half an hour earlier if it weren't for the food and drink breaks. Both engineers left with goody bags of muffins and both agreed that that had been one of the best jobs they had done in donkey's years.

"How about tea and sandwiches on the veranda out back?" Jen suggested after they had seen the engineers off. Henry hadn't been seen all day, but had opened the gates before she had even left her bed.

"You know what I'm still full of muffins at the moment. How about a tour of your small little bijou shack you have here?" Paul opened his palms up to the chandeliers and smiled at her.

"I think I can arrange something. You see I share the same bed as the owner." She winked and smiled cutely.

"Is that on the tour then?" He shot back boldly, hoping he hadn't blown his chances before they had even been on a date.

"There are certain places a girl likes to keep out of bounds." She bit her lip and looked up from his neck to his eyes. "For the time being at least."

"You are the lady of the manor," he bowed, "I am but your humble serf."

"You might regret that. There is a whole basin full of washing up to do."

"I have many regrets in life, Jenny, but being in your company isn't one of them."

"Washing up it is then," she commanded, with a seductive curl of her lips, "come on."

"Coming."

He followed her to the kitchen, then the herb and vegetable gardens and then to the pool room for a game of something he called Snooker. A trip to the library ended the small tour, as she just about resisted the urge to drag him upstairs and tie him naked to her four-poster bed.

They talked sometimes of small things, sometimes touching on their previous marriages, sometimes flirting to the edge of seduction, sometimes commenting on the hot weather.

"So, do I get an invite for dinner?" he asked, looking up and seeing the clock had moved round to six o'clock in the library.

"Is that the time?" Jen craned her neck around to look at the huge wall clock, "Time does fly when you're having fun."

"I haven't enjoyed a day so much in years and had such captivating company."

"Flattery won't get you everywhere at the moment, Paul, but that doesn't mean you have to give up trying," She teased, rubbing his arm for the first time. She sat cross-legged on the desk, with him below her on the wooden swivel Admiral's chair.

He turned his arm and took her hand lightly in his, his eyes fixed on her legs.

"So, dinner tonight?"

"How about lunch at the pub this week first?" She counter-proposed.

"Okay, Wednesday lunchtime about one, I'll be yours all after-noon because the bank shuts at half-twelve that day."

Paul leaned back in his chair and let his eyes wander up her slender legs, up over her body to her pretty face.

"You've got yourself a date handsome."

"I can't wait," he replied and stood up to sit next to her on the desk, close enough to touch shoulders.

"Some things are worth the wait." She gazed into his eyes and her head nearly caved in to her heart there and then. So, she hopped off the desk to try to distance and compose herself.

"Sounds like my cue to leave you, until Wednesday that is. One o'clock at the King's Head, saloon bar?" He stood also. Both felt a little embarrassed and awkward, neither having been on a date in a decade.

"I do have cooking things to do and soaps to watch." She smiled sweetly now, wanting him to leave before it got dark.

"Yes, I have toast to burn and baked beans to microwave." He nodded with a grin.

"Come on. I'll walk you to the door, Mister Jordan?" She extended her crooked arm toward him.

"Lead on, Miss Adams." Putting his arm through hers, they promenaded back to the front door without speaking another word.

* * * *

"He kissed my freaking hand when he left. How gallant is that, Val?" Jen squealed down her phone at her New York apartment sitting friend and agent.

"Jesus, girl, I woodaa let him kiss more den that."

"We all can't be sluts like you, Valerie. Girls like me have to build up to our sluttiness."

"Bitch."

"Ho."

"So, when are you seeing the guy again and will you slip him some tongue girl
friend?"

"Wednesday is our first date. I don't put out on a first date."

"That's why you are all alone in that big house with cobwebs in your silky draws, not in the thick of the action like me."

"I had a fun day and want more to come, so I'll take things at Jenny pace, not wham-bam Val pace, okay?"

"I hear you. You sound really happy, Jen, and that makes me happy too." Valerie's voice lowered to a more sensitive tone.

"Ah, thanks, honey. Look my TV show is on. I'll call you later in the week to tell you how it all went."

"That's if you can drag yourself out of your big ol' sex bed you have there, with bank boy."

"He's no boy, hun."

"Good to know."

"Laters."

"Yeah, bye for now."

Jen closed her cell phone and smiled widely at the TV, only half taking in the farm set soap. She felt like a teen, a new woman and Mrs. Obama rolled into one. A cooking show, with a rather beautiful, dark-haired cook came on one of the other channels, so she watched that until nine.

With a break to get a cool glass of French white wine from an open bottle in the fridge, she curled up on the sofa again and watched an old episode of Grey's on another channel. When she had the internet up and running, she'd splurge big-time on TV's, blu-rays, DVD players, clothes and shoes.

She hadn't had much more than snacks for dinner, so she hurried off to the kitchen to make a cheese and tomato sandwich. The herb garden outside the window looked dark, proper dark since there weren't any street lights for miles around.

She ate her sandwich, texted some other friends in the states and generally slobbed about, her mind always on Paul, making anything that required too much concentration difficult.

She went up to bed at half-past ten and read for a while in her bed, nearly at the end of her book. She needed something new to read, thought about going out to find a bookshop, then silently rebuked herself as she had a library with thousands of books just below her.

She decided to take a drive out to the big supermarket to get in some more supplies, food, maybe even clothes if they had them. Jen turned off the bedside light at a quarter past eleven and just lay on her back in the dark, thinking she could have had Paul lying next to her right now. With a smile on her face she fell asleep, but not for long.

* * * *

The knocking at her front door shouldn't have woken her, but she was only in a light sleep. Apart from owls and foxes the nights were low on noise pollution around Adams House.

Jen sat up in bed and listened, then turned on her lamp and tugged on her dressing gown. *This was stupid.* She'd have a word with this guy at the door or call the local cops out.

She hurried to the landing, turning on every light she passed and descended the stairs quickly. Then suddenly getting a touch of the Mrs. Chongs', she entered the drawing room and picked up an old iron poker from a stand next to the real fire, that had a basket of dried flowers inside for show.

She swallowed hard and headed for the door, as someone outside continued to knock the knocker like a Morse-code machine. Jennifer headed for the door and peered through the peep hole, just as the knocking ceased. She saw no one on the lit porch, no movement, no one running away or hiding.

"This is my house." She cried at the inside of the front door and began to unbolt it. She unlocked the door with her key and pulled it inwards, the cool night's breeze blowing against her body.

There was still nobody to be seen and she scanned the darkness for any strange shapes that shouldn't be there, but saw none. Then she looked down and saw on the metal mat where you wiped your muddy shoes, just outside, a single red rose in full bloom.

"What do you want?" she asked the night.

The night didn't answer.

Chapter Eight

Dates, Dead Men and Retail Therapy

Early on Tuesday morning, Jennifer had cereal for breakfast, went to her study and plotted the shape and content of her new cookbook for two hours.

By ten, she sat in the Aston roaring down the estate road, heading for the supermarket past the train station, full of the joys of another sunny day. It was only one large store, not the hyper-malls back home in the States, but it also sold clothes, media equipment and a vast array of foods. She bought a lot from the Foods from Around the World section and the deli. Fresh fish she bought also, then had to go back to get another cart to buy a blu-ray DVD player and a DVD and Television combo for the kitchen. She eyed two immense wall hanging televisions, but knew she wouldn't get them in the Aston. Once the broadband was up and running at home she could order more.

She left the superstore with a bulging trunk and a passenger seat filled to the windows with stuff. The Aston protested at the weight on some hills, but got her home safely around lunchtime. She had coffee and a pastry before leaving the store and left lunch since she had so much food, clothes and household stuff to put away. Once the food and bathroom things were tidied, she tried on some of the clothes she had bought, while her cell phone blared out Pink.

Paul telephoned later, just to check that she was still okay for lunch tomorrow. She replied that she was, as the conversation skirted around the edge of sexual flirting.

All in all she had a great day. The sun still shone between the white clouds, and it still felt hot and humid. At five she woke up on the sofa. On the television the credits of Dirty Dancing she had bought on DVD were rolling as the music blared out. She had nodded off through most of the film.

Wiping the drool from her chin, Jen headed upstairs for a shower to wash the sleep out of her brain before dinner. She let the hot water rain down on her head and chest, washing the cobwebs away, thinking how nice it'd be to have Paul in the shower with her, with a bar of soap and nothing on but a hard-on.

Shaking her lustful thoughts from her mind, she left the shower to dry, moisturize and dress in her sweat shirt and pants, before rustling up her swordfish and simple salad, pulled from the garden.

She ate dinner, with no wine this time, only flavored mineral water. She did both sets of nails while watching her soap, which was on for an hour today for some reason. Then she spent a couple of hours of trying on new and old clothes, so she could achieve that simple just pulled-them-on-look, for tomorrow's lunch date with Paul. She nearly, well seventy percent, decided on a white, buttoned blouse, with short sleeves, so she could easily adjust the level of her cleavage showing, with the simple undoing of neck and chest area buttons. She was about fifty-five percent going for the knee length skirt, but the bets were off her as she could easily put on a longer one at the last moment, or even ankle length slacks. With her hair held back with a head band and a few bracelets on her wrists, she had the look she was looking for, smart and sexy. She just hoped Paul liked that look and didn't just go for the Hooters slutty look.

She went to bed at half-nine since she was still tired. She flicked through some cookbooks from some British chefs to get a feel for what the Brits liked to eat. Then she picked up a Wilbur Smith tome, she had bought at the superstore about ancient Egypt and read twenty pages, before she turned her light off at twenty past ten. In her ears though, she wore a set of foam earplugs, just to guarantee she had a good, long beauty sleep that night.

* * * *

Jen came too with the now familiar glints of bright sunlight scratching at the edges of the shutters to be let in and fill her bedroom with warmth and morning joy. With a wide yawn a lioness would be proud of, she padded off to the bathroom to urgently answer the call of nature. The light in the corridor caused her to squint until her eyelids were just slits. She walked into the doorframe of the bathroom as she entered.

"Fuck me, God damn it, shit." She swore, clutching her left temple. Now, she was fully awake.

After urinating, rubbing at her head and cursing under her breath, she went to the wall mirror to see and feel with two fingers that she had a small bump there.

"God damn it. Why today lord of all days," she swore, prodding at the little bruise. Wetting a flannel, bought only yesterday, she held the cold wetness to her forehead. "Just the look I was going for, battered wife."

Jen peered closely into the mirror and then pressed the bruise against her cold reflection, hoping to ease the small swelling.

At last Jennifer headed back to her bedroom to pull open the shutters and try to find the tub of concealer she had brought with her from New York.

Jen pulled back the shutters and gasped, finding thirty or so red rose stems placed from one end to the other on the outside of her wide windowsill.

This wasn't Paul or Henry's work, she knew at once, unless they had a ladder of a cherry-picker. This was from another admirer, probably a dead one, almost certainly Cromity.

With trouble she opened her stiff windows and dragged all the roses inside and put them in the bin by her dressing table. Then she looked at the two cuts in her hands from the thorns and cursed again.

"There goes my smart-sexy look, with gardener's hands and a boxer's forehead. She dressed in a sweatshirt and jeans, cleaned up her palms and found her concealer. She'd get properly dressed later. Now, she'd apply a good old layer of slap to cover up her injuries and headed off downstairs to fry up the greasiest bacon sarnie this-old-house had ever seen.

She had just made it to the bottom of the stairs in the hall, when a woman in her early sixties walked out of the drawing room, with an apron on, holding a pocket full of dusters, wipes and polish.

"Good morning, Miss Jenny." She smiled, showing off a very new set of pearly white teeth, a new hair-do and a set of gold rings on her fingers, not many cleaners could match.

"Hi." Jen smiled back bemused at finding this stranger in her house, not sure what to say next. She didn't look like a cat-burglar.

"Now, don't mind me, love. Just get on with what you're doing. I'll clean around yer." The thin, dyed white-blonde lady answered and moved across the hall to polish the telephone.

"Erm, sorry, I don't know your name?" Jen asked her hand on the banisters, as she trotted down and around the bottom of the stairs to face the cleaner.

"Mrs. Wilberforce, love. Sorry. Should have said. Oh, by the bye, me and Fred, that's to say Mr. Wilberforce and I are off to our home in Spain for a fortnight on the middle two weeks of October, so you'll have to fend for yourself cleaning wise for those two weeks, luvvy."

"I don't mean to be rude, but who are you and what are you doing in my house?" Jen tried to sound as gentle and not come across as a total buffoon.

"Now, the late Miss Adams stole the march on being rude, love, so don't fret yourself. I'm your cleaner, luvvy. Olive Wilberforce at your service." Mrs. Wilberforce put down her leather duster and reached out a liver-spotted hand that had seen far too much sun over the past sixty-one years. Jen hesitantly moved forward and shook the woman's hand, which would smell of Mister Sheen for the rest of the day.

"I'm Jennifer Adams. Sorry. I didn't know I had a cleaner?"

"I used to clean for Miss Gwen, your great aunty. She left me a far old whack in her will you see, but old Henry said you needed someone to pop in once a week just to spruce the place up, luvvy. And between you and me, the money is fine, but gods spending all day and every day with Mr. Wilberforce, would tax the patience of even Mary mother of Jesus."

The woman laughed, a shrill, interesting laugh that had more key changes to it than a Queen song. Jen also returned the laugh, as it had an infectious quality to it.

"Well, okay, now, we know who we both are then. I think I'll have to have a word in Henry's ear about keeping me in the loop."

"Probably his age, dear, none of us are getting any younger."

"I was just about to make some tea and bacon sandwiches for breakfast. Would you like any, Mrs. Wilberforce?" Jen asked politely, in an effort to make a good start with somebody in this country.

"Tea, please, Miss Jenny, but the bacon sarnies are out now. I've had my gastric band fitted." Mrs. Wilberforce rubbed her apron at the tummy area and grinned stoically.

"Okay." Jen smiled and retreated still facing the cleaner as she walked backwards. "One tea coming up."

"Milk, two sugars, please."

"Okay, then." Jen smiled and headed off to the kitchen. She filled and boiled the kettle and took out two mugs, when she saw that Henry worked in the vegetable garden digging up some potatoes.

Jen left the kettle to finish boiling, to ask if Henry wanted a cup. Also to ask him to let her know, if she had any other mystery members of staff that might pop out of the woodwork.

He apologized and assured her there was no one else apart from the odd contractor or tree surgeon he had to call on now and again to tend the grounds. So, she had tea with Henry and Mrs. Wilberforce, all sitting on stools in the kitchen, talking about the hay-day of the house and lots of bits of gossip about her relatives, she didn't really need to know.

Jen excused herself, which was like pulling herself out of a barrel of treacle, rather than just extraditing herself from a one-sided conversation. Mrs. Wilberforce really could talk for England in the next Olympics and Henry was no help. He had just slipped off with a grunt half-n-hour ago.

Jennifer checked her broadband connection, but it wasn't working so she had to reply on dial up, to check her emails and website. While walking to the library across the way from the study, she heard the dulcet tones of Mrs. Wilberforce approaching around the bend, singing some Abba tune.

Jen rushed into the library and closed the door, not wanting another long chat with the cleaner, that would surely make her late getting ready for her date. Jennifer saw the winding stairs to the upper levels of the library and took that two steps at a time, then rushed around the shelves of books to a door she hadn't tried before. It was locked, but a key poked out of the keyhole. She turned it and pushed forward, as the library door opened below her.

Jen found herself not more than four doors away from her bedroom. On the same corridor, she turned and hastily closed the door behind her, to find it wasn't a door at all, its outward appearance matched that of the walls of the long west wing corridor.

"A secret door, how kewl is that?" She was amazed how flush it looked and how it merged in with the wainscoting and picture-rails.

With an impressed look on her face, she skipped to her bedroom and sat down at her dressing table. She felt glad to see her bump had nearly vanished, and with the help of concealer it did. Jennifer did her hair and make-up and then slowly dressed, making sure she was covered in deodorant, because of the still hot autumn weather outside.

By the time she headed downstairs for the garage, to jump in the Aston to drive to her lunch date, Mrs. Wilberforce had either left for home or cleaned somewhere in the midst of the great house.

Jen rolled down her driver's window, trying not to break any nails or sustain any other minor injuries. She roared out of the garage and headed down the long drive to the gates.

* * * *

She pulled into the front parking lot of the pub with ten-minutes to spare, but saw Paul waiting outside on a wooden table with fixed benches on either side, a half drained pint of cider in his hand.

He stood up and waved. Jen adjusted her head band and climbed out of the car, smiling back, her skirt showing off her knees and lovely lower legs. She let him kiss her cheek and he showed her toward the table outside the front of the pub near a collection of pots plants and a large tall hedge.

"What can I get you?" he asked, clapping his nervous, sweaty palms together, as she sat opposite to his half drunk cider.

"Dry white wine spritzer, please."

"Okie-dokie, I'll grab a couple of menus while I'm at the bar. The food here is wonderful." He kept smiling and she smiled back as he headed inside the pub to order her drink and curse the use of the words okie-dokie on a first date.

* * * *

"So, how do I go about getting more cable channels for my imminent super-bad-ass televisions that I'm gonna order once my broadband is up and running?" Jen asked an hour into their first date and halfway through her brie, and pine nut with cranberry dressing salad.

"Well the best way is to get a satellite dish and subscribe to one of the digital TV company packages. "

"Satellite? I only want to pick up TV stations and my favorite shows for the States, not talk to Mars." Jen whimsically jumped in.

"But there is an inherent problem with that as your house is a grade three listed building. You probably couldn't do anything that is detrimental to the outward façade of the house."

Jen stared at him blankly.

"What was it Churchill said about two countries divided by a common language? Could you repeat and elaborate, in kinda grade school U.S. English?"

"The government won't let you put a bloody great satellite dish on the front of the house, 'cause it will look like crap. How's that?" He smiled, picking up a chip and popping it into his mouth.

"Much more my level." She laughed.

It seemed to him the most beautiful sound he had heard since his last trip to see Swindon Town and they had won four goals to nil.

"But seeing your place, we might be able to put the dish on the wall of the herb garden or on the blind side of the garage and run lots of cables up to the house. I will investigate for you."

"That really is above and beyond the normal service for a bank manager!"

She pushed the last of her cheese into the rocket salad and popped it between her lips, trying to remain the air of seductiveness, but only managing to drop a red drop of dressing on her delicate chin.

"It is for a bank manager," he stated and reached across the table to wipe the red drop from her chin with a soft rub of his thumb, "but I just don't have bank business on my mind when I'm around you."

"Really?" She squeaked, her heart turning to Jello for a moment. Then she composed herself and changed the subject. "So, do you live locally then?"

"My house is a minute's walk, that way." He pointed to a side road past the garage. "You want to pop around, erm now, if you like?"

"I could do with a cup of tea right now."

"Let's go then." Paul stood up abruptly and knocked his three quarters drained second pint of cider onto the paved front of the pub, which exploded everywhere spectacularly. "Shit!"

"Oops." Jen giggled and then saw the embarrassment on Paul's face and just burst forth into louder and more raucous laughter.

"Thank you so much," he responded sarcastically with a bow and excused himself to head into the pub to get a dust-pan and brush.

Jenny Adams was still giggling when he returned, with said cleaning items.

Yet the moment had somehow been lost and the intensity and sexual longing had given way to a more easy going great first date.

"Do you fancy going for a walk first?" he asked as they reached the gate of his cottage set back down a small side road away from the main road of the village.

They went for the walk, arm-in-arm in the September sunshine, hearts pumping with renewed vigor; their minds wondering about so many things, so many possibilities. Hoping that there could be love a second time around and that second chances could be perfect.

Later they sat on his two seater sofa with an old film playing in the background on the television. He had invited her in for tea after their walk and showed her the range of programs on his satellite system. Jen felt the heady rush of first attraction when she was close to him and felt shocked that the teenager feeling she had when last she dated came flooding back.

"Will you stay for dinner?" he asked a little breathlessly, fiddling with the TV and satellite remotes, one in each hand.

Jen glance at the clock on his mantelpiece over his real fire and felt shocked to see it was already half-past six at night. Outside the light was fading from the sky quickly and she jumped off the sofa.

"God, is that the time? I gotta run." Jen pushed her feet into her shoes and headed for the hallway.

"I'll walk you to your car then."

He smiled, a little disappointed that she didn't want to stay for dinner and then maybe all night. He loved being with her and her odd little foibles just made him want to hug her forever.

"Next time you can come over and I'll make you some lunch, maybe Saturday or we could go for a picnic in the Aston?" She suggested as she waited in his darkening small hallway as he put on his shoes and grabbed a jacket from a coat stand.

"Saturday, I'm supposed to be working, but I have loads of days off due, I'm sure I can swing it. The picnic idea sounds good to me, with food rustled up by such a beautiful and talented woman," he said, closing the cottage door behind them.

Taking her hand, they began walking down the road to the pub's parking lot. They turned the corner and reached the parked Aston Martin.

"So, this is the end of our first date then?" he asked her, wanting more than anything to take her in his arms and kiss her right now; only his British reserve held him back.

"You, Paul Jordan are a lovely man and this has been a great first date." She reached up on tip-toe and kissed his lips softly in thanks for realizing she felt a little uneasy about tea at his house yet and all that entailed. He responded to her kiss and for a while the world shrunk to a very small space indeed.

"Don't forget about Saturday will you and try and swing it with the boss." She stepped back, catching her breath again as her heart fluttered in her chest.

"I am the boss."

"For the moment." Jennifer pushed her body against him, her breasts squashed to his torso for an instant and kissed him quickly.

"See you Saturday, Paul, about ten at my place." She unlocked the driver's side door, climbed in and started her up.

"You will, Jenny."

Paul stood back as she powered out of the pub's parking lot. With a flash of a smile and a wave, she sped off along the dusky road back to Adams House. Paul breathed in and out through his nose, a warm feeling of happiness and longing stirring inside him for the first time since his wife had died. He turned round to go home and bumped into Saul Pike, heading for the pub.

"Sorry," Paul apologized and his nostrils flared at the smell of sweat and urine emanating from the unkempt young villager.

"You better watch your step." Saul stared at him under low hooded eyelids and with a scowl on his beard dominant face, headed off toward the bar entrance.

* * * *

The gates to the ground remained open as she roared past White Lodge, lights blazed from the downstairs windows. From inside, Henry Greenwood watched her speed past with a disappointed shake of his head. He loaded his shotgun and with Purdy in tow headed out into the darkness of just fallen night to close and lock the gates.

It seemed much darker under the canopy of trees as she sped along toward the house. *Did she really have to be concerned every time she stepped outside the doors of her house after the sun had set?* She hated the fact that the dark long nights of winter would soon be upon her and her usual fears and dark moods would return. That was something else she had to order over the internet and hoped they had what she used in the States over here to combat the effects of SAD.

Yet right now she just wanted to get home, drink a glass of Merlot and dream about her new man-friend, while watching her English soap. She shot out from the cover of the woods and slowed her speed by half to negotiate the bridge and curved road that led past the lake up to her dark house, silhouetted against the royal blue early night sky.

As she turned the car left, she thought she caught a dark shape of a man standing between the edge of the east woods and the garage. She gunned the Aston and pulled up in front of the house, with a squeal of heavy brakes and the slight skidding of tires on the stones of the drive.

She jumped out, locked the car and then searched the dark area where the figure had been standing, but no one stood there now, if they had been in the first place. Maybe Henry's stories had just made her extra jumpy about the night, not that she needed much of a push. Scanning the area as best she could in the darkness she ran up to her front door and unlocked it, with the uneasy feeling that someone or something would grab at her while her back was turned.

Jennifer opened the door and slammed it shut without looking back. Then raced to switch on all the light switches in the hall, stairs and associated corridors.

While an exhale of breath and a nervous laugh, saw from the grandfather clock nearby that it was seven o'clock already, so she rushed to the TV room to catch her soap. She turned on the light and the television and then fell back onto the sofa, tossing her car and house keys onto the table in front of her.

Outside a set of dead eyes watched her through the gauze view of the net curtains.

* * * *

After her favorite program ended, she headed to the kitchen and uncorked a new bottle of merlot. She grabbed the neck and turned to fetch a glass from a cabinet across the kitchen, when she saw a dark shape standing in her herb garden.

The bottle dropped from her hand and shattered between her legs sending waves of red wine over her bare ankles and shoes. She stood transfixed, but the figure didn't disappear or retreat back into the night this time. No, he slowly walked down the rough stone path to her kitchen door and she watched him raised his fist to the door.

Knock, knock.

"Who are you? What do you want from me?" Jennifer screamed at the shadow that filled the rippled panes of her upper backdoor. Her perfect day had dramatically turned for the worst in a very short space of time; the time it took for daylight to fade to the menace and uncertain fear, darkness brought to the primitive part of every human's brain.

Knock, knock.

Jennifer Adams could take no more. She grabbed the biggest carving knife from the block and ran over to the back door and unlocked it. She wasn't George's frightened little wife anymore. She was her own woman, back in her birthright family home, with a possibility of new love on the horizon. No Halloween ghoul from ancient history was going to rain on this girl's parade anymore.

She pulled in the back door, and before her, not more than three feet away stood a figure not much taller than her. He had an off-white looking tied shirt and a cloak that seemed not spun material at all, but a wispy cloak of impenetrable darkness.

"I am Captain Silas Cromity, m'lady. Whom do I have the pleasure of address this clement night?"

The gaunt cheek man addressed her and drew from his head a large round hat made up of the same darkness as his cloak. Jennifer dropped the knife which clattered to the floor beside her wine dripping ankles and shoes, and rotated twice slowly. She couldn't take her eyes off his fork beard and the impossible supernatural denizen of the Adams's families skeleton filled cupboard.

"What do you want from me?" She heard herself ask, and felt her lips move, but it seemed to her like an out-of-body experience. Someone else said it for her.

"I just wish to welcome you to this house, dusty-skinned lady from lands far away, judging by the curl of your tongue: be you from Ireland or the Isle of Man methinks?"

"I'm from New York." She found herself replying to the gaunt (not without physical charisma) pale-skinned man whom stood at the threshold of her back door.

"New York, have they perhaps tired of the old one?"

Silas Cromity smiled, and Jen stood transfixed to the spot. Her uncalled for visitor reminded her of one of those unsolicited door-to-door salesmen that catch a person on the step at the front door and are hard to dislodge. "It's across the ocean, the United States of America."

"That would account for the tinge of your flawless skin, though of this United State you speak I have no recollection. Come let me in from the night, my dear and tell the name that wouldst go with such a comely woman?"

Cromity closed the gap to within two feet now and a wide smile pushed up the side of his long pointed moustache.

"My name is Jennifer, Jennifer Chong and you better stop right there, bud, 'cause you aren't entering this house this or any other night."

Jennifer marveled inside her head at the calmness of her voice and thoughts, as not to give away she was born an Adams.

Cromity stepped forward to the cusp of the door frame and Jennifer stepped back two paces on frightening feet and wobbly red wine stained legs.

"Then Jennifer Chong, I will bid thee a goodnight, but I will come and visit thee again. Maybe you whilst let me tarry a while inside your warm, but lonely house. I will tell you how it is I became such a cursed ghast of a man."

With that, the pale countenanced man spun pulling his dark cloak up over his head and merged into the background darkness like he had been nothing but a cloud of dark smoke from a bonfire.

Jennifer jumped forward and slammed the door shut, rattling the window panes in their frames before she locked and bolted the door. She looked down at the knife, her purple-red blotched legs and the glass and wine over the kitchen floor. Her mind couldn't take on even the simplest of cleaning tasks at the moment so she ran from the kitchen up the stairs switching on every light switch she passed into her bathroom to strip off and shower away the wine stains on her calves and ankles. She let the heat take the chill that ran from her tailbone to her nape and dried herself with a large towel from the heater rail which Mrs. Wilberforce must have kindly placed there.

She hurried into her room and closed out the night, blocking the windows with the heavy wooden shutters and scrambled into her bed, still only wrapped in her big towel. Her legs drawn up to her belly, causing the towel to pull at her backside, she just hugged herself and thought of Paul. Should she ring him, ask him to come over and hold her all night in his strong embrace?

She should have, but she didn't. For reasons she didn't know why, unless it was a morbid curiosity about Cromity. Our very human nature to understand everything, tapped at something deep inside her mind. Cromity and Adams, those names had been inexorably linked for hundreds of years. She wanted to know why and how he was still here.

She sank back into her bed, even though the hour was still early and thought of Paul and their date and his strong lips kissing her. Yet whenever she thought she could now sleep, Cromity's face appeared in her mind's eye.

The only way she could find out was to talk to him again, but not inside the house. That Great Aunt Gwen had informed her was her only line of defense. She knew now what it meant to be the Adams lady of the house now, even though it made her feel like Mrs. George Chong again.

She didn't fall asleep until one in the morning, when fatigue finally conquered her fears of the vampire ghost thing she had also inherited with the house. No knocks came at her front door this night, when the grandfather clock in the hall chimed midnight.

Sitting on a bench in the formal gardens behind the conservatory and the vegetable garden, Silas Cromity let a twitch of a tiny smile ghost across his thin, red lips. He didn't believe the words of the retainer who had long lived at the lodge at the edge of the estate; he could smell the Adams blood through the sweat in her pores. Not wholly pure Adams, but of that tainted line. He sensed that she was the last of them too. The long circle had begun again, as it did with every Adams female born to live in what should be his house. This time he would avenge the ills cast upon himself, his wife and daughters for good.

Chapter Nine

The Last Dogs Days of the Indian Summer

When she woke, she felt ninety-five percent positive that the events of last night had only been a nightmare, brought on by her fears of getting close to someone new and living in this huge old house alone. When she found the towel that had slipped off her naked body during the night next to her, the percentage fell to only seventy-five percent.

When she found the light still on in the bathroom and her clothes just strewn upon the tiled floor, it dropped again to about fifty-one percent. She showered quickly and put up her hair and donned no make-up. She hurried into a newly bought t-shirt and skinny jeans and slowly headed downstairs to the kitchen to confirm, what only her rational mind was trying to deny.

On the kitchen floor lay the broken wine bottle and near the back-door the carving knife. Jen thanked the lord that the sun was still shining or she might have easily fallen into one of her winter fugues in that very instant. Instead she hastily cleared up the mess and cleaned the knife in the sink before putting it back in its wooden block.

She put on the kettle, but couldn't stand waiting in the kitchen long enough for it to boil, so she took a bottle of water and a breakfast chewy bar and retreated to the west wing living room. It was far enough away from the frightening memories the kitchen invoked and was bathed in a new morning's sunshine.

Jennifer stood at the window her eyes closed and let the warm rays of the sun clear the mental barriers and nightmares that rattled around in her mind, like wild dogs trapped in a large empty room.

Jennifer breathed in and out like Doctor Gagne, back at home had told her. She used a mental exercise to suck the sunshine and light into her mind and banish all the dark thoughts and her Mrs. Chong self-doubts far away.

Thankfully it worked, and she replaced her dark intruder, with the images of Paul, with all the hope and excitement a new relationship could bring. She ate her bar, drank some water and after getting her phone, she sent Paul a polite happy text, with some risqué unsubtle over tones.

Then she headed for the study, tried her laptop and found out the broadband was up and running. After an hour or so of connecting to networks, finding a provider and updating her virus security, she was away. She spent an hour mostly deleting emails, replying to a few of her friends, most of Valerie's and the odd comment added onto replies to a couple of cooking friends.

The next hour she spent updating her website, adding a quick thousand word blog about England and new food projects. Leaving out all the juicy and insane parts, it was her mad-private life in the end.

Then she rewarded herself with some fun, going to the supermarket's website and ordering some more food, clothes, DVDs and two gigantic televisions and one small one, two sound-systems and CDs; plus she found a website that produced products she had used at home to combat her SAD, so she ordered three.

A raised level of sauciness in Paul's text reply, made her search for something new on the web and she found a place that did nightwear of a more sensual nature up to the levels of sluttiness.

She ordered a few silky things, slips; then moved onto a Basque set. A tight Lycra dress with missing parts where most dresses added material to protect your modesty. Then on a more practical whim she bought a box of condoms and massage oil.

Her finger hovered over the complete order button for a second and then with a weighing up shake of her head side to side, pressed the enter button on her laptop.

Smiling from ear to ear, she then found a large UK computer website from a company her laptop came from and ordered the most expensive gigged up PC she could buy, with a printer, monitor and external memory drive.

With her credit card that now had no upper limit, changed by Paul last week, practically melted from over use, she closed her laptop down. Whistling, something her grandpa had taught her, she returned to the kitchen to make lunch.

She opened the back door wide in contempt of Cromity and wandered around the herb and vegetable gardens for a while soaking in the sunshine. She ate lunch on the veranda that overlooked the gardens and her eyes just marveled at the size and straight line of the formal hedges and borders and low walls beyond.

Paul rang her at a quarter to one, and they chatted in soft

murmuring tones that newly together couples do. She wondered *how long, before they did the our song part, or invented the cutesy puppy names for each other?*

Night and Cromity seemed far away now. She'd make sure she ordered blinds for the kitchen windows and door later that afternoon and more earplugs that would keep the English Civil War corpse from interrupting her sleep.

She worked on the outlines for her new cookbook for two hours after lunch. Then she took a little stroll through the formal gardens and headed into the western woods. She had been walking for an hour when she came upon a rough rectangle of a clearing. At its center were the scattered stone remains of an old looking building. Only the outline, covered with moss and weeds could be seen, but at one end next to a clump of stinging nettles, the stones were slightly more raised, probably where the chimney of a fire had been.

The sun hardly penetrated the green leaves of the thick tree canopy. As she hopped over the remains of a wall into the inside of the building, a cold sensation assaulted her, like all her spinal fluid had frozen. Jennifer wrapped her bare arms around herself and the woods surrounding the remains of the dwelling spun like she stood in the center of a carnival ride.

From the ground the cold emanated. As she closed her eyes to stop the giddiness, a cold collection of female voices began to chant words she couldn't understand. She wasn't sure if it was one voice that echoed and multiplied or many voices.

Jen forced her eyes open. Enduring the nausea that swept her head, she stumbled from the inside of the stone-lined ruin. At once the voices stopped; the trees stopped their spinning and quickly the sick feeling left her. Jen left the area as fast as her legs could carry her. Soon she followed a leaf-mould of a single path out of the woods back into the sunshine. She smiled in relief as she walked onto the road leading up to the bridge over the lake and headed that way also, so glad to be out of the woods.

The bridge was wide and made of stones. She leaned on the walled side and cast a few loose chippings into the carp filled man-made waters below. The late afternoon sun on her face and the plopping sound the stones made as they punctured the skin of the water eased her mind and made her forget the coldness of the ruined dwelling in the woods.

The sounds of padding canine feet caused her to turn to her left and she saw Purdy bounding toward her, tongue lolling out of one side of her open mouth as she did. Henry Greenwood was just emerging from the woods on the east side of the estate and it took him a further five minutes to reach her on the bridge.

Purdy had licked her a few times and obviously now saw her as a proper Adams family member and part of the family, with her enthusiastic tail wagging.

"I see you are fast-friends, now," Henry stated, a bit out of breath as he reached Jennifer where she knelt, stroking Purdy.

"Us girls have to stick together," Jen replied with a pleased to see you smile on her lips.

"Been out walking 'ave yer?"

"Yes and I found what looked like the remains of a small house in the woods; any idea what was once there?"

"That'll be the Witch's house then, Miss Jennifer." Henry replied matter-of-factly.

"The Witch's House, that figures, why couldn't it be like, I dunno, 'the old sweet lady healers place' or something bright and cheery?"

"You're in the wrong place for bright and cheery." Henry laughed, which ended in a small throaty coughing fit.

"So, I have witch houses and ghostly vampires on my doorstep. I could start a Friday the Thirteenth version of Disneyland right here." Jen pointed around the grounds with her hands and arms. "So, what's the story with the Witch house then?"

"Even I ain't old enough to know, rumor has it an old witch lived in those woods before the Adams came along and extended their estate. She was told to sling-her-hook and the house has just fallen down over the hundreds of years since."

"What happened to her then?"

"Look I may be old, but unlike what my sister's kids and grand-kids say, I wasn't around when dinosaurs ruled the earth, you know."

Henry leaned on the wall of the bridge next to her and smiled, sending thousands of lines shooting this way and that across his old weather-beaten face. Jen looked at him and smiled back, laughing softly through her nose. They stood there for a while in silence, just taking in the air.

"How would you like me to cook you dinner up at the house tonight, Henry?"

"As long as I'm back at the lodge for half-six afore it gets dark, then you're on." Henry stood up and stretched his back, as Jennifer glanced at her wrist watch. It was five to five now, so if she rustled something up in thirty minutes, everyone (including Purdy) should be happy.

"Right then," Jen pointed to the house, "shall we?"

"We shall, after you."

* * * *

After rustling up a chicken, with a creamy peppercorn sauce with sliced potatoes and peas, Henry and Purdy left at quarter-past six with their bellies full. Jennifer washed up quickly and took a bottle of red wine, a glass, a bottle of water and corkscrew into the TV room, so she had no need to visit the kitchen again that night.

She went to ring Paul, then just texted instead, thinking he should be the one doing the chasing since she was the hot divorcee lady. She rang and chatted to Valerie for twenty minutes on the landline telling her all about her hot date, but nothing about vampire visitors or witch's houses.

She watched her soap in the comfort of a large glass of wine and made a note to order a nice box of chocolates or a bag of cookies next time she was online. Once her program ended, she fetched the laptop from her study and sat it on her lap, testing the strength of the wireless broadband around her cavernous house. It worked fine and she ordered some chocolate and cookies and things that looked like small cookies, but called biscuits.

Then with a naughty smirk, she looked at the saucy clothes site again and eyed the men's wear section and looked at a few posing pouches that Paul might squeeze into for her benefit. She re-watched Dirty Dancing and didn't fall asleep this time; the chirp of her cell phone came every few minutes or so with some with texts from Paul.

She toyed with the idea of sending a photo of her cleavage to Paul on her cell phone and then decided strongly against it. Maybe after a few more dates, when her sexy new lingerie had been delivered.

She headed up to bed around ten o'clock, had a high density bubble bath and pampered herself and then read for a while, a bit shocked she didn't feel tired after last night. She finally turned off the light just after eleven with ear plugs wedged in deep in both ears and slept through until way past dawn. Of the urgent knocks on her front door and back door she heard none.

* * * *

Friday morning was bright, yet the clouds half-filled the sky for the first time since arriving in England. She headed off in the Aston to the village to pick up a few bits at the shop and butchers and arranged to have the New York Times ordered, via the newsagents. She popped in to see Paul, who gladly took her into his office without an interview and pushed her against the door as soon as it closed for a hasty and urgent groping and kissing session.

"I'm sorry but I have a meeting in five minutes," he stated in a husky voice as their lips finally parted.

"Hey, don't sweat it. I have errands to run anyways."

"Oh, I spoke to the English heritage people, and they are going to send someone out next Tuesday about the satellite dish, etcetera."

Paul kissed her on the tip of her nose and crossed over to a side wall to a mirror to check his askew tie. He changed the angle to reflect Jennifer as she bent over to pick up her dropped handbag. Turning her head she saw that he was ogling her backside via the mirror.

"Hey, caught you looking at my fanny."

"Erm." He began to cough as he swallowed his saliva. In fact he had to go and pour himself a glass of water from a decanter. After a few pats on the back and swallows of water he felt okay again, if not a little pink around the gills.

She left him with another urgent kiss and headed off to the butchers. On the way back to the car she got a text from Paul. Where he gave a quick explanation of the subtle differences between the meaning of the word fanny in American English meaning behind bottom and English English which meant front bottom.

She climbed into her car laughing her head off and texted back that maybe he would get to see both meanings of the word in question real soon. She sent the text, biting her bottom lip and then thrust her phone into her handbag. Then she roared out of the parking lot and headed back home, getting more confident every trip of driving on a different side of the road than she was used to.

Henry flagged her down at the gate and handed over a package that had arrived not more than fifteen minutes ago by a parcel delivery company. Jen warned him that she might have a few more things being delivered in the near future. Henry said he would put a sign up that if no one was at White Lodge to call his phone first or the main house's number.

She thanked him, with a smile and cheery wave and zoomed down the road toward home through the woods. Henry smiled to himself as he closed the gates, but didn't padlock and chain them. He knew she wasn't a full Adams like Gwen, but she had the same smile that would make any man walk over hot coals for her.

Jen snacked in the kitchen while she prepared things for tomorrow's picnic. The internet weather showed it would be cloudless and 22 degrees tomorrow. She made some cold rice and pasta dishes, some Chinese parcels, and even pork pies from an old recipe book. The rest she'd make in the morning, instead she cleaned up and washed her hands. Once dried she grabbed the unopened package and trotted upstairs to her bedroom.

She ripped it open with girlish glee, because she knew from the franked company logo on the back where it had been sent from. Inside she found her ordered silky special bedtime wear, Basque set and condoms. Her oils and a couple of other bits would be sent later, but she didn't worry because she had something to put on to impress Paul when the time felt right.

She tried on the red silky shorts and cammie top and then the white one. The red hid more, but showed off her bust and legs better. The Basque and knickers, garter belt and stockings were stunning, but they were at least two or three play-dates away from bringing that number on. The red would do. She took some of the condoms out and stuffed them into the top drawer of her bedside cabinet, feeling like a Texas ranch whore setting up for a day's business.

Carefully taking her pretty sexy things off, she pulled on her jeans and T-shirt again. She wondered if it would be a good idea, if (and it was still an if) Paul stayed the night, they chose another bedroom to do the deed. The last thing she wanted was Cromity knocking on her door or bedroom window, if she had company. *How do you explain that one? 'Aren't you going to get that?' 'No, because it's just the vampire ghost that came with the house. He wants to come in and murder us!'*

Jen spent the afternoon scouring the best east wing bedrooms, to turn into her sex boudoir for the night. She found one that over looked the conservatory, quite a way from the front door on the second floor. It smelled musty, but not damp. She threw the windows open, checked the shutters and fetched new bed linen. On her second trip she returned with her red silkies and ten condoms she stuffed in the bedside drawer.

"Must remember to take those out again, in case Mrs.

Wilberforce decides to clean up this room anytime soon. She'll think I've started up a freaking brothel," Jen stated to herself as she dusted, polished the place up and plugged in an air freshener to make the bedroom smell like summer meadows.

Valerie rang her later that afternoon, as Jen sat at her laptop in her study; she had won some competition from a credit card company, for a two week cruise around the Caribbean in two weeks time. She didn't even remember applying really, something to do with a travel website she had visited.

Valerie was looking forward to seeing if the crew and Caribbean boys measured up to her high standards and Jen replied that the gutter and hobos upwards were her standards.

Smiling away Jen headed back up to the boudoir and made the bed having left the mattress to air for a few hours. Paul rang her to compliment her on her text, say he'd be around at half-ten tomorrow and that she had to pick a picnic spot for them.

"Picnic spots?" She pondered aloud later after dinner, her soap and dusk. "Maybe on the vampire's tomb, or the witch's house, or the werewolf's brier patch or the zombie lake."

She laughed quickly, a wry smile on her face as she teased her situation, one not many people had to deal with. Yet, the lake seemed a good idea, as long as there weren't swarms of flies and with a bit of shade for the food. A spot flashed in her minds eye and she'd check it out early tomorrow morning before Paul arrived for the hottest picnic date a girl ever gave.

That reminded her to ring Henry and warn him Paul was coming over. He stated he would leave the gates open since he was off to the races with Purdy for the day.

"Just the two of us, with no prying eyes."

Jen smiled and took a sip of water, since she felt sure the wine and good times would flow tomorrow. She headed off to bed early so she could apply a face pack for the night, to make her look even more irresistible than she already was. With earplugs in and a quick read of her book, the lights were out by ten o'clock. If anyone knocked on her door after that, they were going to be very disappointed.

Chapter Ten

Love Blossoms as the Leaves Turn to Blood

Jen removed her face pack, showered, plucked, rubbed, applied and painted herself before eight on Saturday morning. She had toast, eaten over the Belfast sink, as not to drop any crumbs on the flowery dress she had picked for her picnic date with Paul. It was white, flared at the waist and down to her knees, with small yellow daisies stitched along the hemlines. She looked in the mirror and nodded; she had gone for the right look. She'd do.

She put on an apron (one of Mrs. Wilberforce's cast-offs) and made sandwiches, rolls, croissants and jelly and placed them all in a hamper she found in the pantry. With drinks of water, soda pop and wine, which they could plop in the lake to keep chilled, everything was going to be perfect, like something out of Jane Austin, except she didn't have a frilly hat.

Exhaling from running back and forth to her room and the study to collect sunglasses, she then hurried around the linen cupboard upstairs and wardrobes until she found a suitable blanket to put the picnic on. She headed to the bathroom to roll-on some more deodorant and then with another thought she squirted a feminine spray to cool down her panty parts.

She stood on the landing, over looking the drive and watched for twenty minutes, trying to tell herself she really didn't need to pee right now, until Paul's car pulled up in the drive.

She rushed, walked, ran and walked again to the front door. She was about to open it and looked down to find she still had the blue apron on. She pulled it off and threw it under a nearby chair as the doorbell chimed above her head.

"Don't fuck this up and you'll get some loving tonight," she whispered, wiped her hands down her dress and shook and tousled her long, black hair, before finally opening the door.

Paul stood there in jeans and a pale blue polo shirt, holding a large bottle of champagne in one hand, and a bunch of pink carnations in the other.

"For you." He smiled and thrust the gifts forward, nearly

whacking them into her breasts in his efforts to impress.

"Thanks, Paul," She reached up and kissed his cheek. "Come on in."

"Okay."

"Let's head for the kitchen then and I can put these in water." She smiled as he stepped past her, smelling like he had bathed in an aftershave bottle, but it was the effort that counted. She shut the door and they walked in silence across the hall toward the kitchen

"The weather has held nice for us, not a cloud in the sky," he remarked going the safe English route to chit-chat about the weather.

"The sun shines on the righteous, my daddy used to say. Hope you're hungry. I made way too much food."

"Starving Jenny, so you're in luck," he said as they entered the kitchen.

"I think I am," she whispered to herself as she went over to the sink to lean the flowers inside, while she searched for a vase.

* * * *

"Varse." He pronounced slowly, opening his mouth wide as he sat legs to the side on the end of the food strew picnic blanket.

"Vaise." She pronounced back and giggled. Taking a sip of cold champagne Jenny smiled at his rolling eyes and the bubbles went up her nose.

"Here another one 'batt-trees.'" He offered his glass and she chinked it with hers.

"Batt-er-ies," she retorted and laughed again. "Don't worry I'll get you speaking American, my young padawan."

"Will you, now?"

"Yes." She smiled and her eyes glistened like jewels reflected by the autumn sunshine. "Want some more tart?"

"You're more than enough tart for one man, Jenny." Paul leaned forward and her lips met his in the middle, their glasses of bubbly held beneath their respective chins.

"Hey, isn't a tart some kinda English floozy?" she asked with a mock frown.

"Yes," he said, his face still only inches from hers, "but there are different kinds of tarts, my dear Jennifer?"

"Really?" She moved closer to his lips again. "And what kinda tart am I?"

"The kind that needs to be eaten," he bravely said and pushed forward to kiss her, before she could reply. Inside her head Jennifer Adams was the happiest she had been since her first cookbook had come out. She opened her mouth and let his tongue inside. Soon they were lying side-by-side partway off the blanket not caring about grass stains.

The sun shone on the couple as their hands explored inside each others underwear. Her fingers wrapped hard around his manhood; his fingers pushed past her cotton panties and into her inviting wetness. They kissed and groaned in pleasure and for them life became just about as perfect as it could get.

* * * *

"Are you sure?" he asked, lying on the bed in the special east wing boudoir she had prepared earlier. Paul lay on his back and she eased down the fifth condom of the day on his hard penis.

"Yeah, but I think I need some music, if you don't mind?" she asked, her body slick with a healthy sheen of perspiration, as she sat straddling his muscular legs.

"After today I don't mind what you do." He laughed, his throat a little dry, but he wasn't about to ask for a drink break right now.

"Kewl." She smiled and reached across to grab her phone and put on something pop and loud as the clock on her cell read five minutes to midnight

She smiled at him with a lustful face he had never seen before. He reached up to fondle her breasts as she grabbed the base of his cock. Then angling the end of his penis against her butt-hole, she lowered down on his hardness slowly as the pain and pleasure mingled as one.

Neither of them had expected how far they'd share each other bodies, since their simple kisses by the lake. Jennifer discovered the real woman inside her, the Jenny Adams that George had slowly beaten down year after year, until she doubted her every decision. Thank God for Valerie and that cooking competition George had suggested she enter. Ironically his idea had brought the downfall of their marriage, even more than him screwing prostitutes while away on business trips.

Now, she was in charge. She could be as dirty as he. As she closed her eyes, she eased Paul's cock deeper into her back passage. She never did this with George, even though he begged her to. No, she did this for her, because the man below her crushing her breasts and rubbing at her stiff nipples was more a man than George would ever be.

* * * *

Cromity knew she wasn't in her bedroom; he couldn't pick up the scent of her Adam's blood. She wasn't in the kitchen or other rooms of the ground floor either. Only as he crouched on the parapets of the house, did he see a slight reflection of artificial light on the conservatory roof. Climbing down the side of the house like a cockroach in search of sugary foods, he found his way down to the window. His cloak somehow billowed out behind him still like it was made from smoke and darkness itself, even though he was upside down. His eyes fixed upon the crack left in the top part of the shutters and he peered in.

Then he saw her in all her tan-skinned, naked beauty riding on top of a man with such wild lust filled abandonment that it nearly made his cold heart pump again with excitement. As he watched on with a dead man's cold envy, he knew she'd be the one to end his curse. Plans began to form in the undead gray cells of his evil mind, as he watched her movements become more urgent and close to peaking.

Yes, she'd be the one.

* * * *

Jennifer turned over in bed facing not only the shuttering window, but the shape of Paul Jordan, eyes half open having just also woken.

"Hi."

"Morning."

Both smiled the sloppiest contented smile either of them had for a good many years. Paul reached out to gently caress her cheek, and Jen kissed his fingertips and held on tight to his hand.

They both had so many thoughts running through their minds, as the sunlight angled through the top of the shutters, where the years had warped them apart over the years.

"How you feeling?" she asked, just to say something. Things had gotten pretty wild last night and she never knew what he might think of the situation, in the cold light of morning.

"Spent and like my balls have been repeatedly hit with a cricket bat until they retracted back into my body, but in a nice way. But apart from that, pretty bloody fantastic, Jenny Adams. And you?"

"Warmly tender below, but again in a nice way. I'm glad you stayed the night, Paul," Jen said with a flood of emotion that choked her voice and she drew herself closer to his warm, strong body.

"Funnily enough so am I," he chuckled, "will it be like that every time with you?"

"I dunno, no promises, but you never know, why?"

Doubts crept into her mind, *had she pushed things way too far, too soon, because it felt so right at the time. Had she been too slutty? Was the second date too soon for bedroom shenanigans? Was her lovemaking up to the required standards?*

"Because I may need the use of oxygen and Viagra next time."

"I think you kept up pretty well." Jen slid on top of him and felt a twitch of interest between her legs.

"You may kill me, but I'll definitely die with a smile on my face."

He stroked the hair from her face and stared into her eyes. It wasn't only lust on show here from him. It felt like instant love.

Her hand slid down between her legs and she cupped his balls and gently massaged them, a wicked grin on her beautiful face. Jen kissed him, to stop his speaking and then her hot kisses traveled down his chest, belly to his groin.

"Oh my God," he whispered, as Jen worked under the covers.

* * * *

Sunday morning continued as a day of togetherness, from the bed, to the shower to the kitchen to eat a hearty late morning breakfast. Then they drank coffee on the veranda as the warm sun warmed them and their jaws ached from smiling too much, or maybe other reasons.

"Do you fancy Sunday lunch at the King's Head? It'd save you from cooking, as you must be tired after last night?" He winked.

"Sound's cool," she replied, closing her eyes and letting the sun wash over her face. This was surely as Dickens said, 'the best of times'.

"What do you want to do now?"

They had thirty minutes until the roasts were served up at the pub.

"I would like to have our first dance as a couple, does that sound stupid?"

"Not at all, do you want to go to a club tonight or something?"

Paul asked, sipping down the last of his coffee, as he brushed croissants crumbles off his lap.

"No need for that," she said, getting up from her metal chair with a squeal of metal on stone. "Come with me."

Paul stood and followed her beckoning finger as she entered the conservatory and led him around to the double door of the Reclamation Room.

"I didn't show you this the other day, did I?"

"Nope."

"Then mister, I think you're in for a treat." Jen moved forward, each hand on a door handle and pushed both the doors wide open to reveal the ballroom.

"Oh, my fucking word," he stated as he followed her into the cavernous room, with its polished floors and stack of chairs around the edges of the room.

Jen skipped to the raised stage, cranked the gramophone and put on the waltz music again. After the usual crackles the music from another time began to blare out into the silent room. Paul moved forward and putting his hands around her small waist, lifted her from the stage easily onto the floor into a ballroom pose.

"May I have the honor of this first dance, Miss Jennifer?"

"You sound like my gardener, Henry." She giggled. "But yes, I would be delighted."

They began to step, spin and waltz, in a not too shabby fashion around the vast empty dance floor.

"Well, I do declare, Mister Jordan, you dance right fine and dandy for a fellow." She spoke in her southern belle voice.

"I never miss an episode of *Strictly*." He winked and they danced and pranced, until the record stopped.

"Lunch?" she asked, her tummy now rumbling.

"Sounds like a plan. I'm starving after last night."

"Well, we must keep our energy levels up."

They kissed for not the last time today and then head off to get the Aston out of the garage.

* * * *

They greedily had slices of all three roasts pork, beef and chicken, with a ton of roast potatoes, stuffing, and Yorkshire puddings and as much vegetables as the small space left on their large oval plates would allow.

"This is pretty intense, isn't it?" she asked later as they sat outside on the wall drinking, ice clinking drinks, their bellies full to bursting.

"Yes," he simply replied with a few nods of his head.

"Erm, do you want to stay over again?" she asked coyly, not sure if she could stand another night of passion as she had experienced the night before, or that her body could take it.

He paused deep in thought and grabbed her free hand.

"My heart says yes, but my body says I need a good night's sleep before work. Understand I really want to be with you, but I'm still new to this dating lark and being honest is the best way to start a relationship. Which I want with you, but I'm shagged out, Jenny."

"Oh, thank God for that." She signed and chuckled in relief. "I want this to work out too, but apart from the really hot sex," she whispered in his ear, "I think we need to take our time, have our own space too. Not with others; I dunno what I'm babbling on about; but I definitely need a good night's sleep also."

"Motion carried by a unanimous decision. God, I really didn't want to upset you or anything. I want more of last night and picnics and other days out and things. Glad we're singing off the same hymn sheet."

"We are definitely doing that, honey." She leaned up and kissed him again, with all the people outside the pub watching them, but she didn't care one little bit

They stayed at the pub until four and parted like new lovers do, with many kisses and thirty-seven goodbyes, before she climbed back in her car and drove off, not before a last blown kiss.

Of the drive home, she could hardly remember any of it and returned to the open gates of the estate before she knew it. As she closed and locked the gates herself, Henry came out to tell her about his big wins on the horses yesterday.

Tired she drove back up to the house and parked the car carefully into the garage, before locking the place up. She then trudged on weary legs along the crunching gravel to Adams House. The sun shone across the rooftops and tall chimneys and she smiled. She really did feel at home now.

She woke up on the sofa at eleven, the television blaring loudly at her. With an over-loud yawn and stretch of her arms, she rose to go to bed. Her left palm went between her legs and pressed. She felt a bit sore and raw down below now; sitting on wooden pub benches hadn't helped much either.

After the telly and the lights turned off, she padded up to bed, stripped off completely naked and just fell into bed. She just managed to turn off the bedside light, breathed deeply through her nose and fell quickly into a deep, contented sleep.

No coldness from the room next door or knocking on her back or front door disturbed the lady of the house, this night.

* * * *

Monday dawned, with October knocking at the door on Friday and the weather was still hot for late September, but more clouds interrupted the sunshine. Paul texted her before work and she felt a tiny pang of guilt, as Monday's held no work fears for her anymore. He had a few ideas for what to do Wednesday afternoon and if she wanted they could spend the whole weekend together.

Which was an excellent plan, but dating, her haunted house and Cromity's presence, put the slight damper on her plans. She texted back, cleverly sidetracking the problem by asking Paul how big and comfortable the bed at his house was.

Yet, Jen didn't have much time to dwell on such things, as within the space of and hour and a half, all the rest of her deliveries arrived at the gate and Henry's pointing finger showed them where to go to up to the house. With a few tips, she set up her televisions in the right rooms, with the latest DVD players. She put a new PC in the study. She took the black Lycra dress and the massage oils to her bedroom.

The rest of the day she spent loading things into her PC; software, then the new printer. Signing up to the website again, took longer than she had planned. She ate at her desk, before her brand-spanking-new monitor, a sandwich of ham and cheese with a local apple cider pickle. She went through three cans of diet coke and two packets of chips.

She relaxed about four, in front of her near-cinema-sized television on a stand (not wanting to drill holes in this listed building, without asking the man who was coming tomorrow) and watched one of her new DVD's with a glass of white wine.

She had a hall full of cardboard and polystyrene and those white plastic bands that are impossible to tie up. She watched her Rom-Com movie until ten to six and then headed to the kitchen to whip up a steak, because the exertions of the day had left her ravenous, with mushrooms and chunky chips (not fries, Paul had taught her). She ate in her dining room, glad for once to be alone with her lovely meal.

She watched her soap, marveling at the sound and picture quality and felt sorry for the actresses during those large close-ups. Paul rang her twenty minutes later and she curled her legs up on the sofa and gushed like a love-struck teen down the line to him.

He was going to take her to Swindon, the nearest largest town to the village for her to check out the shops, take in a film and have dinner. She agreed instantly, thoughts of Cromity pushed to the back of her mind now.

She made a list of clothes she needed, maybe a few more winter ones, as she planned ahead; something like a business suit, plus a few uptown gowns would be nice. Even if she only wore them in her private ballroom, in Paul's embrace, him in a tux. *Now, that had possibilities.*

She got into a crime show on BBC1 and watched that until ten and then the news, depressing and sad as usual. She took her laptop to bed with her and added a little more substance to the outlines of her new cookbook. She read for a while, put in her ear plugs, switched off the light and fell to sleep in her four poster bed, dreaming of Paul.

* * * *

Cromity stood before her front door, after another fruitless night of hammering on the door knocker and ringing the bell for good measure. None of his efforts raised the new lady of the house from her mortal slumber. Now his century's old patience was running short. She'd listen to him eventually and let him into the house that should rightfully belong to his kith and kin.

She felt safe in her bedroom, behind shuttered windows and locked doors. There were other ways to woo a wench, and Silas Cromity had twenty lifetimes of men to learn them. He'd let her sleep safely in her bed for now, lulling her into false security. He had waited this long for revenge, a few more days or weeks meant nothing to his lost soul.

Heading back to the woods, his resting place during the daylight hours, which his skin couldn't take without burning, he called up to the trees. Down from its sleepy roost it glided a rook and landed on his outstretched left arm, its black eyes staring into his. His thoughts merged with the birds' and seeded a message into its small brain.

With a squawk of acknowledgement, it flew off into the

darkness with a message only black-hearted men could extract. Smiling he headed back through the trees to his holly-covered tomb.

* * * *

The next morning the sun shone alone in a heaven of blue. With no roses or frosty messages from her nocturnal unwanted undead tenant, Jen dressed up in smart blouse and long black skirt for the visit of the man from English Heritage. He arrived thirty minutes late, which annoyed her, as she could have been reading up on recipes and not hanging around her hall again.

Short, with spectacles and clipboard and quite the poshest name and voice she had ever heard, Mr. Marks-Latham entered the house with a polite, if not clicky air to his upper-crust tones.

She showed him the TV room and other living room where she had put her huge screen televisions in and pointed out where on the walls she wanted them mounted.

He instantly said, "No," with a shake of his head and a scribble of fountain pen on the forms on his clipboard.

She showed him to the outside walls of the herb and vegetable gardens as a place to put her satellite dish out of the way. Mr. Marks-Latham said no, with more scribbles to his second form on his clipboard.

Getting past the annoyed stage, she took him over to the garage, where Purdy lay outside bored and Henry in overalls washed the Aston Martin.

"This is another place I had an idea to put the dish, on the blind side of the garage. It's no way as old as the house, Mister Marks-Latham." Jen pointed, through gritted teeth, on the cusp of politeness.

"Is that a Wolseley Hornet?" Marks-Latham asked out of the blue, ignoring Jennifer as he stumbled toward the old sports car next to the Aston and Henry.

"Yes, it is," Henry replied to the English Heritage man, dropping his dirty sponge into a bucket of soapy water at his feet.

"May I?" Marks-Latham asked his clipboard under his arm and his hands poised to caress the vehicles long hood.

"Up to the lady of the house." Henry pointed back to Jennifer as she approached, bemused by the sudden spark of life that had come into the bespectacled eyes of the official.

"Be our guest, would you like to sit in it?"

Jennifer suddenly saw an opening here, every man, however hard, quiet, dull or evil had a passion; she just had to find it and exploit it.

"Really, that would be exceptionally kind of you, Miss Adams."

Marks-Latham opened the driver's side door and stepped in, turned and eased himself into the classic car, with a look of sexual or religious rapture on his face.

"So, about the satellite dish on the side of the garage?" Jennifer asked going around to the other side of the car.

"When was the garage built?"

"Nineteen fifty-six." Henry lied quickly, before Jennifer could tell him the real earlier date.

"Well, that shouldn't be a problem then. I should get the paperwork done quickly enough for permission to come through by the end of next month."

Mr. Marks-Latham rubbed his open palms down each side of the steering wheel.

"That long really, isn't there a way to speed up the process?" Jennifer asked, leaning forward on the hood of the car, the top button of her blouse had come loose in the last few seconds.

"Well, I could try and push it through quicker, but the rules are there to protect these grand old houses and estates."

"A week seems a long time to me, Mister Marks-Latham," Jennifer replied, tossing her hair back behind her head like a model in a shampoo commercial.

"Well, I'll see what I can do."

"Would you like to take the Wolseley for a spin around the grounds first and you could complete your paperwork after that?" Jennifer suggested, standing up and running her hands along the side of the car to where the English Heritage man sat, staring at her goggle-eyed.

"Really!" He enthused, "Well, it does all seem rather straight forward, your request, I could have it all approved by the end of this week."

"Henry, fetch the keys to the Wolseley, for Mister Marks-Latham, would you?"

"With pleasure, Miss Jennifer." He winked at her and turned to get the keys out of the cabinet behind him.

* * * *

Jennifer was in woman heaven, out with her new boyfriend,

who acted as her pack-horse as she bought and bought from the shop and boutiques in Swindon. An early cinema trip and a late meal at a French restaurant proved Paul was a proper gentleman. He bought her some gold earrings she liked, the cinema ticket and for the meal, even though she insisted they go Dutch; she was as they both knew a multi-millionairess now.

She laughed a lot, not only at the comedy they saw, but at Paul's self-deprivating dry humor. When it got to the dessert stage in the restaurant, every time they met eyes, they just burst into giggles.

They exited the small French place at ten and headed arms interlocked back to his car in a nearby parking lot. It was fully night time, but she felt no fear in Paul's company. It was nice to see buses, taxis and street lamps again. They were lost in the hustle and bustle of a night out, in the company of strangers that passed by and it made a change from her solitude.

"How you feeling? Had a good night?" He asked, as he drove back to Oxsteaden.

"Contented, but tired." She replied, wishing she could go to sleep right now. Her skirt waistband feeling a tad tight from all the courses they had wolfed down.

"I'll just drop you off at your place then. I think we both need to save our energy for the weekend."

"Okay," She replied in a tired voice and closed her eyes. The sound of the engine sent her off to sleep.

Paul Jordan looked at Jennifer and smiled. She looked so much younger when she was asleep and there would be plenty of night's ahead for them both.

* * * *

"Wha?" Jennifer spoke as she woke, still in the car driven by Paul, as dark woods shot past outside her passenger window.

"I said, 'sleepy-head, we are nearly home.' Well, your place anyway."

Jennifer sat up straight in her seat and half-recognized the road and the woods they travelled along, but it seemed so different and sinister in the dark. In the trees to her left, a shape, like a man stood. When she craned her neck to look back, she could see nothing.

"What you looking at?" Paul gently inquired, as the car exited the woods and turned to head around to the bridge.

"Nothing." She smiled nervously back. "Just an animal."

"Probably a fox or a badger, get a lot of those around here, they love my dustbins for some reason."

The car crested the bridge and followed the curve of the road past the garage and up the drive toward her front door.

"Here we are then, door-to-door service, how's that?"

Jennifer paused, sucked at her teeth and then looked up from her lap into his eyes.

"I think you should stay the night, saves you driving back home?"

"I thought you were tired?" he asked, unclipping him seatbelt and reaching over to touch her cheek with the back of his fingers tenderly. "I don't want to mess this up, by pushing too much too soon."

"You're not. I just want you to come inside and spend the night with me. Nobody said you were going to get lucky."

"Hmm, I think I'm the luckiest man on the planet already going out with you Jennifer."

"Ew, nice sentiment, but just a little too corny," she teased, her nose creasing up, in fake distain.

"Really, laid it on a bit thick, eh, duly noted."

"If you stay the night, I'll let you sleep in my real fairytale princess four poster bed and bedroom."

"You know, I can't understand why I'm discussing this, come on."

Paul turned off the engine and exited the car. Jen followed and eagerly grabbed his arm and made him run to the front door. She swore as she fumbled for her keys. Just then she finally opened the door and pushed Paul inside.

"Why the rush?"

"No rush," she replied, shutting and locking the front door behind them and then switching on all the lights. "I just want to get my big hunk of man candy into my bed, that's all."

"Man candy! Who's laying on the corny lines now?" he asked, taking her into his safe embrace and kissing her lips softly.

"Duly noted," she replied with a longer kiss of hers and then took his left hand in her right and led him upstairs.

* * * *

The night passed without any external incident and it felt so good to wake up beside someone again, even if it was for the odd night. Paul woke up early for work. After a quick and stimulating joint shower and a rushed breakfast, he left.

A tinge of Mrs. Chong surprisingly hit her, as she was left alone with the breakfast things, while her man headed off to work. It reminded her of her old life a little, but she knew this life was so different to anything she had before. The sex was so much better and intense, than even the best of times with selfish George. She had a proper life too; this relationship with Paul felt more like a partnership. George had always led her around like a pig with a nose ring, until she finally got over the deaths of her parents and started cooking.

George was so pleased at first, having such a pretty housewife to come home to, who spent all day baking and cooking up different foods for him to try. So sure of his lofty pedestal that he put himself on in her life and the person she came to with all her little worries, he was too arrogant to even consider her hobby might be any threat to their happy home.

She had won the competition; he made her enter, for his pride, to boast to the fellas at work around the water cooler. Valerie had been one of the judges and they became fast friends. Still no alarm bells rang in his macho mind. Then the first book came out and he was still proud of his little wifey and mentally patted her on the head. All the while his position as bread winner and king of the marriage were slowly being eaten away without him realizing it. When the book hit number one on the New York Times non-fiction bestseller section, only then the unease began. When she received her TV slot on the daytime chat show, he started going to prostitutes and paying them big bucks to humiliate them and do some hardcore stuff.

When she out-earned him, he ordered her to stop, be his wife again and not some food whore on television. The war had already been lost. When she refused to quit, he, in a rage, when out and paid some poor crack-whore a thousand bucks to beat the living crap out of her.

The seed and strength inside Jennifer had grown now and her confidence, long stifled by George, renewed. When Valerie and she found him a month later in that hotel in Houston with two seventeen year old prostitutes, the war was over. He would grant her a divorce, leave the company her Grandpa had set up without a word. He could keep the house and car, but any funny business or if he tried to contact her again without the use of a lawyer as a go-between, she'd tell all his friends and the cops everything. The pictures on Valerie's cell phone of that night would keep him to his word.

Jennifer plunged her hands into the hot water of the sink, to wake her from her daydream and wash the breakfast things. A ring of the doorbell caused her to dry her hands on a tea towel as she ran to the front door. She could well understand why people employed butlers now.

A delivery guy was standing at her front door with three cardboard boxes banded together. He thrust an electronic pad at her which she signed with a bemused mind, wondering what she had forgotten she had ordered.

Once the delivery man left, she fetched a serrated knife from the kitchen and separated the three boxes, by cutting the bands. She opened the first box and pulled the bubble-wrap aside.

"Oh, it's those things," she finally cottoned on, "I'd forgotten all about them."

She took one box to her study, one to her bedroom and the other she stored in the TV room. She was getting quite a collection of cardboard and crap in the hall now and rang Henry to see what happened to it. She hadn't noticed any trashcans anywhere outside yet.

Henry informed her that all the big bins were kept behind his house and collected on a Friday morning. Mrs. Wilberforce or he emptied the bins into sacks and just brought them to his place whenever it was required. He'd drive up and collect the cardboard in his Land Rover later.

With that mystery solved, she finished washing up. She put some washing on, since she was getting a pile of clothes now, she'd hid in her great-aunt's room last night, while Paul had made a pit-stop to the lavatory.

She picked out a few more recipes and tried a few out with good, bad and indifferent results that morning until Henry turned up. She made tea as he loaded up the Land Rover and fed Purdy with some cold meat from the fridge.

"So how have you been keeping, any trouble from that bothersome Cromity lately?" Henry asked as they stood by his Land Rover sipping at their hot mugs of tea.

"No, earplugs and ignoring him works pretty well at the moment, Henry.

"Well, good for you, miss, but be mindful, he's still a cunning, slippery bastard."

"I try not to think about him much," Jen stated and sipped her tea.

"Got other things on your mind, have you?" He smirked and raised a white over-hairy eyebrow in her direction.

"You don't miss much, do you, Henry."

"It's my job, Jennifer."

"Things between me and Paul are going well, yes." She nodded, a little embarrassed to have been found out so early.

"You've not mentioned old Cromity to him then?"

"Get real."

"Well, he's lived here a whiles. He's probably heard the rumors himself."

"How do I approach that little conversation then?"

"I dunnos, but if you're getting serious and having him stay, so you don't want him opening the door at midnight to old sallow chops, do yer?"

"Thanks, Henry, you have a knack of spoiling even my sunniest days." She joked sarcastically.

"Those days will be ending soon, look at the reds of those trees, miss. Winter's coming and this hot weather won't last much longer. You mark my words."

"Please refer to my previous answer." Jennifer frowned and sipped her tea, while watching a few red leaves fall gently to the ground at the edge of the woods, by the garage.

* * * *

October arrived on Friday, as did a letter from the Mr. Marks-Latham at English Heritage, giving them the go-ahead to put a dish up on the far side of the garage only. Jennifer called Paul at the bank, and he said he'd call the satellite company right away for her.

It was still on the sunny side, but there was a cold breeze that had whipped up overnight, to lower the temperature from short to long sleeve weather.

Jen laid out her white, clingy silk nightwear on her bed, since Paul was stopping over for two whole nights. Then she went down to the kitchen, to try even more old recipes, with the odd call to Henry to ask what certain old words for some ingredients really meant. The ones she couldn't find, she looked up on the internet and by luck found a site that produced some of these old cuts of meat from strangely named creatures and birds.

She decided to try a few of the ones she could do easily on Paul tonight, hoping not to give him an acid stomach and spoil the weekend.

Paul turned up at half-six with a small overnight bag, and she almost immediately plunked him down in the large dining room and showered him with dishes, both old, new and exotic. He ate them all with gusto and said that every dish was fantastic, even though his face and eyes told a different story.

"Look, if you tell me they're all brilliant, how will I know what to drop from my next cookbook?"

"So you want me to be brutally honest?"

"Not brutally, just not every thing is swell, dear. Honest, okay?"

"This isn't one of those tests that woman do, that they say aren't tests, but secretly are, just to catch men?" he asked, putting a fork with carrots and turnips in his mouth and giving her the eye, before he began to chew.

"In defense of women all around the globe I plead the fifth amendment on that one."

"Now, I'm more confused than ever."

"That's the correct state us women like to keep you men in." She smiled her eyes wide and full of cheekiness.

"Well, it's working. I'm happily confused and brain addled by your charm, wit and beauty."

"That's what I forgot tonight. Corn on the cob."

"Oi!"

They both laughed and chinked their glasses of wine together as dusk fell over Adams House.

Chapter Eleven

Dark fall the Winter Nights

The weekend flew by and for both nights of his stay Jen watched the clock as it hit midnight, but with Paul asleep beside her, no knockings came at her front door. In fact no sign of Cromity existed anymore. She relaxed into a life that was becoming more warm and cozy as the days went on.

The satellite people arrived on Monday morning with clouds in the sky, but enough intermittent sunshine to not think it wouldn't last forever. Henry took charge with digging of a ditch to send the plastic tube cover line down to fix to a box just outside the TV room window, covered by old gray stone pots. With the sudden leap from five channels to over three hundred, Jen spent the rest of the afternoon, just watching TV and channel surfing, to see where she could catch her old American favorites and what series the UK was up to.

Valerie rang about four to check up on her and remind her that she was off on the cruise in two weeks time. She had heard back from the BBC, who were very interested in her doing a show for them, maybe in the new year to tie in with her new old English recipes upgraded for the 21st century book.

"I better get working on the project then."

"Yes, it'd help. I'll send the proposal and contracts over to you before I go on my cruise, depending on how quick the Brits are on their end. Did I mention I was going on a cruise?"

"Hmm, let me think only about fifty times in one phone call, Valerie."

"Cruise, cruise, cruise."

"Go away with your vacation taunting."

"Going, chat soon kiddo and do your new man several times for me, wontcha."

"Bye." Jen clicked off her cell phone, shaking her head at it, but grinning at the same time.

Things were going good at the moment, with life, her career choice, her love life. She could only be wealthier if she was the

Queen of England. She relaxed into the back of her sofa and flicked through her new hundreds of channels. Discovering the kid ones, she found one showing old episodes of *Saved by the Bell*, with *Keenan and Kel* to follow. She settled down and relived some of her misspent youth.

* * * *

Jen met Paul for lunch on Wednesday afternoon for a sandwich. Paul had brought her a half of bitter to try. They sat in the gloomy booth at the rear of the saloon, holding hands and exchanging lovers' whisperers and double entendres. The weather outside, though still sunny through the white and gray clouds, had a strong breeze to it that cooled the outside temperature down.

By the time they walked hand-clasping-hand, back to Paul's cottage, the gray clouds had covered over the dots of blue sky and white clouds.

"Looks like rain," Paul commented, looking up at the darkening skies, blown in on strong easterly winds.

"Well, my luck with the weather had to fail sometime."

Jen felt spots of rain on her hands and face as they walked up the cottage garden path to Paul's old front door.

He opened it quickly. They hurried inside as the rain started to fall a little heavier. The inside of his small windowless hallway was as dark as dusk as black clouds came across Oxsteaden to merge with the gray.

"Do you fancy a cuppa?" he asked hanging up his work jacket on a mounted coat-rack, screwed high up on the left wall.

"No, I fancy you." She smiled her perfect teeth shining through the gloom, as her hands encircled his waist. Her raised chin turned up to kiss him passionately.

"Maybe after then?" He gulped slightly, his left arm holding her close, his right playing with the lines of her long black hair.

"After what?"

"After this." Paul kissed her and then taking her hand, led her upstairs to his bedroom.

* * * *

Jen didn't mind the rain. When it mingled with early darkness and the cusp of winter and long sunless hours, she and her body began to hate it. She was convinced she had been an Egyptian

Queen in a former life, with the love of the sun she had, not sun-bathing, but just the thrill of waking to a sunny summer's morn, filled her with an ecstatic feeling that only great sex and food could equal.

Now, she sat astride Paul on his cover-strewn bed, as the heavy winds brought torrents of rain like crashing waves on a breaker against the bedroom window. It seemed that the rain wanted to get inside itself to escape the wind, so she closed her eyes and ground her pelvic bone against his, trying to shut out the noise. Her arms went down now onto his shoulders, her long hair across his chest and neck as she thrust down and squeezed her pelvic floor muscles tight. She could hear his soft grunting and her cries of rising pleasure, like she was experiencing it as a third person.

As the rain slammed hard against the panes, like they'd shatter the old glass at any moment, Jen increased her pace and noise levels, her eardrums filled with the beating of her hard worked heart. Then she could take no more and let out an earthly strangled cry as her orgasm shook her body. She collapsed onto Paul's chest and lay panting.

Outside the wind changed direction and the beating on the windows of the rain stopped as the dark rain clouds were pushed further west toward Gloucestershire and Somerset.

* * * *

Jen stayed the night, but they didn't make love again. They settled down for a quiet night in. He insisted he make dinner, as she watched her favorite soap, even though she was recording it at home. After dinner they snuggled up and chatted over a glass of wine, while music played on Paul's ancient looking stereo system.

He got out some old photo albums, so she could giggle and tease his eighties mullet hairstyles and his clothes.

"So, show me your wedding pictures, too?" she asked, sitting on the edge of the sofa against the arm, her jeans covered legs over his lap.

"You sure, you won't feel all funny about it?"

"No guarantees, as I am a woman and full of jealous hormones, but I think I will survive," she teased.

He shrugged and fetched a large ornate silver-white photo album for to look at. Jennifer had seen pictures of Paul's dead wife before; he had a couple on the sideboard and up the stairs of the cottage. The album was full of happy faces, not least the bride and groom. Paul looked a bit thinner and his hair was longer and styled, unlike the short barbers trim he had now. His wife looked just stunningly beautiful on her big day.

She was third generation British-Asian, shorter than even Jennifer and had just perfect skin, great bone structure and hazel eyes that just sparkled with love that just radiated off the gauze covered pictures. Jennifer wiped away a tear that trembled on the lid of her right eye, unseen by Paul, who like a man was trying to name all the friends and relatives in the background and ignoring any emotional linkage to the pages. He had cried too many times, over too many years over these pictures to let it bother him now, not in front of the new love in his life.

"She's so pretty," Jen stated, with an unnoticed sniff, as she stared at a new photo with the bride out of her white wedding dress and in a traditional sari for the reception.

"She was," he simply replied.

"And it looks like you go for a certain Asian type, in your taste in women?" She noticed and sucked both her upper and bottom lips into her mouth, so none were showing.

"Strange that. Normally I fancy big-breasted Norwegian blondes, but I suppose you'll have to do." He bit his bottom lip in and stifled a laugh.

"Hey," she pretended to sound hurt and punched him harder than she had intended on his bicep.

"Ow," he cried, rubbing at his upper arm, "husband beater-upperer, you."

"Excuse me, I'm not a violent woman, nor am I your wife."

Their eyes locked for a second, though it seemed to them it lasted longer and behind their eyes they considered and thought things that they hadn't believed they could think of again. Both opened their mouths to speak, but no words came out and the moment disappeared. They let it drop, for the time being.

"So, where is your ex-husband, now?" Paul asked trying, to push the word love to the back of his mind.

"Don't know, don't care; probably in some barely legal hooker's bed getting his hundred bucks' worth," Jen spat with a ferocity that Paul had never heard utter from her lips before.

"Ok-ay," He replied and closed the wedding photo album, "Fancy that cuppa now?"

"Yeah, I would." She looked up at him and winked, glad he received the not-so-subtle hint to change the subject from George to anything else.

She lifted her legs off him. Once up he leaned down to kiss her forehead and headed off to the kitchen with a slight case of pins-and-needles to fill the kettle. Jennifer meanwhile picked up the wedding album again and flicked to a large portrait print of Mrs. Jordan. She wondered if Paul and she could ever reach the levels of happiness of his first marriage. Something she hadn't considered since her divorce, would she want to do the whole marriage thing for a second time?

They went to bed late, after chatting more about families, education and funny things people had said and done in their school, college and university years. In bed they just kissed, cuddled up and fell to sleep in each other's arms, something she and George had never done, which made her feelings toward her and Paul's relationship more special.

Outside in the drizzle, a dark figure with a covered hood knelt down beside Paul's car and out from the folds of his black clothes he pulled a long sharp hunter's knife and stabbed it deep into the front driver's side tire.

* * * *

"I've got a flat tire." Paul stated, as they walked out of the gate of his cottage early that morning, since he had to head off to work.

"Bummer, want me to give you a lift?" She teased, since his bank was only a minute's slow amble down the road.

"Funny girl," he frowned, "I'll have to pop into the garage before work now."

She kissed him wet and sloppy on the cheek. "Ring you later, lover."

Paul watched as she moved past his car up to her tires which were fully inflated. She waved and blew a kiss before getting into the passenger's seat of the car. Paul turned and folded his arms. With raised eyebrows, and a sarcastic grin on his face, watched her get out again and go around the car to the driver's side for UK vehicles.

"Shut-up, it's the first time I've done that since I've been here." Sticking out her tongue, she clambered into her driver's seat, shut the door and started up the engine loudly. She waved as she slowly drove past him, her tongue poking out between her lips again, to counter his tongue sticking out. Then she drove off with a blast of her horn down the road, indicating left onto the High Street of the village and headed for home.

Paul looked down at his patent leather black shoes and smiled, then his humor died, when he noticed the tail, hind legs and wet furry behind of a small rat rammed into his exhaust pipe.

"What the fuck?"

After popping to see Dave in the garage, he let himself into the bank and called the local police, having taken photos with the camera on his mobile phone.

* * * *

Paul didn't tell Jen when he called her later about the rat or the slashed tire, according to Dave at the garage. Some village lad probably thought it was funny somehow to damage his car, because he could afford the newest and best models and had a decent well-paying job.

Thursday was much colder than even the previous day and the white clouds let no sun shine on Adams House all day. Least it wasn't raining and Henry felt pleased for the plants and lawns. It cut down the necessity of him having to get the hose out today. They shared a quick brew and Jen showed him her new televisions and her hundreds of channels, before she set down to work on her new book again, only interrupted by a search through her library's upper levels, where she found both a pre-war and Victorian cookbook.

She had a quick lunch and returned to outlining her book into sections and possible chapters: desserts, starters, meat and poultry and vegetables. She already had a few dishes to pop into each section. It was just a case of building them all up, typing them in (the bit she hated) and testing them at least five times.

She leaned back in her chair, put her hands behind her head and yawned. Her eyes felt tired and had enough for one day. She saved what she had begun twice onto a file on her new PC and emailed it to herself as an extra back-up.

Jen went upstairs to fetch a cardigan as her bare arms felt a little cool, trying to look into the distance as much as possible, to settle her vision down. She had a sudden urge for something fattening and comforting and headed down to the kitchen to handmake the dough for a large pizza. She had tomatoes, basil and oregano from the garden and for buffalo mozzarella and olives in the fridge. She felt intrigued to try the buffalo cheese to see how it differed from the mozzarella she ate in America. So, she made the dough from scratch and left it on a large, wooden chopping block and covered it with a dish towel to shape out later.

She made herself a cup of Lady Grey tea and drank it in the kitchen just staring out the window into the herb garden. Because of her minimal lunch she already felt hungry after her tea so decided to give in and make her pizza right now. Lucky for her the wide, old oven heated perfectly around and her dinner came out perfectly. She had made some garlic bread also, by chopping up a few leaves of fresh basil finely and mashing chopped garlic and large knobs of butter together. Then she smeared it liberally over some toasted French bread.

It tasted delicious, and she amazed herself by polishing it all off in one sitting. She sat back in her kitchen and rubbed at her sated belly.

"Glad Paul's not around tonight with my garlicky breath."

With a click of her fingers, she popped some parsley from a pot on the window sill and chewed on that. Then she poured herself a long tall glass of milk, grabbed a container of cookies and headed to veg-out in front of the telly.

Paul rang her after her soap finished, because he knew what was good for him and by then she had finished off half the biscuits too. The conversation was short, but pleasant, because she had a headache coming on. Jen popped a couple of aspirin, but that didn't help too much. She headed upstairs at nine for a soak in the bath and an early night.

* * * *

Friday came with early showers and like the tugging ache in her belly lasted the rest of the day. She put on her granny panties, fished out her women's products and dressed in her sweats all day.

Now this was always an interesting test of a new relationship. Especially one that had begun with an early start to the physical side: to see how a man reacts to a woman's time of the month. George, one of his only redeeming attributes, thought the most natural thing in the world, very unnatural and hardly touched her when she started. This she had found slightly odd for a seemingly intelligent human being, but had been glad in her heart of hearts. During those awful dinner parties which were more about showing off your trophy wives and business, than food, George's business chum's wife told her; (not that she wanted to know) that her hubby made her give him oral sex on every day of her period like it was somehow her fault.

Jen felt very glad those days and those fake coffeehouse friends were long gone out of her life. Now she'd see how Paul reacted, to a non penetrative weekend of fun, but she hoped against her hormones that he'd be cool about the situation.

"God, I forgot, how much hard work new relationships were," she said, heading slowly downstairs to the kitchen on the wet Friday morning, "and God, I need some chocolate."

She tried to do some more work on her book, but her heart wasn't really in it. So, she sat in the TV room and watched some old movies, with one of her Light Therapy Units set up on the table beside her, to bring fake daylight to the dull washed out day.

She felt glad she had started today, because the first day was always the worst with her. She had time to let nature take its course. Paul wasn't coming over tonight, because he had booked Monday off to do something special. So he would stop over Saturday and Sunday night instead. Which was just about right for them at the moment.

Jen finished her chocolate and fetched some salt 'n vinegar crisps, which she had come to love as much as her English soap opera. She then had a sudden urge to watch hardcore porn, for some reason, but the thought of period masturbation, dulled this hormone induced idea very quickly.

So she pulled her knees up to her aching belly, stretched her cardigan over them and flicked through to the music channels, to try and find some songs to cheer her up.

* * * *

Paul rang her at nine on Saturday morning and told her to dress up warm and bring a waterproof coat and hat, preferably not pink. He'd be around to pick her up at eleven, not ten, as they had arranged, because he had another surprise idea to immerse her into English culture. As long as it wasn't drinking anymore pints of that awful brew called bitter, she didn't mind.

He arrived on the dot of eleven, so the grandfather clock's chimes told her in the hall. She wore an old, long suede jacket and a long, red scarf around his neck.

"Where are we going?" She asked after getting into his car and kissed his cheek.

"Swindon Town." He replied with a smile and zoomed off down the road toward the lake bridge, even before she had time to fasten her seatbelt.

"What are we gonna do in Swindon then, shopping, food or something else?" Jen hoped the first two were involved as she had seen a lovely pair of shoes in a shop window on their last visit.

"Definitely in the something else column, but they do sell food and clothing too, in a shop."

"You're being very mysterious. Why not tell me exactly what we are going to do?"

"Because my most beautiful girlfriend, women like surprises allegedly and if I did tell, you might not want to come?"

"Oh," she wondered, "it isn't anything too physical or demanding on the body, is it?"

"No, why are you feeling a bit fragile today then?" He turned to ask, checking the lane before exiting her grounds.

"Yes, in a way?"

"In a way, cryptic women's language, men don't understand." Paul grunted in a Neanderthal voice.

"Let's just say certain very enjoyable activities are off the menu for this weekend."

Paul slowed down to let a tractor pass on a narrow bend.

"No darts in the snooker room?" He asked, a vague look on his handsome face.

"What?"

"Well we had a go of darts last weekend and I enjoyed it, but I felt that you weren't so keen?"

"What are you talking on about?"

"I dunno, what are you going on about? I'm a man I don't do hints." He smiled at her, while doing bunny fingers on the steering wheel when he said the word hints.

"I'm on my period, so no sex for you this weekend, bucko! That straight enough for you?" A little, frustrated anger had crept into her voice. *Was he really this dumb?*

"Is that all," he began, "blimey, my lower appendage will be glad of the rest. He hasn't worked this hard in years, hard being the operative word."

Even though her lower abdomen protested, a bellyful of laughter burst forth from her mouth. He joined in, not because he thought it was that funny, but her wild laughter was infectious.

"God, I love you," She said without thinking, when her giggles had died down enough.

The air inside the car stopped, time stopped and the world around them spinning at millions of miles an hour also ceased. Jennifer cringed and closed her eyes, wanting to sink into the seat. She hadn't meant to say those words. If she did, she wasn't really sure of their meaning.

Then she took a deep breath and looked across at him. He beamed back at her like the cat that got the cream. Though he didn't say anything, he didn't have to; his eyes told her everything she needed to know.

Jen put her hand over his left one that hovered on the stick shift. He turned it and gave her hand a quick squeeze, before they travelled on to Swindon in happy silence.

* * * *

"Oh?" She stated as he led her through the throng of people toward the football stadium.

"Club shop over there, and burger van over there." He pointed in two different directions along the front of the grounds.

"I've never been to a soccer match before," she called into his ear.

A group of young lads walked past chanting a very rude song, very loudly.

"Then, Jenny Adams, you're in for a right treat." Grabbing her arm, he led her toward the turnstiles, while pulling two tickets from his jacket pocket.

At least, it ain't raining. Men and their sports? She pushed her way through the revolving gate, as a young man took her ticket from behind an enclosed ticket booth.

For the first quarter of an hour of the match she had pleasantly enjoyed watching the fit, young men in their shorts run about the field. With half 'n hour gone, she continued asking questions about the positions and the rules. When Swindon Town scored with five minutes to half time, she cried, "Yes, we fucking scored a goal!"

As the home crowd went wild around them, Paul hugged her and whispered in her ear, "I think I love you, too."

At halftime, Jen made Paul go and get her a scarf and a beanie hat in the home colors. She scanned the program he had bought her, while he was away. Swindon won 2-1 in the end. They had a kebab, while walking back to where he had parked the car. To Jennifer, it tasted like the food of the gods and she had forgotten about the dull ache in her belly.

It was dark when they returned home. They rushed inside, as it had begun to spit with rain. Jen ushered Paul into the kitchen to make her a cup of tea and she headed to the nearest toilet to change her tampon and liner. All refreshed she joined him in the kitchen as he whistled a footie anthem, while putting the teabags in mugs.

Jennifer came up behind him and wrapped her arms around his waist and just pushed herself into his thin pullover, taking in all the odors of his body. They turned and kissed, long and deeply, his hands grasping her backside, which felt so nice.

Chapter Twelve

The Tale That Has To Be Told

Saturday and Sunday night, they spent just holding each other and kissing, joking and talking and getting to know each other more and more.

Monday's surprise was a trip to a local stable and an hour long horse riding lesson. Both of them had never been on top of a horse, let alone ridden one. It was a great day out; the sun shone a little, glinting on the puddles of water the horses trotted along on the way around the stables.

Jen had to use the facilities quickly since horse riding made her flow more than normal. They ate at the King's Head, in their favorite snug, both wishing Paul didn't have to go back to work tomorrow.

When he dropped her home, she had a happy but tired look on her face. She rubbed at her numb buttocks as she climbed out of his car.

"Catch you Wednesday for lunch then, honey," she said, rising up on her toes to kiss him.

"Can't do lunch Wednesday, babes. Area manager is down, and I have to entertain him for the day," he replied, huffing out a long breath over his bottom lip.

"Your loss."

She kissed his nose and with a cheeky grin sauntered over to her front door, knowing he was watching the seat of her jeans wiggle as she exaggerated her seductive saunter.

"I'll call you tomorrow, Jen." he stated, getting back into his car.

She waved, entered her house and watched him drive off down the road toward the woods. Singing a happy tune to herself, she switched on the lights, since it soon would be getting dark. She wandered off to fetch her laptop and check her emails over a cup of coffee in the drawing room.

* * * *

Having drunk too much tea that night, she had to hot foot it to the toilet at half-past twelve to go pee and change her thick liner. On the way back to her bedroom, the blaring toilet light ruined her night vision. Her feet felt the unnatural coldness coming from her late great aunt's room again. Luckily she had her longer trouser pajamas on, but her feet felt like blocks of ice, by the time she had reached the door to the next bedroom along.

She flinched at the feel of the icy, brass door handle. So, she grabbed it quickly to turn and open it, pushing it inwards as her other hand reached out to turn on the lights. She saw her breath first thing as a puff of a cloud before her face and then the writing on every pane of every window in Gwen's old bedroom.

Hear my tale. I beg of thee.

She turned and saw a white face framed behind the far window. Cromity, pointing one longer finger down and around the west wing to her front door.

Jennifer screamed and ran from the room. She had thought that this nightmare that had dogged her line for hundreds of years had vanished, but she had been sorely mistaken. Jen locked her bedroom door, turned on her light and climbed into bed, fumbling for her cell phone. She had Paul's number up on the screen ready to dial, but then stayed her finger. *What was she going to say? Come over quick. A vampire-ghost wants to chat?*

She had only just found him. No way she wanted to make him think she was some insane girl, who sees dead guys. She didn't want to risk losing him. So, she stayed up until four, when she finally fell to sleep again, with the light on.

Late the next morning, she headed down the road to White Lodge to speak to Henry Greenwood, the only person she'd talk to about Cromity, or else be called a crazy foreigner.

Henry was in for a change and showed her into his living room, dominated by a huge brick fireplace and a color print of John Wayne, in his halcyon cowboy days.

"Fan of The Duke, are you?" Jen asked, sitting on the blanket covered two seater sofa, pointing up at the dominating framed print.

"My matinee hero, when it meant something to be famous." Henry looked up at the ceiling his eyes half-closed slits, as he thought. "Fancy a brew?"

"Yes, tea would be lovely."

Jen put her hands on the knees of her jeans as Purdy padded

in and jumped up to sit next to her. The dog did a one-eighty turn and collapsed down to rest her chin on Jennifer's left thigh, begging with sad eyes to be stroked, which Jen duly obliged.

"Maybe I should get a guard dog," Jen stated as Henry returned to the room eight minutes later carrying two cups of tea.

"One of those scary buggers to keep Cromity away won't work, he has a way with weak-minded animals."

Henry put down the two cups on a coffee table before them and then collapsed, much like his canine companion into his old, favorite leather armchair.

"Not worried about Purdy then?"

"She may look dopey as hell, but she's cleverer than thee and me put together."

"I don't doubt it for a second," Jen said, giving the dog a good, vigorous stroke.

"So, you having trouble with old bony-chops again?"

"Yes, how did you guess?"

"Well, I'm pretty sure you'd rather be visiting your young fella than me at home unless you had another reason to. You didn't just pop down heres to chew-the-cud and visit this old man."

"No flies on you, Henry."

"So, what's Cromity been up to now?"

"I thought I'd seen the last of him, but up he pops last night out of the blue, wanting me to listen to his tales of ancient woe. What do you think I should do?"

"Listen to him."

"What? Are you for real?"

"As long as you are strong enough not to feel any sympathy for his old dead bones and don't invite him in, you're safe. Once you have let him tell his tale and showed it hasn't bothered you, he'll hardly bother at all."

Henry reached down and picked up his cup of tea and began to sip at the end of the cup.

"Is that what Great Aunt Gwen did?"

"Yes, she was stronger than many men I've met, even to her dying day. God rest her soul. She didn't give in to his words and ways. 'Twas easier for her being a spinster en'all, but your young man complicates things. So, you have a hard choice to make, tell your bank manager friend all about him, or listen to Cromity, but never ever reply to any of his questions. That's how he reels 'em in."

"This is a big change in what youse told me before?"

"That's because I didn't think you'd last the week, Jennifer, but I see you're made of the same stuff as your great-aunt and a true Adams."

Jennifer absently stroked Purdy's head, while looking up at the actor with his ten gallon hat and Winchester rifle, deep in contemplation.

"What would old John Wayne do?"

"Probably get the hell-outta Dodge. Maybe that's what you should do, Jennifer. Grab your fella, travel the world and forget about Adams House and its ghosts."

"The old me probably would have, but I'm not that person any-more. This is where I want to be more than anywhere in the world at this moment in time, and no old sack-of-shit undead thing is gonna scare me off."

"Good for you, Miss Jennifer."

Henry looked at her with pride. She didn't look like Gwen in features at all, but the blood inside her veins was the same, for good or ill.

* * * *

The rain fell heavily the next day and Jen only received an odd text from Paul, in between work and taking care of his area man-ager. Jen put on a brave show, with her light boxes to fight the gloom and loud, happy pop music on her music systems to ward off her thoughts of Cromity. She typed up a few recipes, linked parts to her new book in the morning and spent the afternoon cooking up some recipes. Late afternoon, she searched the net for locally produced food sources for her old and new recipes and or-dered some exotic fowl and meats from gourmet farm produce websites.

She ate some of the food she had cooked earlier, in her dining room, because she didn't like being in the kitchen too much after dark, even with the blinds down.

She watched her soap, then a Nigella Lawson cooking show on BBC2 and was taken with her beauty and elegance of ease while she cooked up various dishes from her with ingredients from her immense store cupboard. She watched a news program about the American president, and the stars and stripes behind him, gave her a pang of homesickness.

Coupled with the fact that she felt concerned about facing Cromity: could she really just stand there chatting with him, like he wasn't an evil monster? At nine, she had decided to face him, but by ten, her resolve had flushed down the toilet like her urine from the many nervous trips she had taken that night. So, she crawled into bed, put in her earplugs and eventually fell to sleep just before midnight.

She awoke at seven with the dawn and rushed into her great-aunt's cold bedroom. The temperature was rising slowly. The driblets of water running down the glass erased the writing on the panes of glass, but the message still read clearly.

Hear my tale

Jennifer wiped at her top lip and sneezed because of the freshness of the room. Then she turned on her heal and left. She headed straight for a hot shower and dressed up in warm clothes for the day. It looked bright outside at least, but the temperatures had dropped down to more seasonal norms.

She had some cereal and then an idea came to mind. Pulling on her boots, she headed up to the secret room in the attic and one by one hauled the portraits of Cromity and his family downstairs. In the shed by the wall at the end of the vegetable garden, she found a wheelbarrow and a bottle of white spirit. Patting a large box of matches in her coat pocket she put the portraits in the wheelbarrow and headed into the woods.

It took longer than she thought, but eventually she came to the clearing again, where stood Cromity's burial mound, encircled and crowned by ancient gnarled holly bushes. Onto these bushes she hefted the portraits one by one; viscous looking thorns instantly punctured two of them.

Jennifer then pulled the plastic bottle of white spirit from the bottom of the wheelbarrow and squirted each picture in turn with the flammable clear liquid.

"Don't mess with me, dead boy. I'm from New York," she said aloud to the mound. Lighting four matches at once, she tossed them from nearby onto the first family portrait. It caught light with an instant silent flow of blue flame that turned to yellow as it caught. She repeated the lighting with the next two portraits.

Then she stood back as the flames and smoke rose up from the frames and canvas, as the paint bubbled, popped and eventually turned to dark ash. The bushes underneath were still wet from yesterday's rain and the morning dew and hardly scorched at all.

"Now, what you going to do?" she asked softly to the burial mound. She turned and wheeled the barrow back to the shed, before Henry noticed anything was missing.

Later that night, she received her answer.

* * * *

The rain stayed away all of Thursday, but it felt cold and fresh outside. The leaves on the trees turned brown in places no longer red. She chatted with Valerie in the afternoon, who was thinking of what not to wear in the bikini department on her Caribbean cruise.

She spoke loving words to Paul. All the while, she just wanted to tell him about Cromity, but felt too afraid. She stayed dressed and watched a crime thriller film on until a quarter to twelve on one of the lesser channels starring Andy Garcia.

The hallway outside her bedroom already felt chilly, but more so than the rest of the house. She pressed on into the cold-spot and opened her great-aunt's bedroom door, with her outside coat on and turned on the lights.

No faces pressed against the windows and no writing stained the cold glass, so she glanced at her watch and sat on the edge of Gwen's death-bed.

At the stroke of the echoing grandfather clock in the hall, to signal the arrival of midnight, the room grew even colder. A light frost crept up the windows from the bottom to the top, pane by pane, until this unnatural occurrence blighted all.

Jennifer exhaled a nervous cloud of breath in front of her eyes and watched as unseen fingers began to write on each pane simultaneously. Jennifer stared in shock as the supernatural phenomena happened right before her tear-filled eyes.

When the words were finally finished, a deeper fear gripped her heart. Knowing what she had done to burn his family portraits as an act of strength, had only made the situation worse. She looked from pane to pane, window to window, seeing the same message again and again, turning her blood to ice-water.

Hear my tale or you will suffer

Jennifer ran from the bedroom in tears, her peripheral vision catching a glimpse of a pale face pressed up against the window at the near end of the corridor.

"No, go away, leave me be."

She cried and ran from his face down the corridors, sweeping down the stairs as quickly as her feet dared. Once her soles hit the parquet flooring, there came from the front door the booming knock of brass on brass, louder than any mortal could make it sound.

Putting her palms over her ears, she ran past the stairs and drawing room, past the pantry and utility room into the kitchen. She skidded to a halt at the sink, just as all the blinds suddenly rolled up by themselves, untouched by human hands on their draw-strings.

Jennifer reeled back with a cry of surprise. For there Silas Cromity stood in the moonlit herb garden on the gravel path, caped in his impossible cloak of night, watching her.

Anger rose up in Jennifer now, an anger that had started to boil when she and Valerie had burst into room 722 of the Houston Hyatt Hotel and caught her husband having sex with two skinny, underage hookers.

She hurried to the back door, unlocked it and pulled it in so fast that it banged the door into her big toenail on her right foot.

"What the fuck do you want from me?" She called into the silent night, as Cromity walked slowly toward the backdoor, a confused look on his strangely compelling countenance.

"You have me vexed child, should not I be the one full of wrath at the crimes thy family hast done unto mine or how thee burnt the last vestiges of my old life on my very grave."

"It was a message, not to mess with me, Cromity."

Jennifer felt amazed how her Adam's side was coming to the fore. She hoped her grandfather would be so proud of her.

"Desperate men do desperate things. I merely needed the chance to meet with thee again in person and tell my tale. This I ask, as a damned spirit cursed to walk this earth without the comforts of home and family, wishing to bring this agony of mine to an end. I want thee to listen and listen well to my life's tale. If you can see in your heart a way to end my suffering, this is all I ask of you, m'lady. No other motive have I but to end this torturous existence, and you mayest look upon this living corpse in a different light."

Jennifer turned on her heel and headed back into the hall, where she grabbed a chair, carried it back to the kitchen and placed it five feet away from the open door. Then she sat and crossed her legs and arms in a defensive posture and bore her eyes deep into the soulless eyes of the accursed revenant before her.

"Tell your tale and then don't come back again, ever!"

"I will do as you ask and not return unless you call for my presence."

"Well you have seven hours until the sun comes up, buddy. I suggest you get on with it, unless you want the sun to tan that white dead skin of yours."

"Yes, the sun is my greatest enemy, m'lady. I could not see it even if I wanted to end my life, but all these things you will learn in good time. Let us begin at the start of everything, when I had everything a man could ever want, then lost it because of your forebears."

Chapter Thirteen

Cromity's Tale

On the night of the third of September in the year of our Lord sixteen-fifty-eight, I knew the dream and hopes of a better England died. I served well as a captain in the Civil War under John Thurloe. When Oliver Cromwell, our Lord Protector died, it seemed the will of the parliamentarians and the church died with him.

It only took a couple of short years before the restoration, and we had once again a king to rule our affairs. All our past deeds were to be forgotten and the followers of Cromwell left to their own devices. Yet the promises made by man, even before the witness of God can be easily broken.

I lived here, Silas Cromity, withiest my wife and two daughters, so kind and dutiful. No man could praise the Lord Almighty for better. The house then was not like this made of brick and mortar, by old and made from solid English Oak. My lands were but a quarter of the lands you now own, but I was happy. I had done my part in a great venture and my rewards were simple, to be at home in peace with my family who loved me, as I loved them. Yet, all that was about to change.

The head of the local militia, a man I had known good and true for many years, came a knocking on my door around this time of the year. With sad eyes, he handed me a royal proclamation, signed by the local magistrate, It said that because of the crimes I had inflicted upon men of Royalist stock during the war, I was to be evicted from my home and lands. Also I did not leave by the ending of the next day, with only what my arms could carry, my family and I would be imprisoned.

I foolishly stood my ground, knowing that this was wrong before the eyes of God. The next day, he came. Sir William Adams rode upon my track with twenty men of arms behind him.

He ordered me to leave his house and take my family to safety. If I refused, they would suffer. I was a dullard, rigid in mind and thinking God would not forsake me on this day I needed his strength most. I tried to resist them.

I was beaten to a bloody pulp; my possessions thrown out on the grass for all the villagers to take the best spoils. My wife, Sir William, the craven blackheart, took against her will to his bed-chamber and I was thrown in gaol for seven long years.

I will not bore thee with the suffering that befell me in there, but I would bore it a hundred score years and more, if I knew that my family were safe and well. A kindly man of the cloth, I had known many years before learned of my plight and paid the gaolers to set me free. Yet such a dirty scurrilous state I had fallen into, he hardly recognized me.

I travelled a long way back by foot to my home, as my prison had been far away in Newark. I stole food and begged more from priests and monks, but my will to find my wife and daughters pressed me on, when my belly ate at my very insides, wanting sustenance. Thin and ill of body, I finally returned to Oxsteaden Village dressed in a cloak stolen from a washing line in a nearby village.

The place was in turmoil, for Black Death had spread west from London and strangers were not welcome. Yet, I sought refuge in the church on the hill road away from the village and its blight. The old sexton remembered me with fonder eyes than any man had showed me for more than half a decade. He gave me food and water and a place to stay, though it only be the barn where he kept a few beasts of the fields.

Of my family I pressed him hard, but he would not answer until I had consumed broth and bread.

"Where ist my wife and daughters?" I enquired, the pain in my heart aching for news of them.

Yet, that ache would soon become an unbearable agony that would tear my wretched life to pieces, as if they had been hung-drawn-and—quartered. Of my family the kindly sexton told me this and all hope of redemption left me that day.

The very magistrate, once a friend, had taken in my family and in the beginning treated them well. Yet, when his wife died, his attentions turned not to my wife, but my young daughters. The eldest he begat a child with against her will and outside the vows of wedlock. Finding herself with child and with no husband, she packed a few items and ran off into the night never to be seen again.

My wife left the magistrate's house with no food or money and no shelter to be had and ended up in the poor house, where she died two years ago of the Black Death. Of my youngest child, she was forced into doing vile deeds for pennies. They had only just buried her last wook, dying of the pox that sweaty godless men had defiled upon her.

I visited their pauper's graves and wept until, there were no more tears in my body. I headed toward my former home to vent my rage upon any Adams that I could find. Pity my luck for they found me first in the west woods. Sir William's son even though I did no harm to him, his sword thrust my innards, felled me and they left me to die on the forest floor.

I awoke to my surprise in a hovel, deep in the woods, my side bandaged. An old crone stood above me feeding the foulest of devil's brews down my throat. A fever took me and of that night, I do not remember much except the vile chanting and croaking of the old woman's voice, calling up such devilments and spirits of the underworld a man of God like I, had no idea existed.

"Do you want to live Cromity, to get revenge on the crimes put upon you and your family?"

I said that I did and revenge on the Adams was all I had left and I wasn't going to leave this world until I had my fill. Little did I know then the curses and spells the witch had laid upon my ailing body, or the evil potions I had imbued to regain my strength.

Her son had died also at Sir William's hand, after he had professed his love for his youngest daughter. So burning with evil and malcontent I gritted my teeth in my sallow cheeks and headed off to the house that once had been mine. It had grown in size and stature since my enforced absence. Stealthily I broke inside and set brands from the fire around the newest rooms of the building afore I had apprehended by servants of the house.

They beat me and dragged me outside, but the damage had been already done. Sir William's wife and daughter couldn't be rescued from the blaze, as its wooden beams and walls caught like a fire bug and took half of the house before they could dowse the flames from the nearest well, helped by a storm of rain that thundered swiftly.

Of, I this happened, beaten again and tied behind a cart horse I was dragged to the eastern woods where lay the stone tomb of my late father. Inside with his mildewed bones I was put and the stone tomb covered. A month I lasted drinking my piss and blood and gnawing my father's bones, to give me any life or chance to kill every Adams left.

Yet eventually death curled its bony fingers around my neck

and took my last breath, on which a whispered curse of revenge carried. That wasn't the end, for I went not to heaven or hell's inferno, but another place on a green hill where dawn and dusk transpire in less than a day. Mostly I was alone, but sometimes I had company of sorts in this limbo place; once a changed man came, a creature of blood from far across the Alps and learned me things a corpse man could do, that no living man could.

Others times I was alone; lately a younger tall, dark-haired man was there with me, but he saw me not, or just did not want to speak with me. Of this place I got to only in the hours of the day, for the sunshine would surely turn my skin to ash and my bones to cinders; this the trapped creature called Ripev once told me.

Yet when night fell, my body returned from the shadows, and I could walk and talk and be near enough the man I once was in life. I found the old house had been torn down and replaced with a new house, the first Adams House.

Sir William had long turned to dust in his grave by now and new blood, just his descendants lived there now. Of these was a sickly daughter, frail and pale as the silvery moon, she spent much of her life in her bedroom, reading much and dreaming of a life where she could be active and whole like her siblings. She had somehow reached her twenty-forth year, still frail, without suitors or chance of marriage. To her I listened, every night we would talk and laugh and she'd write poetry about her love for me and how she wished to be my wife.

She gave me permission to enter. I took her virtue, which she willingly gave to me and her blood, for it was the only kind my revengeful stomach can take. She died in my arms, still swearing her undying love for me, even though I had taken what little strength she had from her into my own.

Sickened by what I had done, I broke the oil lamp by her bed, lay down beside her and covered us both in that oil, then set us both alight, to go to whatever judgment St. Peter had in store for me. The pain was terrible and all turned black. Yet the next day, I was whole again and left my tomb of stone, earth and holly to seek what had befallen the house.

Only a quarter of it remained and still members of my enemy's line survived and by the house was once more leveled and built again, to the place you sleep in now. Yet my portrait, taken by a villager long ago, remained and every Adam's girl was warned from an early age to recognize me and not to let me into the house under any duress.

Here I remain until the curse is lifted or the Adams bloodline runs dry.

Chapter Fourteen

Life and Death Go On

Jennifer woke the next day like she watched a good scary movie the night before, and it had seeped into her subconscious and inflicted itself into her dreams.

Friday, she pulled open her shutters to find that the sun had returned brightly this morning and on her window ledge laid a single red rose. Her mind was empty, her thoughts wouldn't come or she didn't want to deal with the things that she had learned about the great Adams family line.

Cromity had sworn to keep away, unless she called him. She had no clue what would happen next. She expected closure after hearing Cromity's sad tale about what happened to him and his family. Even though he promised not to return, unless asked and she and Paul could carry on their romance without fear, something nagged deep in her mind.

What if she had a daughter? Would she have to warn her about the vampire-revenant that lived in the woods; would the circle never end? She had a shower and some of her doubts and questions flowed out of her pores down the drain with the hot water.

By the time Paul arrived, just before it darkened, her thoughts turned only to him and how they would sleep all night in the safety of each others arms. She heated up an Asian-fusion stew she had molded from the old cook books and one of her mother's recipes. After a hard week at work, Paul wolfed it down.

They cuddled up and watched TV, kissing now and again like new lovers. Then he taught her how to play snooker. They leaned over, with his body and arms guiding her. She definitely found it more fun than the game they were playing.

When it came to bedtime, she re-entered the bedroom dressed in her night things. A heavy waft of feminine spray came up from between her legs to mask other odors. She joined him in bed. They kissed and held each other tight and talked until the small hours about everything and nothing.

No knocks came upon Jennifer's door that night to her relief or the next. When she bid farewell to Paul on the cold, rainy Monday morning, she felt In control, like at no time other in her life.

As she tried to work on her new cook book in the study, questions kept popping up into her mind about the cursed creature that resided in the woods. She wondered if there was any way to stop the curse and let him rest in peace, without something awful happening to her or the house. She also wondered about his limbo existence. *Did he feel any pain or remorse for his acts?*

The wind outside changed direction and the rain tapped at her window. Yet it wasn't too dark and morose outside. She resisted the urge to get her light boxes out. She felt stronger now. This year with the love of a good man in her heart and a new book and life to pursue, she'd try and do without these crutches.

Not in the mood to write, she drummed her fingers upon the desk and rose, pushing back her chair. Jennifer headed to the kitchen and began trying out four new recipe ideas that had come to mind from her research and imagination. One tasted superb, one okay, one gross and one an affront to all that was good in cooking today.

It tasted so bad she had to have a shot of brandy to take the taste away, followed up by cookie dough ice cream just to make sure. She rang Valerie for a long girly chat in the afternoon, but Val just sang about her Caribbean cruise on the phone to her every five minutes or so. Jen smiled, looked out at the rain failing outside and called her a Bitch!

Day followed day and the dreariness of an English winter started to seep into her being, yet only at the edges. She felt stronger now, a new woman. She kept herself busy. If she was leaning toward boredom and loneliness, she texted or phoned Paul, or visited Henry and threw a stick for Purdy to chase after. She saw no shade of Cromity. The questions she had for Cromity faded, as her love for Paul grew into a mutual co-dependency.

The cold, white cloud filled days didn't worry her at all, or the fresh sunny days. A walk through the leaf shedding trees gave her joy. She had the fun of buying a new wardrobe for the change of season. She loved looking out across the due covered grass that stretched to the woods. Sometimes a low lying mist would be there when she awoke, and she gazed at it from an East wing upper bedroom. If it was a sunny start to the day, it would slowly rise up through the bark boughs of the trees and evergreens and cast shadows across the misty wet lawns, a breathtaking sight to behold.

She felt blissfully happy. The nights drew in now and the darker rainy days became more frequent.

* * * *

On the weekend that Valerie left on her Caribbean cruise, Paul took Jennifer away for a weekend in London as a surprise. He knew that she'd miss her friend, so they took a train that Friday night, ate out at Leicester Square and saw the latest blockbuster film. In their hotel room overlooking the lights that marked the curve of the River Thames, they made love on every piece of furniture that they could comfortably manage.

Saturday they did some sightseeing aboard an open-top double-decker red bus and saw a matinee musical of *Dirty Dancing*. That night they went to a club and danced until blood flowed from the blisters in her high-heeled shoes and Paul's old football injured knee stiffened.

They walked the dark streets back to their hotel at three in the morning. Yet people still milled around, on the buzz of London life after dark. In bed after a long, slow sensual bout of love-making, Jen curled her arm around his neck, looked deeply into his eyes and without fear said, "I love you, Paul."

"I love you, too, Jen. I feel like the luckiest man in the world to have found you."

"Aw, sweetie." Jen pulled him down and kissed his lips softly.

* * * *

Back home, at the remains of the Witch's cottage, two figures, shaded by the darkest of moonless nights stood conversing in low murmurs. One dead, one alive; one spoke to give orders, reveal plots and put into motion acts of revenge that would finally end his curse.

The other figure dressed in dark clothes left and returned the way he came through the trees, while Cromity's smile couldn't be seen behind the cloak of night he wore. He looked down with his dead eyes at the remnants of the witch's abode, remembering how he had throttled the life from her in this very spot hundreds of years ago.

* * * *

They returned from London on Sunday afternoon and Paul just dropped her off at her front door, because if he came in for a while it would only make their parting far more difficult.

She knew as he waved and drove off that she wanted to spend every single moment of her life with him. If he had asked her to marry him on their London weekend away, she'd have said yes in an instant.

She pulled her overnight bag into the hall just as the rain began to fall outside. A text came through from Valerie on her vacation cruise. Smiling at the smutty report from her best friend, she closed out the rain as her front door boomed shut from her push.

* * * *

From White Lodge Henry emerged from his front door with a frown. Paul's car had just roared out and woken him from his nap in front of the football on television. Grumbling as the rain really started to come down, he closed and barred the gates to the estate, while Purdy sensibly watched from the dry doorstep.

* * * *

Two days later after stopping at Bermuda for a day, Valerie stood on the starboard rail of the ship, watching the sun set over the sea. She wasn't much for Mother Nature and walks in the park. She loved the beach and couldn't help wondering at the shear, gorgeous sight happening before her eyes.

"Beautiful," A clipped English accent spoke from directly behind her, though she hadn't heard anyone approach.

She turned from the captivating sunset, to find a handsome, white man somewhere in his early thirties standing before her, in a sharp, linen jacket and jeans.

"The sunset is awesome, don'cha think?"

"Who says I was talking about the sunset?" He smiled thinly, with a cheeky turn to his lips and a glint in his eyes.

"Flattery will get you everywhere." She smiled, her lustful one, just for such situations.

"Then perhaps, you would like to accompany me to the bar, so I can buy you a cocktail. We can get to know each other better?"

"Sure, why not." She smiled widely at him. "I'm Valerie by the way." Valerie pushed forward her hand held at a limp feminine angle for him to shake. Instead, he took her hand in his and kissed it.

"My name is Mister Vaine, but you can call me Jonathon." He smiled widely and putting a gentle arm around her waist led her toward the bar and ballroom area.

* * * *

"Do you want anything done especially 'cause I won't be in for a fortnight? Fred and me are away to our holiday home in Spain," Mrs. Wilberforce said that Thursday. She popped her head around the study door, as Jen worked on her book.

"I don't think so," Jen replied, racking her brain. She had enough spare sheets for twenty-odd beds and could always bed hop if she felt too lazy to change hers.

"Right, I'll be off then. See you in two weeks."

"Do you fancy a tea before you go?" Jen asked, standing up from the desk, with a slight pins-and-needles sensation in her left thigh and buttock area.

"Now normally I would jump at the chance, but I've left Fred to start the packing. I'll probably have to re-pack both our suitcases, while he pops down to the shops. If I don't keep an eye on him, he will turn up with twenty copies of the *Racing Life*, a pair of Speedos too tight for him and two t-shirts. Men, eh?"

"Yeah," Jen smiled back, the image of Paul made her feel all warm inside. "Have a great vacation."

"Oh no problems there, dear, you take care. I'll see you in a fortnight."

"Bye." Jen waved at the closing study door before she realized what she was doing. Then she glanced at her watch, nearly one in the afternoon. Her stomach suddenly woke up. Leaning over her desk, she saved what she had been working onto two different drives and headed off to the kitchen.

The house's ambient temperature grew colder by the day. She now noticed the creaks, groans and rattles of the old central heating system as it came to life each night now. Luckily she had invested in a whole new range of winter clothes, coats and skirts and accessories to keep out the English winter chill.

She was halfway through eating a peanut butter and jelly sandwich, when the phone rang in the hall. It always made her jump, mainly because it didn't ring that often. She normally gave out her cell phone number to contacts.

She wiped the corners of her mouth and swallowed down her piece of sandwich as she jogged to the phone.

"Adams House, Jennifer Adams speaking, how may I help you?"

"Is Jennifer Chong there?" a sad, older woman's voice asked with a Philly accent.

"Yeah, that's me, or was until the divorce, but I'm babbling. How may I help you?"

"This is Valerie's mother, Eloisa. We had a call from the American Consulate in Bermuda last night...there's been a terrible accident..."

Jennifer went cold suddenly from the tip of her painted toes, up her legs, until goose bumps covered her skin and a numb feeling hit her throat. She listened to the words and sobs from the other end of the line. Somehow her brain took them in on autopilot, but the rest of her body had shut down.

Her best friend had fallen over the rails of the ship at the dead of night, only witnessed by a deck hand on his way off duty. He had seen her as she tumbled past him two decks below, from where a shoe, with a broken heel had been found by the rail. No one else had seen her that night since dinner. By the time the ship had turned and sent a boat out to look for her, no trace of her could be found.

She was missing, presumed drowned.

Jennifer managed to say the usual platitudes, as one did to the recently bereaved and promised to call again tomorrow to see if the Bermudian Coast Guard had any more news. She managed a half-sob of a goodbye and had to slam the phone down quickly, before heaves of sobbing shook her body.

"Nooooooooooo," she screamed to the chandeliers of the empty house. She felt the trickle of warm piss down the inside of each leg of her jeans as her body let go. She fell to a crossed-legged position on the parquet floor.

Valerie was gone, her brave crutch that had helped her become the Jenny Adams she had always wanted to be. The person who held her in the elevator after they had caught George in Houston; the woman who gave her the number of the best divorce lawyer in town and had found her a publisher for her first cookbook: was gone forever.

Jennifer pulled at her long, black hair; the pain of tugging at her roots caused her to feel better somehow. She cried a pall of salty tears for the woman who had turned her life around. She hadn't even visited her new house yet, or met her new man. All the things in her life that would happen to her, she'd never get to hear about them or be part of them.

Jen managed to get up and race to the hall lavatory, just in time to throw up her lunch into the white porcelain throne. There she stayed for over an hour, the urine in her crotch turning cold, as she lay curled on the floor.

She had to call Paul. She needed him with every fiber of her body now, but not in this state, so she headed up the wide stairs in a crouched position, like an old, withered lady of tender years. She entered the shower room and turned on the water, fully clothed; the icy, cold water shocked the breath from her chest. As the water soon heated, she began to undress under the water, the cuffs of her blouse and the legs of her sodden jeans the hardest to pull off. Soon she had an inside-out pile of clothes before her on the shower room floor, by the drain. The hot water cleansed the tears from her face, but couldn't stop her jaws from aching or heat the icy pit in the center of her stomach.

Sitting on her bed in her dressing gown, letting that dry her body, her wet hair just left to lay down her back, she called Paul at work on her cell phone.

Within fifteen minutes or so, he knocked on her front door, but she couldn't leave the edge of her bed to answer. Not the knocking, she couldn't answer the knocking and let the darkness in. Paul ran around to the back of the house, which was quite a run. Weaving through the formal, vegetable and then herb gardens, he found the backdoor stood open.

"Sorry, I wanted to get up, but my legs refused to budge..." she began to explain.

He burst into her bedroom and rushed over to envelope her in his arms as the sobs and heart-wrenching tears began to flow again. He lay on the bed and held her tight until she fell asleep in his arms. Only after she had been asleep did he pull his arms from under her and closed the shutters as the afternoon faded into early evening.

He turned on the bedside lamp and held his breath. Jennifer murmured Valerie's name in her slumber, but didn't wake.

Paul left the room on tip-toe. From down the bend in the corridor, he phoned an international line and waited, eyeing the bedroom door as the call went through. At last his call was finally answered.

"Hello, can I speak to John, please?" he asked into his

mobile phone, hoping that Jen wouldn't wake up and overhear his conversation.

Jennifer turned over in her sleep, patted the warm bed twice, but didn't wake.

Chapter Fifteen
Darkness All Around

Jennifer woke to darkness and for the first time in years, it terrified her. She still wore her dressing gown and the covers were scrambled around her ankles. She sat up and wondered why she hadn't changed for bed last night. *Hadn't Paul come over?*

Then her mind clicked into gear and she remembered. The bedroom's darkness faded a little as her tear swollen eyes became adjusted to the gloom. Yet the gloom wouldn't leave her whatever light filled the room, even though the sunniest October day since records began blossomed outside.

It was a new day, Friday, she thought; but Valerie was still gone from her life forever.

She was sitting up hugging her knees when the bedroom door opened. Light from the passage entered the room, sending the dark blue shadows into a browner hue.

Paul stood in the doorway with a tray, with two cups of tea on it and some toast, butter and jam. "I was hoping to surprise you." He smiled thinly at her, but it wasn't a real smile at all. There was no joy in his thin lips today, only sorrow for the woman he loved.

She tried to smile back, but it was even a paler imitation than his. She patted the crumpled covers beside her, giving him permission to join her. He put the breakfast tray at the end of the bed and carefully sat on the right hand side, moving slowly as not to slosh the tea from its china cups into the saucers.

"Thanks for staying the night, but shouldn't you be going to work?" She managed to speak through the lump of raw emotion wedged in her throat.

"I've rang in to take the day off. In fact, I booked all next week off, also."

"Why?"

"To take care of the woman I love in her time of need. I'm so sorry, Jennifer. Is there anything I can do? Do you want me to grab you a piece of toast?"

"Toast." She sniffed with distain and looked down at the tray,

"Sorry, no, but I'll take a cup of that tea."

"Okay." Paul reached one, picked a cup and gave it to her, before he took the other for himself.

She took it from his hands without looking at him. She sipped at it quickly, trying to ease the painful lump in her throat and try somehow to figure out what to do next.

"I took the liberty of phoning an old friend, John at the High Commission in Kingston. He said he would give his Bermuda colleagues a call for me, to see...well...what was happening."

"Thank you." She patted his leg briskly, then gulped at the hot tea, trying to concentrate on that and not break down again.

"If you need another help, lawyers in the states to contact, or someone to keep an eye on your apartment out there, just say the word, okay?"

"Not now, Paul, please." She spat the last word as tears began to roll down her cheeks once more. She let him take her cup and put it on the tray with his. Then he held her close and didn't say another word for thirty minutes.

Paul telephoned Henry to let him know what was going on, and the old gardener drove up to the main house with Purdy in tow. Jen washed her face and styled her hair. She dressed and came downstairs at one, the same time she had received the call from Valerie's mother in Philadelphia.

She looked upon the home phone with disgust now as she shuffled past and headed for the drawing room, to have a coffee and nibble a couple of cookies. Purdy sensed her mood, came and laid her head on Jennifer's lap. She felt glad of the silent company and the fur to stroke.

The men left her to it after a while and headed in the kitchen to chat about football and the state of the nation, anything but death. It was an even more silent day, in the large silent house on the rise above the lake and it would be for many more days to come.

* * * *

From the edge of the lake, he watched the lights that shone from many windows of Adams House and smiled. Winter had only just begun to bite at the occupants, but he didn't feel the cold. He felt nothing at all, but the burning anger of revenge in his black heart.

Yes, it would be a very cold winter indeed.

* * * *

The days passed so slowly for Jennifer for the next week. Still no body had been found. With each day that passed, it became clear that the sea had claimed her best friend and wouldn't give it back for burial. Nor was there ever likely to be one, which was hard for Valerie's friends and relatives to bear. They had no final act to say goodbye and move on.

Paul and to a lesser extent Henry had been her rocks during this time of bereavement, and they had her eating proper meals again by the middle of the next week. Some of her strength and will flowed back into her, but not all. Jennifer knew she'd never be the same person again, maybe ninety-nine percent, but never whole again. Something in her died the day she heard about the loss of her closest friend.

She added to the long list she had, grandparents, parents, Lou at College, even George to an extent. George wasn't dead, but the person she once had loved had died. By Friday of the next week, she sent Henry away and Paul back to his cottage; she had things to sort out. If she didn't do them herself, she'd end up being Mrs. Chong once more, over reliant on others and that couldn't happen again.

She kissed Paul and told him not to come back until Sunday lunchtime, so she could have her own space to deal with things. First, she called Brian in Valerie's office to ask him to represent her now and then Valerie's PA, Gail to ask her to pop into her apartment now and again to check everything. She spoke to Mr. Kowalski at her apartment building to let Gail in, to find her packers and transport agents to clear her stuff and ship it over to England. Once finished, he could put the place up for sale.

Even if she didn't settle here in the UK, she knew she could never live in that apartment again, because it'd just remind her of Valerie too much. At least here in Adams House, she had no constant reminders of her friend. She'd stay here until the pain and emptiness left her and all that remained was the excellent times they had spent together.

She even phoned Valerie's mom and they had sobbed their hearts out over the phone. They'd have a memorial service sometime in November if she wanted to come. Jen said she'd come and felt so sorry for her: not only to lose a child, but not have the legal closure, a funeral, a place to draw a line in the sand.

Sitting at her desk in her study, she opened the folder containing her new cookbook manuscript and added a blank page in between the cover page and the first chapter.

Dedicated to the Memory of Valerie Jones

Then she saved it, closed the file and shut down her PC for the day. With a quivering lip on the verge of tears once more, she headed for the pool room and poured herself a large glass of twenty year old whisky and downed it in one gulp. The burning liquid did the trick and melted away the lump that had returned to her throat. Outside the rain had come again and dark clouds made the afternoon look like a sunless dusk.

Cooking held her salvation, plus the love of a good man and the help of an old gardener. She flung herself into her new book with gusto, wanting it to be the best it could be, for Valerie's sake.

The days grew shorter still and before she realized it Mrs. Wilberforce had returned from her holidays with pictures already developed and a bottle of something strangely alcoholic in the shape of a fish as a present from her and Fred. Her stuff from her apartment was on its way by cargo ship and the place up for sale, which brought no sadness to her heart. She hadn't lived there long anyway. Paul still stayed over on a Wednesday night, Friday and Saturday, an arrangement they liked as if it gave them still an air of independence and time to miss each other.

Suddenly Halloween passed by, and the clocks went back an hour due to Daylight Saving Time. She disliked that it now darkened around half-past four. She used her box lights more now; yet the odd, frosty, but sunny day did lighten her heart a little.

So it was a shock on a Thursday night, just in the new month of November to hear knocking on her front door at eleven o'clock. She pulled on her cardigan over her long pajamas and kicked on her slippers, before she rushed downstairs to the front door.

Through the keyhole, standing in the glow of the outside lamp stood the smiling face of Silas Cromity once more. Jennifer in anger unlocked and pulled open the front door to face him.

"You said you would not come back unless I asked you too and I ain't!"

"Ah but you have, m'lady. Do not treat Captain Cromity as some dullard. I heard your voice as plain as day, in your dreams."

"I don't think so, bud." Jennifer moved to close the door on the dead man and keep out the knowing cold of the night.

He verbally interjected. "You wants to know if I can talk to your poor Nubian maid, lost so far away at sea?"

"What?" Jen asked, pulling open the door again, as the draught whipped through the thin cotton of her pajama's legs.

"Do I not make myself plain, sweet Jennifer Adams? She is sadly deceased and so my part, so art I. In your nightly thoughts, where your mind wanders every road heaven can show, you wish to know if I can talk with her and I can."

Jen watched as Cromity crossed his arms, revealing his white, laced-up shirt underneath his dark cloak, which billowed out behind him, even though there was no wind.

"This is a trick, right?"

"No, wandering conjurer am I, no Merlin, I can speak with her and ask any question your heart such desires."

"Where is…her body then?" Jennifer asked, not really believing this process could do any good or that Cromity told the truth.

"In pieces, in sharks, in fish and nowhere at the same time, it's a real bitch."

Jennifer jumped back a step as Valerie's voice flowed from the lips of Silas Cromity. "Val, is that you?"

"Jenny, it's me. Is dat you? 'Cause this dead dude says I can speak through him with you?"

"Oh God, Valerie, it's me. It's Jen. What happened to you?"

"Too much drink, too many handsome men, not sure, it's kinda hazy. I remember staggering up on deck pissed outta my gourd, then my heal goes over and I follow right over the fucking rails."

"Why didn't you swim, or did the sharks get you?"

"Swim, hun, I hit my head on the way down. I hit that water and knew no more. Now I'm fucking shark bait."

"I'm so sorry, Valerie. I miss you so much."

"Least I went out with a bang or two." The voice from beneath the distant waves laughed, through Cromity's lips.

"So, you met someone on the cruise then, same old Valerie?"

"Yeah, Johnny was real sweet, and he came from…" Cromity began to cough and splutter. From his mouth onto the step issued a torrent of water that no human's stomach could hold. Cromity moved back, bent over, spit a small fish from his mouth onto the step between him and Jennifer.

"What happened?" Jennifer asked, looking down at the fish gasping for a return to salt water and the sea.

"I do not know. The sea used me as a vassal. With your wenches mind and soul flowed the very waters her remains lie in. I am sorry, m'lady. Me' thinks I cannot do this act for yea again."

"You can't bring her back?"

"Not unless you want all of God's oceans channeled through

me onto your step I think not. I must leave you now and rest for this has vexed me to the very core." Cromity turned to leave, his black cloak billowing around him and floating up to cover his head like a hood.

"Come back again at this time on Sunday night, okay? I want to know more about Valerie and about you, if you promise not to harm me or try to get into this house."

"How many nights is it until Sunday, for days and the movement of the sun have no meaning for me?"

"Three nights from now, visit me again, Cromity."

"I will and maybe in time, we try and contact your friend again, or mayest-be others that you have loved and since lost to the reapers' blade. With my hand on my heart I promise not to do anything to you that you do not so wish or desire."

With a wave of his pale hand, Cromity's cloak covered him and he moved off into the night and merged with the darkness. Jennifer shivered as he departed then used a spatula to flick the now dead fish into the garden, then closed and locked the door to keep the cold night out as well. Next time she'd dress-up warm for her nocturnal talks with her dead lodger and wondered if it could be really true that she could talk to her family through the dead man and what would be asked in return for such favors.

Jennifer headed first not to her warm bedroom and covers, but the pool room to pour herself another whisky to warm her from the inside out. She lay in bed for an hour pondering the chance that she could speak to her parents again, just to say goodbye. *What questions would she want to ask them?*

She woke in the night; it was still pitch black outside. With a nagging ache, she padded to the bedroom door and pulled it open. It was cold in the passage outside her bedroom door and moonlight glinted through the window at the end of the corridor, sending reflective light onto the floor and walls.

"Erh!" Jen lifted up her right foot from a wet patch of carpet before the toilet door. "Don't tell me the plumbing is shot to shit?" She opened the toilet door.

Wet footprint-sized puddles of water led up to where a drenched figure of a woman stood. Her left leg passed through the toilet like it wasn't there.

"Valerie?"

It was her, her best friend, water drenched hair lying over her face obscuring parts of it. She mouthed something to Jennifer, but no words came, only a continued stream of water.

Then she vanished, but the wet footprints remained. Jennifer hurried downstairs to use another toilet. Then she came rushing back upstairs with her mobile phone, turned on the toilet light and took pictures of the wet footprints.

Shivering Jennifer returned to her bed, not sure what to think. Thoughts wouldn't come. Her brain had closed down for a while to prevent any mental damage.

Jen pushed her thumbs into the bridge of her nose and pushed up along her plucked eyebrows to relieve the tension building up there.

"Come on, God. Give me a break here. Two ghosts, most people never even get to see one."

She checked her mobile and looked at the pictures she had taken, but when she zoomed in closer on the frames, no wet footprints could be seen anywhere.

"Oh great, no evidence; I must be going fucking nuts then."

Sleep wasn't forthcoming so she dressed at four-thirty to examine the corridor outside her bedroom door and the bathroom. No traces of any water or dampness could be found, with her on her knees patting the floor.

She put on her trainer socks and runners and headed downstairs to the kitchen turning on lights as she went. Once there she unbolted the backdoor and called gently out into the night at first, then louder.

"Cromity...Cromity!"

With a loud yawn, he flowed over the garden wall like smoke from a bonfire, until he stood not more than three yards from her, separated only by the backdoor frame.

"You summoned me, m'lady?" He bowed and his cloak slipped back to lie in the shadows to show what would looked like a man in fancy dress to her, if she didn't know his true ghastly nature.

"I saw Valerie. I felt water on my feet where she had walked. What is going on here, fella?"

"Once a fine wine is uncorked, it must be drunk with haste or it will soon turn to vinegar."

"What the hell is that crap supposed to mean? Why is Valerie's ghost here in my house?"

Jen scratched at her temple, her forearm and then put her hands on her hips giving them something else to do.

"I called the soul of your dead friend from her final resting place to here as you requested. What you didn't ask if there was a price to pay for such an ungodly act?"

"What do you mean?"

"She was dead, her soul at peace, you called her back to this mortal coil and now she is haunting you, hating you for trapping her very soul here. I may be the devil himself, but this act I would not do, even if it was my family I could bring forth. She is in torment, Jennifer Adams, plain and simple."

"Fuck!"

"Is that a request, m'lady?" Cromity asked with a twitch of a smile under his moustache.

"No! Definitely not." Jennifer turned around and paced up and down her kitchen floor. "Can we send her back, to be in peace?"

"I hope so," he nodded, "but I too have my price."

"You aren't stepping in this house, not on my watch, mister, so forget that."

"I know that will never be with one so strong in mind as you, much like your great-aunt you are, pains me to speaketh these facts. No, I wish to strike a bargain as such, one hour of your time I request, once a week to talk to you on the world today and other matters."

"One hour, but why? What's in it for you?"

"I am a tortured soul curse by a witch's revenge to walk the earth at night until the end of eternity, pity I do not seek, just a cure for the worst part of my existence."

"And what is that?"

"I am lonely," he said simply with an honest sadness his pale thin cheeks easily portrayed.

"Lonely?"

"I am trapped in an infernal limbo in my daylight hours and forced to wander the night, trapped by the boundaries of this estate, tied to this house like a limpet stuck to the keel of ship. Yet, this is not the house that I once lived happily with my family. That is long gone. Still I must remain; the taste of blood and revenge no longer seems important after hundreds of years every day the same, never changing and never dying. How I long to join my wife and daughters in death's cold embrace, but there is no end for Silas Cromity, Jennifer Adams, no peace, no rest."

Jennifer blinked and found she had been staring into his pale blue eyes. Her feet had moved her within a few centimeters of the threshold of the door.

"If you send Valerie back to rest in peace, I'll grant you one hour a week, starting on Sunday night at eleven."

"Then I must be away. To do this foul deed we have not many

hours before the cock crows for dawn."

Cromity turned and Jen watched in amazement as his cloak flowed up from the dark shadows near the ground and covered him in darkness once more. One step, two and he disappeared again, like chimney smoke that wafted up into a dark night's sky.

Jen closed and bolted the door, then turned and leaned her back against it.

"I'm so sorry, Valerie. I miss you so much. I didn't mean to cause you pain. I hope you can hear me and rest easy now."

Jen blew out a cheek full of air and headed out of the kitchen. In the Belfast sink the tap gurgled, rattled and shot forth a steam of salty water and a small toe ring.

* * * *

Jen played darts and snooker until the sun came up. She couldn't focus on something more constructive and the sounds the darts made thudding into the board or the whack of the snooker balls sounded hard, noisy and good. She played music and sipped at another glass of whisky, having found a taste for very pale single malt in the decanter.

When the sun had risen, she headed back to the kitchen to make a bacon sandwich and a pot of coffee. She found the toe ring in the sink as she filled the kettle.

She held it up to the cold morning light that entered through the kitchen window. It looked very much like the one Valerie used to wear, but these things were a dime a dozen to buy and all looked much the same.

After breakfast she took the toe ring to the study and typed in a question on a search engine, *Things that ghosts leave behind?*

Several things came up; she clicked on one which sent her to a ghost-hunting forum where someone else had asked a similar question.

Ghosts sometimes leave things behind in the real world, maybe as clues to their identities or what happened to them to make them a spirit. These objects are called Apports.

She then typed in *Apports* and read up about them. *Was Valerie trying to tell her something? Was it already too late to find out, had Cromity sent her back to rest in peace at the bottom of the sea?*

Jen put the toe ring in her top desk drawer and shut down her PC. She wanted nothing more than to do some baking now, maybe a nice cake or cookies for Paul, since he was coming around to-night to stay over. Maybe she'd give him something more too. He had been a real rock for her over the past few days since Valerie's death, and she really yearned for his hard cock inside her for some reason.

Shaking her head, she went to the kitchen and pulled out the bowls and ingredients to bake a cake and some cookies, or bis-cuits as Paul called them. She needed to forget about the dead for a while and concentrate on the living.

* * * *

When Paul did turn up, it was already dark and she saw the headlights of his car from the east wing sitting room window. She rushed to the front door, flung it open and ran out to greet him. He just locked his car, when she jumped up into his arms. His hands reached around her bottom to hold her up as she kissed him urgently.

"Did you miss me then?" He finally asked when she let him up for air.

"Carry me inside, and I'll show you how much," she replied saucily and winked.

Paul reached down to collect his bag, nearly toppling her and him over, but righted himself and carried her into the house. She kicked the door shut with her foot and they crashed open the door of the drawing room and did things the old pictures on the wall hadn't witnessed before.

* * * *

"And I baked," She stated as they lay naked on the long sofa in the drawing room, recovering from their hot, hard and fast bought of love-making.

"Well, you certainly can cook," He replied, then kissed her lips and then her left nipple.

"Come on," she urged, slapping his bare backside, "plenty of time for more of this later. There are cakes and cookies to be tried."

Jen scrambled over him, giving his balls a quick rub as her body moved over his.

"I think I've died and gone to heaven," he said, without think-ing. Ninety-nine times out of a hundred, it would have been okay.

"Don't ever say that. I dunno what I'd do if I lost you, Paul."

When he saw the sadness in her eyes and the tears welling at the edges of them, he jumped to his feet and crushed her in a naked embrace.

"Sorry, I didn't think. God, I can be a prick sometimes."

"I kinda like your prick." She laughed through her tears. "It's okay, really. Damn it. I nearly got through a whole day without blubbering too."

"Sorry." He took her face in her hands and kissed her wet cheeks.

"Forget it, just think cookies."

"Biscuits," he corrected her.

"Whatever." She smiled up at him with love welling in her heart.

"And for the record, Jenny, I'm not going anywhere, okay?"

"Okay."

* * * *

Jennifer woke up on Saturday morning with Paul snoring gently beside her and cursed herself. She had planned to get up in the middle of the night, but she had literally been too shagged out and slept right though to half-nine. She got up naked as the day she was born and pulled on her silky robe, before she headed out of the bedroom door, promising herself once again to oil the Goddamn hinges one of these days. The hall felt dry as a bone and in the lavatory, she found no wet footprints. She headed down to the kitchen. Nothing new lay in the white sink, so she put the kettle on to make her and Paul a cup of tea.

On Saturday, they had another football day, and Jen felt glad for the crowds and noise, even though Swindon lost the game two-nil. Jennifer enjoyed the game, if not understanding all the rules and thought it was hilarious that Paul was in a bad mood on the drive home back to Oxsteaden.

She cheered him up with a Thai curry and a special pudding that not even he in his grumpy mood could resist. It also helped her. Trying to cheer his mood made her forget her worries for a while. It felt cold and dark outside, but warm and snug in the house holding onto Paul on the TV sofa.

She thought about telling him, in that instant about Cromity and Valerie's ghosts. She even opened her mouth to speak, but didn't know how to begin. Even if he didn't call the local mental asylum to come get her, he would just think it was part of her grief process.

"Catching flies are we?" He joked looking out the corner of his eyes as she lay on him open mouth like a goldfish.

"Let's go to bed."

"But it's only half-nine?"

"I said, let's go to bed."

"Gotcha, lead on, Macduff."

"Race ya?"

Even though she had a head start, he caught her half-way up the stairs to the first landing and that became their temporary bedroom for a while.

* * * *

"Have you been bothered again by your friend's phantom?"

Jennifer sat on a kitchen stool, facing the open backdoor on that Sunday night, dressed in her warmest new coat, fiddling with a crucifix in her left hand pocket.

"No, thank you for that, I suppose."

"I am wondering, what you are holding in you left hand, hidden in the folds of your clothes?"

"Just this." Jennifer brought out the crucifix and showed it to Cromity, like Peter Cushing in all those Hammer films, her grandfather used to enjoy.

"The image of Christ, our Savior. Long I held onto my religion, but it seems I am beyond saving."

"Does it bother you to see it? Here catch!" Jennifer threw it through the open doorway, and Cromity caught it in one pale hand with ease.

"It only bothers me, because I know no place remains in heaven for me, m'lady." Cromity leaned forward bending down and placed it on the outer part of the step.

"Do you eat?" Jennifer asked another thought popping into her brain.

"Nay, the only thing I can hold down is Adams blood, mores the pity. What I would not do for a roasted shoulder of beef or a suckling pig to feast upon, but those things are for the living."

"Do you still lust after my blood then?"

"I seek now only the means to end this torment that has gone on for so many years. Only sunlight can kill me, but this old body of mine can never see the rising of a new dawn."

"Have you tried then?"

"Yes, on several occasions in the beginning. I would stand on top of my tomb of earth and holly and wait for the dawn, but every time, my body was taken from this place to the plane of limbo and would never return until dusk. I cannot die, m'lady, not by musket shot or fire or the deepest of thrust blades of cold sharp steel. Nor can I live, for this is not a life I would wish upon even my vilest enemy."

Cromity's thin, handsome face looked down at the crucifix on the doorstep, a mournful look of sadness across his white face.

"So, even I'm safe then?"

"My enemy died hundreds of years ago. You have but a small part of the same blood running through you, and you are not my enemy, Jennifer Adams."

"So, what are we going to do? Carry on this Mexican stand-off together?"

"I do not understand your entire meaning, m'lady, but I reckon a truce like the one I had with your great-aunt is in order."

"A truce it is. Look I'm bushed, until next time, Silas."

A look of wonder and shock crossed the old ghost's face at the mention of his first name.

"No one haft spaken my Christian name for years untold, it is both strange and comforting you chose to use it now, Jennifer Adams." Cromity swept off his black, large round hat and stepped back to bow low at her, which caused her to giggle. "You mock me now?" Cromity replied with a wide grin on his face.

"Never, just I don't get many people bowing at me that's all."

"I find that hard to believe with one of such exotic beauty. Goodnight for now, Jennifer Adams." With that Cromity walked backwards into the herb garden, until he became one with the night.

Jenifer picked up the crucifix from the door steps, before she closed and locked the backdoor. She unzipped her large coat and stared down at the Christian symbol.

"OK, crucifixes are off the list. What next, holy water and garlic?"

Jennifer turned off the kitchen light and headed off to bed, wondering why the hell she was playing at talking to the vampire-revenant that she inherited with the house.

Chapter Sixteen

Blurred Edges.

Jennifer shot up in bed, gasping for air: the images from her nightmare still clutching onto her thoughts for dear life. Paul murmured something incoherent beside her and sat up in bed also, his arms enfolding her in a lasso of safety. With dawn an hour away, she could smell the odor of his breath against her cheek, with the remnants of what she had fed him last night for dinner.

"You okay?"

"Yes, just a case of night terrors, nothing to worry about."

"What were you dreaming about?" He tried to stifle a yawn, but failed.

"One of the bedrooms of this house, not this one, blood streamed down the walls like one of those chocolate fondue fountains. A woman dressed in a white cotton shift or nightdress kept pointing to the bloody wall, but never spoke."

"Sounds gruesome, but understandable after what happened to you lately." Paul shifted on the mattress to avoid a painful crease and get into a better position to hold her to him.

"Are you sure you don't want to go back to America for the memorial service?"

"Not this again, please, Paul. I've said my goodbyes, and it's not like they have a body to bury, so drop it. Okay?"

Jennifer pulled away from him, climbed out her side of the bed and headed for the door.

"Sorry, I didn't mean to push you."

"I know, I'm going to make some tea, on my own, do you want one?"

"Yes, but not for another hour, okay? Some toast would be nice and bacon and eggs. Can you do a Full English?"

Paul watched her open the bedroom door her, small but perfect body framed against the lighter corridor and smiled at the silhouette of her raised middle finger.

"I'll take that as a no then?"

She closed the door gently, a grin across her face and headed downstairs for a brew and maybe a butter and jam covered scone, or two.

* * * *

She was startled to see the face of Cromity, looking at her through the window as she turned on the kitchen light. She looked behind her up the passage, past the pantry and utility rooms, but Paul hadn't followed her downstairs. She hurried to the backdoor to unlock and open it.

"What are you doing here? We have an arrangement. I've got... company?"

"Forgive my intrusion, m'lady, but you called me did you not?"

"Fuck no!"

"Ah, I see you were asleep at the time, caught in the evilest of dreams. I have a warning all the same. There are many ghosts in Adams house, and not all are connected to me. This woman with the walls that run with blood like a cascading waterfall, she is filled with anger long held in and could do you harm and the ones you love."

"And you are the Virgin Mary on that account, aren't you?"

"I am what I was cursed to be. She chose to remain in this house after her death to punish all living souls. It is worrying to me that she has entered your dreams, Jennifer Adams. She is trapped within the room where she perished, which is a slice of luck for thee."

"Do I look like Sigourney Weaver to you?"

"I know not. I have not heard of him or seen his countenance to compare?"

"'Cause I'm pretty sure I'm not and I didn't sign up to be in a Ghostbusters movie." Jennifer turned away from the backdoor, her hands going into her black bed-worn hair.

Cromity watched her from the dark doorstep. Even in her night things and with her just woken up face, she radiated a beauty that touched even his undead heart.

"You are a strange one indeed, Jennifer Adams, but our lovely moments together make the everlasting night more bearable."

"That's me alright lovely and strange."

Jennifer turned to face Cromity again, a wry smile on her lips, as her hands fell to her side. Her smile turned to a look of confusion, when she saw Cromity kneeling, the top of his boot just touching the back doorstep.

"What are you doing down there?" she asked, inching closer as the harsh electric lights of the kitchen cast deep shadows across his sallow face.

"I wish to state, for all ears to hear, even our lords and maybe Lucifer in his fiery planes of hell that if my heart still beat, it would beat for you, Jennifer Adams. When you first arrived, I only thought of doing harm to thee and ending my curse, but now I would live a thousand such years as these in torment, just to spend one night in your warm embrace."

"What?"

"I love thee, Jennifer."

"Oh God!" Jennifer had to find a stool to sit down upon, her just woken up mind trying to get her head around what the fiend at her back doorstep has just uttered unto her. The coldness of the last hour of night flowed through the door and up her legs.

"Hey, Jenny, I will have that cuppa now," Paul said from the passage.

Jennifer jumped from her chair and shooed Cromity away with flapping hands, before she closed the back door and spun around just as Paul entered the kitchen scratching lazily at his private parts.

"What you been up to? It's colder than a witch's tit at dawn in here."

"I was hot, then I heard a noise outside and thought it might be raccoons."

Jennifer pushed herself away from the backdoor and met Paul in the middle of the kitchen floor.

"Raccoons, in England?" He stared down at her half-asleep with a quizzical look on his unshaven face.

Jennifer saw the look and cursed her crappy attempt at lying. *Raccoons? What a dumbass!*

"But checking, it was just a fox, silly me. You know us Americans, huh?"

"Let's have a look then," Paul said, trying to move past her, but she blocked his way again.

"It saw me and ran off. Do you fancy some tea then, or something more fruity?"

"Fruiter than you, is that possible?" He asked, pulling her into his strong embrace, as something twitched against her belly.

"Well, well, look who's perky this morning."

"Must be the cold air in here."

"Nothing to do with your sexy goddess of a girlfriend?"

"Could be?"

"Whom you love and adore above all others, until death do you part?"

Jennifer knew her new sexy side could have such an effect on men. She always knew she was pretty to a degree, but never in her life had she felt so sexy and wanted.

"I love you, Jenny."

Jennifer stared up into his handsome, clear eyes, but a shiver ran down her spine. *What was with the men in her life this morning*? She only needed Henry to turn up with a bunch of flowers and her day would be complete before it had begun.

"Will you marry me?"

Jen suddenly felt that cupid had punched her hard in the stomach and she forgot to breath. She even saw stars before her eyes and for a second, thought she was going to faint dead away. Paul steadied her in his arms, searching her face for any facial signs of a positive reply. Her mouth hung wide open, and she closed it after a much needed intake of breath.

"I know it's a shock. We've only known each other a couple of months. It may be crazy and stupid, but I love you, Jennifer Adams. I want to be with you for the rest of my life."

"Yes." *Who had said that*? Her minded whirled and then finally worked out it had been her. Her heart had somehow bypassed her brain and replied on automatic for her.

"Really?"

"Yes," she said again with more conviction, as her brain caught up and decided this was a very good idea. A totally insane and mad one, but a good idea all the same.

Outside, in the lessening shadows, the sky turned from navy to a lighter blue. Silas Cromity had heard every word uttered inside. With a rage he hadn't felt for hundreds of years, he fled back to his resting place, consumed with jealousy. Evil intent returned to his long laid out plans.

* * * *

It didn't hit her until she was scrolling through her numbers on her cell phone. She had been so wrapped up in her happiness that she had wanted to tell Valerie right away. She had forgotten that she was dead. A hiccup of emotion, followed by a rain of tears burst from her eyes at an alarming rate.

Thoughts of *Alice in Wonderland* nearly drowning in her own tears sprang to mind. *How could such a happy event fill her with such utter sadness and gut wrenching grief?* She rushed up to her room and cried her eyes out on her four-poster bed for over an hour.

With a raw feeling in her throat and an ache in her jaw from sobbing, she decided to have her second shower of the day, only three hours after the first. The hot water cleansed away her tears, but couldn't help the sadness that the weight of her whole body burdened her with.

She felt alone in this cold, drab house, all alone and without Paul, who was at work, feeling so small and worthless. Her malaise didn't lift even through lunch, where she only pecked at one of her sandwiches she had prepared. It rained again outside and the wind rose from the west all of the sudden, hitting the exposed house, like nature was telling it, it had no right to be there.

Leaving her lunch on the counter, she headed upstairs to the east wing first floor rooms. She opened seven doors before she opened the one she wanted. It looked bare except for a fireplace in one corner, a window in the other and a large, floral wallpapered wall facing her.

She noticed the room from her dream last night. She felt sure of it. The wind whistled down the chimney of the fireplace, making sounds like the bagpipe player was being strangled with his instrument.

The door behind her suddenly banged shut with such a force it rattled the window panes in the room and Jennifer both jumped and spun around in the same movement.

"Fuck me," she exclaimed with her hand on her hard beating heart, "must be the fricking drafts in this place."

With a hard swallow she moved closer to the faded blue floral wallpaper and looked up to the top-left corner, where a brown stain, covered a large patch where the weather over the years had gotten through to dampen it.

A faint scratching noise caused her to turn her head to the left to see a line being gouged into the thick flock wallpaper a few feet to the right at eye level. She edged back to the center of the room and watched in morbid fascination as the line continued down until it was three inches long. Then the top of the line was joined from top to bottom in a round semi-circle to form the letter D.

It seemed like someone was using a nail, someone not visible to the naked eyes, to write on the wallpaper with a precision that Jen felt sure she couldn't match. An O followed the D and then after a gap an N. Jennifer could see her breath billow out before her, her thick cardigan had kept off the initial chill that had settled on the old room.

Jennifer looked on as the invisible hand wrote on and on until it finished the whole sentence.

Do not trust him

He does not love you

He is after something else!

"I know he is just messing with my mind. I don't trust Cromity, and I won't ever let him into this house."

Oh, if only her therapist she saw after her separation from George could see her now, he could write a book just about her.

More writing began to appear a foot away from the three line already expertly gouged out of the wallpaper.

Not Cromity

"What are you going on about?"

Not Cromity

"I don't get it. Who do mean? Who are you?"

Paul

"That's bullshit and you know it. I ain't taking this crap from some unknown ghost who carves stuff on walls. I'm outta here."

Jennifer turned and walked toward the door, but behind her the scratching continued. She knew something else was being written behind her back. She didn't want to turn around. She just wanted out of this God-damn room, even Cromity had warned her about.

Her hand held onto the door knob. It felt icy cold, so she used her sleeve to cover her palm to turn it and pull it slightly ajar. She opened the door, but then stopped in the threshold and gave into to temptation.

I'm Gwyneth Adams

"No, you're fucking lying," she screamed at the wallpaper, as a sudden deluge of blood began to run down the entire length of the wall written on and covered it over in blood-red liquid.

Jennifer ran from the room, down the stairs and out of her front door in the pouring rain. She didn't stop until she had made it to White Lodge, where Henry opened his front door, to find her soaked to the skin, sobbing with grief and exhaustion on his steps.

He took her in quickly, stripped off her cardigan, put a bath towel around her and sat her down in his chair by the fire. Purdy kept her company as he fetched her a brandy, which warmed her from the inside out and loosened her petrified tongue.

* * * *

"This one, miss?" Henry pointed at the closed door of the room.

Jennifer just nodded in reply, clothed in fresh dry clothes from her walk-in wardrobe.

"Well, I've heard tales told about this place, something to do with a suicide years ago, before I was even born. One of the servant girls found her, lying against the wall with her wrists slit.

"Who?"

"Erm, what was her name? Now she was an Adams, yes Katherine Adams, back before the Great War."

"Did Great Aunt Gwen ever come in here?"

"Not sure, miss, probably not, this place had a tainted feel about it ever since, it's damp and cold too, not the ideal place to spend the night."

Henry winked at her, then turned the handle and slowly opened the door. He stepped in first blocking her view as his old eyes that had seen much in Adams House and the grounds over the years, surveyed the wall in front of him.

"Can you see the writing?" Jennifer asked, coming in behind him.

"No, miss, but I think we may have a burst pipe somewhere in the floorboard above."

Jennifer rounded him to see that no etched writing showed anywhere on the wallpaper, though it looked sodden and stained brown everywhere.

"But it was here, I saw it," Jennifer exclaimed, moving closer to touch the wallpaper. It felt so wet the piece she touched fell to the floor revealing moist bare wall behind it.

"Well, you don't have to convince me, Jennifer. I know this house can play tricks on you. Try not to let the ghost who did this try and worry you. That's what they love to do, mess with yer head."

"So, you don't think it was Great Aunt Gwen then?"

"No fucking way, if you pardon my French. She is at peace; she ain't got no reason to be haunting you, Miss Jennifer. My advice is forget all abouts it and give this room a wide berth from now on."

"No way am I coming in here again, ever."

"Good for you. Now, I better go fetch me tools and check up in the room above for leaks. Will you be okay now on your own, or shall I leave Purdy with you?"

"I'll be fine. I'll make us some tea."

"That's the spirit."

True to her word, Jennifer Adams left the haunted room and never entered it again, though the words the ghost had written on the wall stayed with her and circled her mind for some time to come.

* * * *

The following Saturday, Jen and Paul headed to Swindon, not for the match but to an old jewelers'. In old letters above the door, a sign read, D'Lacey & Sons.

There Paul bought her an engagement ring to befit her beauty. She picked the one she wanted, not cheap, but not in the break the bank state of things. There were more expensive and excessive rings on show, but a huge rock on her tiny, tan fingers wouldn't suit her or the person she was. It was hard for Paul, knowing his new fiancée could buy the entire shop without denting her bank balance, let alone the most expensive item of jewelery there. She in turn bought him a very expensive gold watch, which she asked the jewelers to engrave: *To Paul Love Jen*, on the back.

They had a pub lunch in town, and Jen couldn't help moving her be-ringed left hand across the beer-stained circled table and looking down at the new addition on her finger.

"It's the one you wanted, isn't it? 'Cause I could have got you a bigger one or more blingy thing if required. I'm not a poor man."

Paul reached across and took her hand, interlocking his fingers through hers, his eyes also on the ring. He stared deep into her eyes, and she stared back at him.

"It's perfect. I know it might be a bit odd for you that I've got a ton of money, but I know in my heart of hearts that you are marrying me for the right reasons."

"The hot sex."

"Yes, the hot sex."

They both smirked and squeezed at each other's joined fingers, and with their other hands picked up their drink and clinked glasses.

"To the future Mrs. Jordon."

"To me."

Jennifer laughed, and he found it sweet and good to hear.

"Look, once I've done my time and stayed at Adams House the required length of time stipulated in my great aunt's will, we could go anywhere, do anything for the rest of our lives."

"You would give up the house. Why? It's enormous."

"Its big, maybe too big for this girl, maybe get somewhere that would be our home, one we make together, not somebody else's old place."

"Sounds like a plan to me, love." Paul raised his glass and took a long drink of beer.

"Somewhere where we could raise a family." Jennifer said tentatively in a quieter voice, her eyes on her ring again.

"Sounds like a plan to me, how many do you want, five or six?"

"Erm, let's try for one first and see how it goes, babes."

"Sounds like a-"

"-plan to you, I know." She frowned and patted his forearm.

"You know me so well already." He smiled widely back at her. "Now down to important business, the honeymoon: I was thinking Bali or Bermuda?"

"Ahem, ain't you forgetting something; the wedding?"

"Yeah, I suppose that traditionally comes first, eh?"

"In most cultures, yes?"

"So, what do you want: a big church, white off the shoulder princess dress, white doves and rice?"

"Been there done that. How about a nude, skydiving wedding?"

"An idea to ponder or an underwater one?"

"Or we could run away to...where do couples run away to get hitched in Britain?"

"Gretna Green."

"Is that like Vegas?"

"I'm thinking not."

"We have a lot to sort out, the date even?"

"Yes, but first I'm going to get some cheese 'n onion crisps, do you want some?"

"No thanks fiancé."

"Good thing is we have a great big house for a reception, and I know someone who's a wiz at catering."

"Who?"

"You, just knock up a quiche and some pineapple on sticks, while you're having your hair done on the big day."

"Suddenly I've lost my appetite." Jennifer shook her head and laughed through her nose. She felt so incredibly happy at the moment. She was away from the house and all the crap that happened there, with a man who loved her, and he wanted babies. Her only sadness was both her best friends and all her family wouldn't be there to see it.

* * * *

"Well, you did warn me?"

Jennifer stated that Sunday night, sitting in her kitchen on her stool, with a jumper, long johns and a coat on. The back door stood open with Silas Cromity by the threshold, as a cold wind circulated around the kitchen.

"Curiosity is hard to resist, Jennifer. I myself would have undoubtedly done the same. You are without doubt the bravest woman I have ever met."

"Flattery will get you everywhere, Mister Cromity, but I'm not brave. I'm just me."

Cromity nodded and his eyes lingered on the gold band with a diamond that encircled her ring finger. "I see my declaration of love was too late and only a dead dullard like me couldn't see that you would want to be with a man with red, strong blood pumping through his veins."

"Come again?"

"You wear a ring as a sign of your betrothment to the money lender from the village." Cromity pointed to the diamond ring, and she lifted it and finally understood his words.

"Yes, we're engaged now. Sorry, Silas. I should have told you right away. I do find your feelings very flattering, but I don't think it would have worked between us, you being the undead sworn enemy of my family and not around much during the day."

"Do you hate me, m'lady?"

"No, not at all."

"Do you see me as one friendly to know? Do you like my company?"

"I won't lie. This is so very freaking odd, in so many ways, but I like our little conversations. It's like talking to a living piece of history, but I do enjoy them. You were right about that ghostly, white lady."

"You are too kind, m'lady."

Cromity did one of his usual hat sweeping bows and it made Jennifer giggle. What the hell was she doing, cheating on Paul with a dead ghost-vampire guy, well not cheating exactly, but they had some kind of strange relationship at some level that couldn't be defined in any usual terms.

"So, are there any other ghost and specter about the place?"

"Many, m'lady, some you will never see, some that hide from the living, but I see them all. Some are lost, some burning with anger at the manner of their deaths, some just full of sadness."

"Do they talk to you then?"

"Talk, no. Shout and scream at me like I am Lucifer himself, yes."

"So, you have no friends then?"

"The dead have no friends, Jennifer Adams, only regrets."

Chapter Seventeen
Douse the Glim

Jennifer woke crying.

It was the first day of the last month of the year and she had just dreamed that Valerie had shambled up the aisle to halt her wedding to Paul. Her skin had a livid green tinge to it, and her left arm was missing at the elbow. White bone could be glimpsed through the torn flesh of her lower legs. She was dripping wet from head to toe. Valerie's corpse raised her remaining arm, her fingers just bones that the denizen of the sea had fed upon. Jennifer had turned to Paul for help.

Standing beside her in a morning suit, Silas Cromity smiled at her, before he burst forth with a raucous laugh that echoed around the church. Wider still his mouth opened to unnatural ends, and from this gapping maw slithered a black, smoky snake, with red eyes and long, poisonous dripping fangs that launched forth at Jen's neck.

This had been the catalyst for her awakening into another dark morning of hopelessness and despair following her from her nightmare. She was alone in her large four-poster bed, even though at half-past seven outside, dawn only just started to show on the horizon.

Fearing more night terrors if she tried again to sleep, Jen swung her legs out of her warm bed, feeling the cold cusp of the winter's morning curl up around her ankles. She showered with extra hot water, but this did nothing to lighten her mood. She dressed and put on no make-up and went downstairs for a light breakfast.

The light of the day didn't want to show itself today and black clouds of impenetrable dark filled the sky as far as the eye could see. This was as bad as she had felt in at least a year; the winter darkness enveloped her on these types of days. Her mind felt trapped, and a dark fog encircled all her worst thoughts and nightmares inside, not letting any good news or sunshine in.

She did no work on her book today and the grim look never left her face. It was almost like her top lip had grown suddenly heavy and nothing would help. She texted Paul, but he never replied to her texts. After an hour, she had half convinced herself that he was going to dump her and his love and engagement ring were a lie.

Crying again through despair and desperation, she didn't remember her light boxes until lunchtime. She set them up in the TV room, one each on an occasional table at either end of the sofa, before she watched a *Friends* box set. This helped lower her angst to manageable levels, but she ended up thinking less about the comedy and more about her best friends she had lost during her life.

She skipped lunch and wandered around her large lonely house in search of something, though she wasn't sure what. She even wished that Cromity would visit, just for the company, but it was still daylight of sorts and his curse prevented such actions.

She was in the library, leafing through a book by someone called William Hope Hodgson, when her phone rang.

"Hiya babes, sorry, I missed your texts. I left my mobile at home and only just gone and fetched it. Been right busy today it has. How are you then?"

Suddenly she felt very silly and cursed her mind for playing tricks on her. A smile appeared on her face and most of the fog around her mind lifted in hearing her finance's voice.

"I love you so much, Paul." She managed to croak out; her voice choked with emotion.

"I love you too. What's wrong? You seem a little down, Jenny."

The love and concern in his voice lifted her spirits even more, to a state where she mocked herself for the weakness of the morning's morose attack.

"Just the dark and the weather, but you make me better, Paul Jordan; you're my light in the darkness."

"Tell you what, I'll leave at three today. You drive over to my place, do your cooking thing and spend the night in my bed. That old, gloomy mansion is enough to get anyone down, okay?"

"Okay," she replied, wiping away the silent tears that had fallen onto her cheeks; tears of relief, not sadness.

"Get your arse in gear then, woman, and I'll see you very soon."

"Woman, hmmn I'll let that slip this once."

"Okay, woman."

"Okay, now you are officially in deep shit, Paul Jordan. Wait until I get my hands on you later?"

"Can't wait; see ya, lover. Gotta go now, bye."

"See you later."

When the conversation ended, Jen smiled at her cell like it was an expensive jewel or an ancient talisman of good omen. She looked down at her clothes and shook her head.

"What the hell was I thinking? Off to glam up for my man."

She headed upstairs to her bedroom, to put on something alluring, try on some new shoes she got the other day and put on her war paint. SAD and sadness weren't going to rule her new life; she was Jennifer Adams and could do anything.

By the time she drove the Aston out of the garage, the dark clouds had been blown away eastwards and the cloud cover broke up to let some winter sunshine spear itself through in gaps. Feeling like this morning's despair had happened to someone else she set off for the village and Paul's cottage.

* * * *

Paul winked at Gloria Glover, his assistant at the bank as he left. She smiled back; the wink meant thank you and the smile meant you owe me one. The sunlight outside shone suddenly, and Paul raised his hand to his eyes to stop some of the glare from the heavens. The clouds white and hopeful covered the sun, and Paul lowered his hand as he reached the curb.

Someone crossing the road bumped into him, knocking him slightly side ways, and he saw only a bearded youth in a hoodie next to him.

"Watch where you're fucking going?" Saul growled from under his hood already a few steps away from the bank manager.

"Oi, don't talk to me like that, you little prick!"

It wasn't eloquent or befitting his stature in the community, but it felt like sometimes he had to fight fire with fire.

Saul a few yards away now, stopped and turned on the spot with a wide, cocky grin across his half-hidden face.

"How's your car? Did the rat turbo power help?"

"You did that? Wait 'til I tell the police."

"That was just the starters, mate. Main course is next, and your yank girl is desserts."

Saul saw Paul coming and ran off quickly, his more youthful and longer legs easily getting the better of the bank manager. The youth disappeared out of sight in moments, while Paul jogged to stop as a few people on the street stopped to stare at him.

Cursing under his breath he headed across the road and up the lane to his cottage, swearing not to tell Jen about this little encounter as she had sounded so down on the phone after lunch.

* * * *

Jen already waited for him, leaning against her classic sports car dressed in black leather trousers, a dark blue t-shirt and a cropped black leather jacket.

"Wow, you look like a movie star."

She sidled up to him, hips swaying, put her arms around his waist and reached up to kiss him long and deep. "What type of movie star?"

"Erm, action hero, hot sexy, beautiful film star?"

Not sure what had prompted her change of look or where she was going with her questions.

"How about porn star?" She leaned up and whispered in his ear, then turned and headed through his gate and up the path to his cottage. "You coming?" She prompted from the front door.

He stood on the same spot, thanking his lucky stars.

"I'm sure I will," he replied. Taking his door keys out, he opened it hurriedly. They tumbled into his cottage, shedding clothes, before the door closed behind them.

After a long urgent bout of hot passionate sex, they lay within the crumpled sheets of his bed, the duvet somewhere on the floor covering their discarded underwear.

"Do you think Adams House is too big for me?" Jen asked, her fingers circling in his chest hairs as they held each other close.

"We could always fill it up with kids."

"Hmmn, not sure I could manage fifty odd rug-rats with these hips."

"Then we can get something smaller, nearer town, or travel the world a bit. The world is our lobster."

"What if we were to head back over the pond to the States?"

"I have little or no family or ties here, Jen; I'd follow you anywhere, my sexy wife-to-be. Or we could spend winters somewhere hot and sunny and summers over here, which are pretty much like winters anyway."

"Any idea on a wedding date yet?"

"June the twenty-first next year."

Jen sat up on her elbow, so she could see his face, which he turned to look at her.

"Why then?"

"Dunno just picked it out of my head, the longest day, summer solstice, on beach somewhere hot and far away from here."

"Okay sounds like a plan."

"Now you're nicking my lines," he stated and reached around to tickle her ribs.

"Paul, stop." She laughed and wriggled under his torturous tickling fingers.

"Make me!"

"Now you're going to get it, buddy."

"I bloody well hope so."

Outside at only four o'clock in the afternoon, the night had come again, as giggles and tickling turned to hot, passionate love-making once again inside.

* * * *

From the fields behind the bank manager's back garden, Saul watched the house from the safety of the darkening shadows. Paul bloody-out-of-towner Jordan would get his come-uppence soon, he had been promised.

* * * *

Jen drove back to Adams House the next morning, which looked dry, bright, but colder than a witch's tit at dawn. Friday morning, Paul had to be in work at the bank, but he would be coming home to her at the house tonight and staying over for three, not two nights.

She felt alert and raring to go this morning and waved at Henry and Purdy by the side to wood road through her estate, as she roared back up to Adams House.

"Gets more like her great aunt every day that one, Purdy." Henry commented, and Purdy barked her agreement from next to the large sycamore tree by the road side. Henry pulled the long aluminum ladder from the grass and set it against the thick trunk of the ancient tree. Then he pushed up the extension and locked it into place. Purdy watched in fascination as Henry Greenwood pulled and slid the ladder along the trunk to a bough as thick as Henry's body.

A yard along the bough a crack had developed and it hung right over the road. It could be fatal if it fell onto a passing car. Henry put his saw over his shoulder and started up the ladder like a man half his age. The way the ladder wobbled always made him feel uneasy as he climbed, but once at the top he had no fear of heights.

Henry used his knees for balance. He un-slung the saw and using his left hand, which was just as dexterous and as strong as his favored right, began to saw at the crack.

It took a good forty minutes of sawing and resting to cut off the offending limb of the old tree. It cracked and fell down wards. Henry had to saw at the smallest bit of wood to send it all falling half onto the road and the grass beneath him.

Henry smiled with satisfaction with a job well done and slung the saw back over his shoulder. Just then out from the woods swooped up a building of at least fifty or more black rooks right at him. He raised his arms to defend himself from the black squawking assault, when he lost his balance. He tumbled from the high ladder onto the road with a bone shattering impact.

Purdy bounded forward barking at the rooks that had swooped up and away over the east woods. She bent down her head and began to lick the face of her prone master, whose left leg had a jagged bone poking out from a tear in his brown cords.

Her barking and sad mewls didn't rouse him, nor the nudging of her nose to his wrinkled forehead. The smell of exhaust smoke still lingered on the road and Purdy suddenly bounded off, up the road toward the main house.

Jen had only just entered the hall after putting the Aston Martin back in the garage and locking it up, when she heard barking from the porch. Blowing out her cheeks she did a U-turn near the bottom of the stairs and returned to the front door to open it.

An agitated Purdy stood on the steps barking at her and twisting this way and that.

"What is it, girl?" Jennifer asked in a kindly voice, thinking of all the Lassie and Littlest Hobo reruns she used to watch on TV as a child.

Purdy bark three times at her and then turned tail and ran five yards before she stopped, turned and barked at her again.

"What's the matter?" Jen asked, knowing somewhere in her brain, that the dog wasn't going to answer her.

Purdy bounded up to her, barked and repeated the retreat run.

"Do you want me to come with you Purdy?" Jen asked, shaking her head. "I can't believe I've just said that."

The bitch barked at her, wagged her tail and fled off for ten yards this time, stopping and hoping the silly human would follow her.

"Okay, okay, I'm coming."

Jennifer popped back into the house to grab her handbag and house keys, before she made sure she had her cell phone, closed the big front door behind her and jogged after the anxious animal.

"God, I wish I was in better shape." She huffed as she followed the dog over the bridge and entered the road that led through her private woods. After a while she made out the scene ahead, a fallen branch lay half in the road, with a ladder next to it and a crumpled body not too far from that.

"Oh, dear God, no, Henry, Henry!"

Jennifer put on a burst of speed that she hadn't matched since Mrs. Wilmington's gym class in high school. Her shoes pounded toward the prone, unmoving figure of her grounds man, when she noticed something disturbing. Purdy was at her side now, glad that her injured master had been found when a growl rose in her throat as a large black rook landed on the piece of blood smeared bone protruding from Henry's leg.

Jen scooped up a stone from the road and whizzed it at the bird. It missed, but it had the required affect as the rook flew squawking off into the sky and disappeared from view over the woods. Jen kneeled down jarring her knees hard before Henry's still body. Her brain ignored the pain of her scraped skin.

"No, no, no, don't do this to me."

Jennifer raised a shaking hand to Henry's neck, trying not to look at the odd angle of his left leg and the protruding bone. She still felt a strong pulse. *Thank God*. She reached into her bag, pulled out her cell phone and dialed 911.

Nothing happened, no emergency services answered and panic set in as she didn't know the dial code for the British emergency services. With no other ideas, she called Paul.

"Just can't keep aw-"

"-Paul, shut the fuck up. Henry's fallen out of a tree or off a ladder and bust himself up real bad. I dunno the number to call for an ambulance?"

"Shit, don't worry. I'll call them for you. You stay there with him, ok. I'll ring you back."

"OK, but hurry."

When the line died, Jen placed her cell phone on the road, took one of the old man's liver spotted hands in hers and held it tight, praying that he'd be okay. Purdy lay by his head, trying to dig her way into the stones of the road, mewling for her master. From the boughs of the tree Henry had been working on, a single rook watched the proceedings with beady, black eyes.

Paul rang back to inform her that an ambulance was on its way and what followed was the longest quarter of an hour wait for the paramedics to arrive. Luckily the front gates were still open from when she had driven through and they soon got Henry into the back of the ambulance. Jennifer rang Paul to tell him which hospital they were going to and got in with him. Jen tied Purdy to the tree branch and Paul promised to come and take her in when he arrived. In fact his car drove into the grounds just as the ambulance with all lights and sirens wailing turned onto the road.

Henry didn't regain consciousness at all during the drive back to Swindon. The paramedic in the back dressed in yellow and green informed her that as well as the obvious broken leg, he had broken his right arm and taken a nasty hit to the back of the head.

When they rushed Henry into a cubicle in A&E (Accident & Emergency, the UK version of an ER), Jen gave a nurse as much information that she had on Henry, which wasn't much. Then she stated she'd cover the costs for a private room and the best treatment.

"Everyone gets the best treatment at this hospital. Try not to worry." The nurse had replied and left Jen in a waiting area, next to a drinks and snack machine and rows of seats filled with the less injured cases, waiting for treatment with their worried friends and relatives. Jen didn't even know if Henry had any relatives, or how to contact them if he did.

After twenty long minutes a young, tired-looking Asian junior doctor approached her. "Did you come in with Mister Greenwood?"

"Yes, I'm Jennifer Adams, his friend. I found him." She didn't know why she added the last bit and just put it down to stress and worry.

"Good job you did. He has many injuries, the broken leg, arm and a shattered elbow, plus two broken ribs. This added with the knock he took on the back of the head would be bad enough, but with his age if he recovers fully, will take a long time to recuperate."

"Can I see him? Will he survive then?"

"We are taking him up for emergency surgery right away, miss. Check his skull for fractures, his brain for any swelling and set his broken bones. The leg will have to be pinned in several places and this will take many hours I am afraid. If you want to go to the canteen or ring someone, you will have plenty of time. I'll get one of the nurses to take you to the surgery waiting area in a moment.

Try not to worry. He is very strong for his age; most patients his age would not have survived the fall I think."

"Thank you, doctor."

* * * *

An hour later she rang Paul from a different waiting room. He took Purdy back to his cottage and had locked up the house and White Lodge, before he closed the gates.

"How is the poor thing?"

"Purdy, not good, she's lost and confused without him and pining. I'll pop to the shop and get her some dog food in a minute. How are you holding up?"

"Worried sick about Henry, but I'm holding up okay. I've just been concentrating on him really."

Jen stared out of the smeared window of the hospital onto a parking lot and some lesser buildings below, wondering why these things kept happening to people she cared for. *Was she cursed or something?*

"You hang on in there. If you need me to come pick you up, just call, okay?"

"I will, hun, love you."

"Love you too."

Jen exhaled and let the cell phone drop to her side, watching the people trying to park or leave or pay for a parking ticket to stay.

After one vile tea and two slightly better coffees and four hours of surgery time, someone finally came to speak with her.

"Miss Adams, I'm Mister Reynolds, Mister Greenwood's surgeon, can I have a word?" A tall, gray-haired man with dark rimmed glasses offered her his hand after joining her in the waiting room.

"Is he okay?"

"The surgery went well. He's a very hearty man for his age and fit by the look of him, that held him in good stead. Good news was there is no swelling to the brain or any fractures either. He has one tough noggin. Saying that he does have a severe concussion that will give him a belter of a hangover for a few days, but we will give him pain relief for that. We patched up his elbow and set his arm and screwed and bolted his leg back together. His elbow will need another surgery at a later date, once he has regained his strength for another op. With a lot of TLC, he should make a full recovery, but I warn you it will take six to eight months minimum before he is anywhere near his old self again."

"Thank you for saving his life, Doctor Reynolds. Can I see him now?"

"Not yet. He's in our recovery room and then will be taken to a private room as your instructions. A nurse will come and fetch you then, say about half n' hour and he should regain consciousness around the same time. It will be nice to have such a lovely face to welcome him back to the land of the living."

"Will he be in the hospital for long?"

"At least a couple of months I should think. Try not to be too worried when you see him. He has a few bumps and bruises that will soon go down and half his appendages are covered in plaster and bandages."

"Right." Jen nodded, just for something to say and the smiling surgeon left her alone with her thoughts, dark as they were.

* * * *

She rang Paul again for something to do and tell him the news. Purdy had eaten a little food and now laid by his open fire, with a sullen look to her chops and eyes.

Forty-five minutes later, a nurse ushered her into a clean, white room with blue pattern curtains. When she saw Henry lying in his hospital bed covered in white plaster, bandages and linen, she had to choke back the tears. She felt the hair on her legs stand on end as she approached the side of the bed, near a blue PVC-covered low chair. He looked so old all of the sudden.

She touched his good arm and his wrinkled eyelids fluttered open under his bushy, gray eyebrows.

"How's Purdy?" He uttered his first words of concern.

Jen smiled at the humility of the man lying in slings, with a tunnel covering his left leg. "Pinning for her master, but don't worry Paul has her. I'll take her in until your back on your feet again."

Jen pulled the low chair toward her calves with an awful squeal and sat down not letting go of Henry's warm right hand.

"They say I busted up my leg pretty badly and my arm don't look too chipper either. Bloody birds."

"Birds, I don't understand, Henry?"

"A building of rooks flew right at me they did, knocked me right off me perch so to speak."

"A building?"

"That's what you call a flock of rooks, miss, like a murder of crows, bit silly if you asks me."

"Well don't worry, I'll get Paul to get that company you use for bigger jobs to check the place once a week until you're fit enough to come back to work."

"But who's going to keep an eye out for you, Jennifer?"

"I can take care of myself. All you have to do it concentrate on getting better."

"Watch out for that Cromity, miss. Don't trust him an inch do you hear."

"I hear. Look I better be getting back, but I'll come and visit you tomorrow after lunch, ok? You get a good night's rest."

"Don't look like I have much choice, do I? Not looking forward to going to the toilet like this."

"I'm sure the nurses will bring you a bedpan" She rubbed his good arm standing up to leave.

"Best fetch me shotgun and put me down now."

"Hey none of that talk, doctors say you're gonna make a full recovery. I'll be here to kick your butt to make sure you do, okay?"

"If you say so, Gwen." Henry murmured. His eyes closed since he couldn't resist the anesthetic that still would remain in his body for a couple of days.

Jen patted his hand and left the private room. She got a taxi back to the village and Paul's cottage, since there was no point in him coming to Swindon to go all the way back again.

Purdy sprang up from the mat in front of the fire and nearly bowled her over as she came through the living room door. Then she let her paws slide down Jen's body and went into the hallway, but nobody else was there.

"Purdy, come here."

Jen knelt on the floor and offer her hand to the dog, her hand that had held Henry's in his hospital bed.

The dog sniffed for a while, then wagged her tail, picking up the recent scent of her master, even though it was masked by sharper antiseptic odors.

"He's going to be alright, gurl, but you'll have to be patient and stay with me for a while, okay?"

Purdy stared deep into Jen's eyes, and then pushed her nose into the startled American woman's armpit. Jen sniffed back a few tears and held onto the warm body of the bitch for dear life.

* * * *

"So, you wanna stay here for the night?"

"Seems the best plan of action, then we can take Purdy back with us to Adams House in the morning."

"Will she be okay down here on her own?" Paul asked looking at the dog as she slept by the dwindling fire in the hearth.

"Hope so." She yawned."God, I'm bushed. I really need a good night's sleep."

Jen stretched out her arms high, before Paul deftly picked her up in his strong arms and carried her up to bed.

"I could get used to this?" She purred.

"Not with all those bloody steps in your house," Paul exclaimed. They entered his master bedroom, laughing out of relief rather than humor.

* * * *

Silas Cromity stepped over the fallen ladder in the grass, swept his cloak around him and walked on up the road until the house without a light shining in any window came into view.

As he reached the bridge, a nest of rooks flew out from the treetops and circled around the chimney of the many roomed mansion.

"Soon, my friends, soon."

Chapter Eighteen

Nothing Left to Give

Following a phone call, a huge container truck pulled up outside Adams House a week later. Jen and Paul watched on as the driver and his mate pulled back the curtain-sided vehicle to reveal pallets of storage boxes full of her stuff from her apartment in New York. They put it all in the hallway, offering to unpack and take it to whichever rooms she required, but she wanted to unpack her personal stuff.

She tipped the men from the freight forwarders anyway, before she and Paul began to cut the clear wrapping and white plastic strips that bound the boxes to the pallets. Jen didn't help the slow and laborious job, by pouring through every box, before sending it off in Paul's aching arms to various places around the house.

She had many boxes just stuffed full of books, half of them cooking ones, the rest modern fiction and classics. She took these to the library. By the time darkness fell before four o'clock, they were bushed. Purdy wandered in, took one look at them curled up in each other's arms on the sofa and turned tail and headed to her den, one of the drawing rooms covered in cloths in the east wing.

It had been over a week since Henry's fall and he was getting better every day and his elbow fixing op was scheduled for tomorrow. Christmas was coming, not like Jen felt that festive, but every commercial on the television told her it was coming and what she should buy. She had bought hers the previous Saturday in Swindon; the couple had split up for a couple of hours to shop and came back laden with goods they hoped their other halves would love.

Jen just wanted it over, because she knew that then the nights would slowly get shorter. She had a wedding to look forward too, Henry would come home and she could forget the pain of losing Valerie. A new year all clean and unwritten would be Paul and her year; they could leave the darkness of winter behind and maybe Adams House for a sunnier life.

The winter darkness, long nights and Cromity's friendly, but not natural presence, ate away at her. If it weren't for Paul and Purdy, she felt she'd just be buried under a weight of gloom and tear that she never would see the sun again.

Some days she could write her cookbook, sometimes she could only huddle up alone on a sofa with her light boxes blazing away, trying to keep away the despair and darkness.

Adams House wasn't to blame for her SAD; she had picked that up on her way through life. The death of someone she loved deep in her heart punctuated it every few years. Every time that had happened, it stole a little part of her life energy. Even though she kept bouncing back not letting it win, she never fully came back from the abyss of despair; some tiny part of her happy soul remained behind for eternity.

Her grandparents, her parents, Louisa at college, George's soul-destroying marriage and now Valerie this year, it seemed to her that Cromity wasn't the only one cursed.

She knew what she had to do; she had to stop talking with Cromity, cast off her dirty dead little secret and forge a new life in the sun with Paul. She wasn't sure Cromity had evil intentions toward her anymore, but talking to a four-hundred-year-old dead guy, wasn't healthy in anyone's book. Paul would be back at work and his cottage tomorrow. She urged herself for her own sanity's sake to tell Cromity they could no longer speak anymore and to stay away from the house at night.

Now that the decision to ditch the undead from her existence had been made, she felt more positive, just get her through Christmas and into a new year and everything would turn out fine.

* * * *

"...And then the butcher doth cried, I only have a penny left." Cromity burst into a guffaw of unhinged laughter and Jen joined in too, even though Cromwellian humor left much to be desired.

"Silas, look, we have to talk."

"Speak away, my lovely. Your voice is but like a cage full of nightingales singing at dusk."

"This has to end."

"What, my bawdy quips, I know they are not to everyone's taste?"

"No this, our little chats. They have to end tonight. I'm getting married next year and I want Paul to live here, with me and me only."

A sudden sadness fell upon Cromity's face and the color from his laughing, faded to a pallid white of the corpse he really was.

"Have I done aught to upset you, Jennifer Adams?"

"No, not at all, I kinda liked our conversations, but I've had enough of living with the dead. I want my life to be full and I think I can have that with Paul. I don't want to upset you. It's just, this isn't real. It's like a nocturnal dream."

"A nightmare more like. I understand, I really do and somehow even my dull thick dead brain knew this day would come. I'm sorry, Jennifer Adams. I truly am and if you regret your decision or need my help, just call out. I will ever be at your side."

"That is very gallant of you, Captain Cromity."

"Then fare ye well, m'lady. Hopefully one day our paths will cross again."

Jennifer said nothing as Cromity faded backwards into the darkness of the herb garden and fled back to his tomb, crying blood red tears of sorrow.

She closed and bolted the door, glad that the freezing night air was gone. She rushed up to her room where Purdy waited at the end of the bed.

* * * *

Her visits to see Henry in hospital felt very tiring, not to her body, but to her mind. She felt cheerful enough in his presence, but the hospital wasn't the thing to cheer you up, when your mood was underlined with dark sullen thoughts.

She ordered a few Christmas decorations, not that she really liked Christmas that much anymore. She had to make an effort because it'd be her first with Paul, but it usually was just a reminder of all the people she had lost. Paul had no family to invite for Christmas lunch, only a few distant cousins that he kept in touch with at this time of the year only, with an annual yuletide card.

The winter solstice only one week away, a date she circled red on her calendar because, after the shortest day, the night times would slowly begin to shorten. Friday night, Paul was out at the private rooms of the King's Head for his work's Christmas meal. Jen had been invited, but she insisted he go alone and let his hair down. If he was hung over tomorrow morning, just give her a call, and she'd come and ply him with headache pills and TLC.

She turned on lots of lights around the house and watched her soap, behind curtained windows. She read for an hour and then put on a latest release chick-flick movie, which she enjoyed more than she thought she would.

She received a text at ten from Paul saying he had only had one drink, lots of food and wanted to come over later to in his words, give her one.

By ending the text with *luv U* and lots of *XXX*, she concluded that he lied that he had only one drink.

She texted back to tell him to have a few more drinks, enjoy the night, asleep in his own bed, and she'd be over tomorrow, following it with her own long list of *XXXX*'s.

She grinned at Purdy, sprawled on the sofa next to her. "Men, eh?"

* * * *

Paul Jordan waved off the last of his inebriated staff into the night and partners cars. He pouted deep in thought, staring at the pub, to the lane that led up to his cottage and nice warm bed. The amount of drink inside him kept off the chilly night's air, and an idea popped into his booze-addled brain.

He promised Jen that he wouldn't drink and drive, but he could still walk to her place. It wouldn't take more than twenty minutes. So, he pulled up the collar of his coat, put his head down and headed out of the village down the road toward Adams House. He checked his watch under the last street lamp in the village, and it said a quarter past eleven, just in time for bed he thought as he skipped over puddles on his way to his fiancée's arms.

* * * *

Knock, knock.

Jen woke from her sleep as the knocker at her front door pounded, and her bell rang and rang, by someone's insistent hand. She turned on her bedside lamp to see that it was a quarter to three in the morning. Grumbling she pulled on her dressing gown, kicked on her slippers and headed out of her bedroom. *Was it Cromity up to his old tricks again or Paul in a plastered state, wanting drunken fumbles with his fiancée?* Whichever it was, they'd get a piece of her mind waking her up at such an hour of the night.

She felt the chill of the house and her dressing gown made a swishing sound as she paced down the west wing first floor corridor to the landing. She swept down the stairs and had a sudden urge for a cup of Earl Grey and some scones. She rubbed at her rumbling tummy and then her bleary eyes, before she crossed the parquet floor and turned on lots of lights.

"This better be good," she muttered under her breath as she unbolted the large front door and then turned the locks.

With a long breath in through her nostrils, she pulled the door inwards to see a police car parked not many yards away and two police officers, one male and one female standing before her.

The male officer asked for her name. The freezing night's air flowed inwards out of the dark to envelope her. When the female officer asked her if she was the fiancée of Paul Ashley Jordan, the strength sapping cold entered her body and began to gnaw at her bones.

Later she could only recall certain words, like incident, hit-and-run, abandoned stolen car and dead before the ambulance could even reach the scene. She felt as an out-of-body experience, like it wasn't happening to her, not again. She felt like she hovered just above her head as the police woman sat next to her, repeating words she had spoken a dozen times before to the recently bereaved.

The older policeman stood near the fire in the drawing room, asking if there was anyone he could call. There was no one. She had no one left. Purdy laid on the sofa, her head on Jennifer's lap, somehow feeling the pain emanating from the woman's body. She noticed that she wasn't crying and wondered why. *Was it shock or had she no more tears to give*?

The police stayed until Mrs. Wilberforce rushed over at half-past eight the next morning. Later that day she drove Jennifer to the police morgue to identify Paul's body. They called on funeral directors on the way back and set certain wheels in motion. Since an accident or intention killed Paul, his body may take a couple of weeks to be released for burial. Later that day numb from head to toe, she sat in her drawing room, clutching a death certificate, a cup of tea slowly going cold on the table before her.

Gloria Glover led a sunglasses wearing delegation from the bank to her house to say if she needed any help with the funeral, just to give her a call. Gloria burst into tears then, and Jen found herself putting her arm around her to comfort her. Still no tears would come.

Mrs. Wilberforce and her Fred stayed until three, vowing to head up to the hospital to visit Henry for her and pass on the sad news. Jen nodded and led them out, knowing that nobody wanted to stay in and around Adams House after dark.

She closed and locked the front door, but turned on no lights as the day turned so quickly and easily to night. Jen headed upstairs to her bedroom and for the first time since last night turned on her cell phone.

She felt shocked to find one message on there, from last night from Paul.

Leave the lights on and your panties off, I'm comin' to kiss u goodnight love Paul XXX.

The time of the text said eleven thirty-two, sent ten minutes after she had turned her cell phone off for the night and gone to bed. Only now did the tears come in cascades of wails and cries of injustice and mortal grief.

Outside a fox howled and Cromity rose once more in mortal form from his tomb. He swept off his hat, tears in his dead eyes and said a prayer for the recent dead.

* * * *

She rose at five on the morning of the funeral, the twenty-first of December, the shortest day of the year. She cooked, baked and chopped the food for the wake. It kept her occupied; it kept her focused on things that didn't involve cold, wet earth, graves and caskets.

Mrs. Wilberforce, Fred and Gloria Glover turned up as one at nine, to silently help and churn up urn after urn of hot tea. With the food covered in plastic wrap or tin foil and the drinks provided by the King's head, ready and waiting in the ballroom, they set off at ten for the local church on the hill on the other side of the village.

The singing she couldn't manage but the odd verse or two. She let others speak kind words about the man she had only known for a few months and loved like no other man before. The burial itself felt torturous to the point that Jennifer wanted to scream and curse God's name to the heavens at any given moment. Then it was over, words spoken, earth thrown on the brass plate of the coffin. Mrs. Wilberforce led her away; Henry sadly was still too incapacitated to attend the funeral.

Jennifer noticed something as she handed around the food at the wake. In the Reclamation Ballroom, like a switch had been flicked, the sullen faces now began to smile and chat away on subjects of cars, Christmas and holidays for next year. She drank some red wine. By two, people hugged, kissed her and said their goodbyes, with promises of help that they didn't really want to keep.

Gloria, Mrs. Wilberforce and Fred stayed until three to clear up and asked her over for Christmas lunch if she felt up to it. Then they left too. She felt a relief that no one on earth except her could comprehend. In the hall, with the front door locked behind her she began to undress, casting off the black funeral skirt, stockings, the white blouse and black jacket. Her bra and panties fell upon her new, black leather shoes as she let the cold draft from the recently opened door, run goose bumps up and down her slender body.

Naked except for her engagement ring and some drop earrings, she padded on bare feet to the kitchen and began to peel a large bulb of garlic and popped the individual cloves into a large bowl. Once the bulb was fully peeled, she added a large chuck of cold, hard butter from the fridge and then began to pound at the two with the pestle. Hard at first, the butter resisted for a time and slipped from side to side to avoid its inevitable fate. After what seemed ages, she had a buttery, garlic mush. Then she added some chopped parsley. She cut a huge long loaf of bread on an angle to make oval portions and turned on the oven. As the oven heated, she smeared the garlic butter over the bread very liberally and then popped the two into the oven for fifteen minutes. While the garlic bread cooked, still naked she opened the backdoor, letting the freezing air into the warm kitchen to steam up the windows.

On her stool she sat, next to the timer, watching the dark quickly pass through dusk into night. When the timer pinged, she put the garlic bread on a wire rack on the counter next to her and waited for the dark blue sky to turn to night's black. She didn't have to wait long.

Already her legs felt numb from the cold, matching the numbness of her heart and the emptiness of her stomach.

Silas Cromity flowed into view. The harsh lights of the kitchen caught his white shirt and matching face, a look of shock on his countenance. He swept his hat down over his eyes and looked upon his boots.

"M'lady, it is bitter with cold out this December night, surely thou would kind more warmth and comfort in frocks and other warmer garb."

"Look at me, Cromity." Jennifer stated in a voice without tone or inflection that might have come from his graveyards lips, rather than that of a living person.

Cromily let his hat slip down and slowly raised his eyes up the body of the naked mistress of the house. Of aught he expected tonight, this and what to follow didn't even enter his darkest imagings.

Jennifer pushed herself forward to the edge of the stool and with her right hand spread her legs and parted her lips with the fingers of her right hand.

"Is this what you desire, Silas, you dead fuck, because I have nothing left to live for. Was this your plan all along?"

"Cover yourself, Jennifer Adams. What has transpired to make you act in the fashion of a common harlot?"

"Everyone is dead or gone, and once more, I am alone, like you are. Didn't you want this? Isn't this your dead heart's desire? To take me and drink my blood?"

"Who is dead? The grounds man? I have not seen him around these past nights. Did old age creep on him at last?"

"He is in the hospital, but my Paul is dead. I want to join him. Want to make it happen? Want to taste me here and end your curse?"

Cromity watched aghast as the grief stricken lady of the house pushed a finger deep inside herself in a wanton act he had seen only whores perform.

"No not like this. Do not sully the memory of a good man with these whorish actions, Jennifer Adams. I wanted you, yes and still do, but I want to go to your arms with love in your eyes for me, not disgust and pity."

"Jesus-Christ, even the fucking dead turn down a chance to screw me. That really makes a girl feel good about herself."

Passion, color and anger and grief returned to Jennifer's face slowly and she leaned forward off her stool and kicked it spinning to the floor with a crack behind her.

"If you are willing I would be with you, but not tonight, not on the day you buried your true love. Let me have some semblance of honor. I will give you time to think, and ponder on this, Jennifer Adams. I will come each night waiting for your answer, but have a care once invited in, there will be no turning back. Call me after the night has fallen, bid me enter and I shall be yours in body and soul. Together we will end this bloody curse that has blighted two families for centuries and all will be at peace."

"Coward."

"You do not know what you say, girl. Grief has made you take leave of your senses.

"Coward!"

"Say not these words!" Cromity snarled back in anger, showing his true nature for once.

Jennifer picked up a piece of garlic bread and threw it at the vampire-ghost at her open, kitchen doorway.

"Coward." She spat with fury and launched piece after piece of garlic bread at the dead man, until he retreated into the darkness and out of range. Jen threw the tray through the open doorway and then collapsed onto the cold, hard floor sobbing painful retches of grief from her throat.

"Think a while and left grief run its course, but if you still want this, call me and I will come to you, Jennifer Adams." Silas Cromity's voice drifted along the cold winds of the night into the kitchen.

Feeling the cold that bore into her bones, Jennifer fled the kitchen for the safety of her warm bedroom and the comfort Purdy's fur and hot body brought to her.

Her mind whirled thinking a thousand different thoughts at once, toward the edge of madness itself. Luckily fatigue and nightmare-filled sleep finally overcame her and brought her back from the edge of her demented precipice.

Chapter Nineteen

The Dead of Winter

Dawn when it came of sorts brought little light and even smaller comfort to Jennifer. She could see no light at the end of the tunnel of darkness that surrounded her and still welcomed the idea of Cromity ending her misery. Her will had been sapped to such a low ebb that no other course of action seemed viable. She had reached the end of her rope and knew in her heart that she couldn't bounce back again from the never ending grief that had become her existence.

Tonight she intended to call Cromity from his tomb and put an end to her life and the curse once and for all. Then, only then, peace and happiness could return to Adams House, for a new family.

This being decided, she could get on with her last day on earth. She showered and dressed in the long winter dress that Paul had bought her. She polished her engagement ring and ate breakfast for the first time since Paul had been killed.

She went to the study and wrote out a will leaving the whole place to Henry Greenwood to do as he saw fit and the rest of her money to her SAD charity in the States. She picked flowers from the conservatory and drove to the church to lay them on Paul's freshly covered grave.

Lunch back at home was a one of her mother's Korean recipes, cooked and eaten with fondest and recalled love. Soon she'd join them all, either on the other side or the nothingness of non-existence; either way she'd be free of pain and loss forever. The next two hours she spent in her bedroom readying it for Cromity to come and end things.

She wandered the ground floor of the house's east wing, going into every room to say farewell. The hours ticked to dusk, when from down the corridor she heard the smashing of glass on a large scale. She picked up the skirt of her dress to run down to the conservatory to find a shabby-looking young man standing before the broken pane of glass at one side.

The light started to fade, but she could see clearly it was the young man she had encountered at the café in the village when she first arrived. He looked damp in his black hoodie top, green-stained denims and off white sneakers. Blood dripped from a cut up his long sleeve on his right arm, in which hand he held a small hammer. The intruder saw her looking at the blood and pulled up his sleeve to show a gold watch attached to his wrist, Paul's gold watch she had given him.

"What do you want, because I ain't got nothing left to give?" Jennifer snarled at the intruder racking her brain trying to re-member the young bearded man's name, as his wild, erratic eyes bore down on her.

"I think you do, miss high and fucking mighty lady of the man-or. Well, I'm going to take a piece of you, before the police catch up with me. It's going to be long and painful for you and enjoyable for me. 'Cause I don't care anymore. He promised me life ever after like him if I killed that cunt of a bank manager of yours for him, but when I saw him last night, he just laughed at me and called me a foolish boy. I fucking hate him, 'cause he did it all for you, Miss bloody Adams, to get you to invite him into this house and suck the blood from you and end his curse. But he won't die, you stupid American twat. He will be reborn as a man, you see. That was his plan all these centuries long."

"You killed Paul?" Jennifer asked quietly, as her body began to shake with anger, like a volcano building up to erupt.

"I did and now, I'm gonna kill you. That will fuck his plans up good and proper."

"Why? Why you stupid son-of-a-bitch? Why?"

"'Cause it has to be him that sucks your blood. If you die in here without letting him in, well, he'll never be able to taste your blue Adams blood. When they take your body away, he'll still be trapped here on the estate forever."

"Got it all figured out, haven't we, little man, but I see one little fault in your little plan." Jennifer sneered at the poor excuse of a human being that had taken her Paul from her. New strength and hope and confidence pumped through her veins, because she had nothing left to lose. People with nothing left to live for were the most dangerous to face in life and death situations.

"What that's, you little bitch? Not that little doggy of yours 'cause I sorted her out a little earlier in the day."

Somehow Jennifer had forgotten all about Purdy. She had let her out for a run and dump at lunchtime, and her mind had been on others things since.

"No, but you'll pay for that too."

"What then?" Saul sneered, moving from one foot to the next ready to pounce and sort this woman out for good; all this bravado was putting him even more on edge.

"Silas Cromity, I, Jennifer Adams rightful owner of this house invite you inside to end this curse forever."

"No!" Saul looked around in fear and ran at Jennifer.

She turned and ran back up the east wing corridor. She skidded around the corner as Saul raced past her just missing her by inches. She ran along the next corridor into the hall with her attacker only a few yards behind, across the darkening hall under the archway into the west wing ground floor corridor. Past the Drawing Room she flew into the Pool Room and ran around the billiard table. Saul appeared at the doorway, blocking her exit and pointing the hammer toward her, with a smile.

Jen pulled three balls out of the middle pocket and threw them one after the other with all her might at the intruder. One left a dent in the door, one hit his arm and glanced off while the last hit him on the corner of his left cheek and nose.

Saul howled with pain, as his nose began to bleed profusely all down his face, chin and black top. Jen grabbed a snooker cue that leaned against the wall, as Paul's killer jumped onto the table. She swung it at him as he jumped down at her, hitting his ribs. The young man caught the cue under his arm pit, pulled it from her grip and caught her with a blow of the hammer head onto her right shoulder, causing her to fall and slide down the wall in pain.

A swift kick to her stomach doubled her over on the carpet holding her shoulder with one arm and her belly with the other.

"Now, shall I beat your head in first or let you be awake when I rape you?"

Jennifer looked up at the wild eyed young man with fear, hoping for the blow of the hammer first to take her from this cruel world.

"Neither," another voice spoke from behind Saul as a long rapier blade burst forth from Saul's left breast, skewering his heart in one single death stroke.

The youth fell dead without a word next to the billiard table's thick legs and across Jennifer's feet. A hand reached down to her, cuffed by a frilly shirt and she looked up at her savior, Captain Silas Cromity.

"I apologize for the lad. Servants are so hard to come by when you are trapped inside a tomb all day and can only wander the grounds by night."

Jennifer let herself be lifted to her feet, the pulling on her arm hurting the place on her shoulder blade Saul's hammer had hit.

"I hope you are not too gravely injured, m'lady."

"I'll survive." She smiled at him with an ironic shake of her head.

"Good. We wouldn't want to dampen such a joy filled occasion as this. At last I have been invited into Adams House by the rightful owner, well rightful if you do not include myself."

"I should thank you, I suppose, for saving my honor from this scumbag." Jennifer smiled seductively at Cromity and gave the dead intruder a hearty kick to the groin area.

"And how would you do this, Jennifer Adams?"

Cromity smiled lustily back at her, his once human desires coming to fore, as she noticed color had come to his once deathly pallid face and lips.

"Carry me to my bed, Captain Cromity, and you'll find out."

Cromity dropped the rapier on the green baize of the billiard table and easily swept Jennifer's light frame up into his steely strong arms.

"What would you have me do, m'lady?" Cromity asked, turning her to get through the room and turning to walk back toward the hall and staircase.

"Make me feel like a woman for one last time, before you take my Adams blood, is all I ask."

"Why would you want this from me, the creator of your downfall, the creature of the darkness who took from you all that you love."

"It'll be better to die in the throws of passion with my heart beating like it is alive, than cowering before death eyes closed and afraid. I am no longer fearful of you, Silas, or what you can do to me. Just let my end be something tender, not dark and alone."

"This I will do for you, brave Jennifer. For all my ills toward you, I hold still a candle for your affections. Maybe, somewhere in the great beyond, we will find each other again and burn the blackness of night away with such a passion of love and fire that no God or devil could stop asunder."

It was dark now through the large windows above the landing, as Cromity's boots trod softly along the floor, holding his ultimate prize in his arms before him. All those years and plans and schemes of death and killing were coming to final fruition.

"Is Purdy okay?" Jennifer asked the vampire, the question popped into her head, as he carried down her west wing corridor to her eventual death.

"Yes, locked and muzzled in that large shed by the woods. It seems young Saul had a higher regard for dogs than their owners."

"Good." Jennifer smiled to herself as Cromity kicked open the door to her bedroom. She felt glad Purdy and Henry would be okay after all this was over.

Cromity laid her gently on the bed as if she was only an infant. Jennifer shuffled herself to the center of the bed.

"Undress me," she stated in a husky voice. Her hands and arms stretched back under the pillows. Her back arched close to Cromity as he clambered onto the bed. Cromity sat over her legs and pulled his shirt and tunic from his body, revealing a firm but wiry, strong chest and arms.

Under the white canopy of the four poster bed, Cromity reached down and grabbed the top of Jennifer's dress at her cleavage and with strength beyond normal men just ripped it open down her body until it lay in two tattered halves at her side. He snapped her bra apart with ease. His head lowered to suckle her freed breasts and dark nipples.

His lips felt cold upon her breasts, making her nipples hard and erect, even though her thoughts were less than sexual. His dry, dead tongue ran down her body until his beard touched the top of her panties. These went the same way as her bra, causing a brief Indian burn to her inner thigh as he tore them from her like some ravenous pack animal.

His dry rasping tongue licked at her slit, fingers rude and probing entered her, and she adjusted her position on the bed for ease of their entry. One entered deep into her anus and she closed her eyes and drifted off into the darkness that beckoned to her, into a null place, much akin to Cromity's limbo words, but for the barely living.

Then his invading fingers disappeared. She peered down to see Cromity's britches untied and his shining, hard and thick manhood, looking like it was carved from marble.

He smiled wickedly at her and her eyes darted once more to the pure white canopy above, as she parted her legs and waited for the inevitable. There was no love or mutual respect here as Cromity thrust hard into her, knocking the wind from her stomach. It caused her to rise up from the bed to avoid the pain. Icy like the instruments' her doctor used in her last gynecological exam;

his dead meat pushed deeper inside her, feeling like a sword going into her tummy.

Then he rose above her. His thrusts caused waves of pain and nausea to rise up from her thighs, vagina, up her body to her throat, which he suddenly grabbed with evil tight fingers. One of her hands rose to grab his wrist, but she might as well been trying to pull a steel cable apart with her bare hands for all the use it did.

"You're hurting me." Jennifer managed to say, as the vampire's hand held her tender neck in a constant grip. His thrusts below continued at a fast pace.

"You silly little harlot, you do not expect to make a pact with the devil and not feel the pain he has endured for all these centuries. You are an Adams, and I will lay upon you such vengeance and wrath not only our Lord Almighty could match. My servants killed your Blackamore friend on her boat trip. My winged friends cast down your servant. Saul, the simpleton, murdered your beloved. My manhood will rip through you this night, until you beg for death. Then I will bite into your tender neck and suck every drop of your Adams blood from you and end my curse forever."

"Fuck you, corpse boy!"

From under her pillow she turned on a switch. The extension hidden by sheets and pillows looped up behind her four poster bed. Above her, under the billowy white sheet she had tacked three sets of box lights for her SAD condition that mimicked natural sunlight. They blinked on. This very day, she had tied them on with rope, before she sewed and knotted them in place. She added black masking tape to the corners for extra strength.

Silas Cromity turned and laughed at first. *What harm could these lights do to him? Had he stood not in front of these magical lanterns before with no harm?* Then his skin began to burn, skin that hadn't seen natural light in many centuries. His white skin turned from white to red, to brown and bubbly black in a few seconds. He tried to pull back off the bed, but Jen wrapped her arms around his scorched body and clamped hard upon his cold invading penis with her pelvic muscles. He was trapped like a fox within a vixen. His skin burnt without flame or combustion, turning layer by layer of skin and tissue, bone by evil bone to wafts of ash that floated up to the virgin white canopy.

Jennifer felt no pain from his inhuman combustion. His blacked sightless face bit down into her shoulder, but soon hair, skull, face and finally teeth succumbed to the harsh natural lights above. The weight upon Jennifer turned from that of a strong man to the feeling that old dry newspaper just lay upon her naked body.

She looked down and saw that black and gray ash covered her and the bed. She saw no physical sign anywhere, well except one of the fiend Cromity.

Jennifer rolled off the ash-covered bed and fell to the bedroom carpet with a knee jolting whack. She ignored the gray dust that had once been Cromity, which covered her naked body and reached down between her legs. Her finger tips inched into her bruised vagina around the vampire's hard cold cock that still invaded her.

"I cannot turn up at the local ER and ask them to pull an undead penis outta my pussy."

She grunted, trying to keep the bile from rising in her throat long enough to complete this vile task and rid herself of the creature that had ruined her life forever. She winced stretching herself and reaching inside, scratching at the tender walls of her sex as her nails finally pulled the icy phallus out of her and tossed it on the bed. It sizzled like a sausage tossed into a frying pan, then burned away into nothing, but gray ash.

Jennifer collapsed onto the carpet and threw up a great torrent of vomit, blood and bits of carrot. Her body and stomach cramped in so tight she vomited again and she soiled herself as well.

Once the dry heaves had ended, she curled up in a fetal position, lying in her own cradle of filth. Her mind stretched to its very limits. With her body in traumatic shock, she fainted dead away for a while. When she woke, the box lights hidden under the canopy of the four poster bed had timed out and turned off like she set them to do after thirty minutes.

She lay in the darkness, covered and surrounded by crud, drying liquid and odious smells, but couldn't move. Her mind a blank, her body parallelized not by injury, but by self-preservation. She knew somewhere in her grief-addled brain, if she rose too soon, her mind might not get up with her. Better to lie here for a while and process things. Let the dust of the dead vampire settle and see what the new day brings.

* * * *

Jen sprang to a sitting position on the floor as the light from the edges of the bedroom shutters showed the dawn of a new day at last. Jen crawled from her bedroom and across the hall to the shower. She rose only to turn it on, then collapsed onto the floor, before she let the warm water cleanse her sullied frame. She shower-gelled her sore behind and poked soapy fingers deep inside herself to make sure nothing of Cromity remained in or on her body. She left the shower without toweling herself and headed downstairs in the pale light of the sunny late December morning. She crossed to the cleaning cupboard where Mrs. Wilberforce kept all her equipment.

Then wearing yellow rubber gloves and nothing else, she vacuumed up the remains of the vampire-revenant and sucked up everything that lay upon the floor. Using a knife and scissors from the kitchen, she cut up the carpet that surrounded the rights side of the bed where she had spent the night. This, the bed sheets and the dust-bag from the vacuum cleaner she put into three separate bin bags.

She then showered and scrubbed herself again, inside and out, before she dressed, tying her hair into a wet pony tail. Like an automaton she took the sealed bin bags down the hall and placed them by the front door, then fetched a spade from one of Henry's sheds.

She did the same to the billiard room and dumped Saul's body into a wheel barrow, before she pushed it deep into the east woods. She spent the rest of the day burying his murderous corpse in a deep grave. Luckily the soil was easy to dig from all the recent rain and no frost clung to the earth this morning. In she threw the carpet from the billiard room and the cleaning things she had used to mop up any trace of the intruder. She scattered dried leaves over the hole and headed back to the house as the light faded once again into premature night.

She felt filthy and put all her clothes and sneakers into the washing machine on a sixty degree setting. Then later that night, she took the three bags from her hall and buried them in an overgrown wooded section of the local church's graveyard. Even if they were found, it would only contain the ash of a man who had been dead for centuries and an old bit of dirty carpet.

Once again she washed her clothes and sneakers, before she placed them together in a bag. Then she put a brick inside and tossed it from the bridge into the deepest part of her lake.

She slept the rest of the night in Great Aunt Gwen's bed, with the shutters open. No knocks came upon her door that night, the rooks had flown away and the dead once again stayed dead.

Chapter Twenty

Inheritance

"When did anyone see them last?" Detective Inspector Milner asked, walking through the open doorway of the lawyer's office, with his junior colleague behind him.

"Sometime before Christmas, they kept to themselves the people above said," Detective Sergeant Atkinson replied, following his superior into the office of Rardin and Keene, on a chilly late January morning.

They passed members of the scene-of-crime team in their plastic white suits with hood and kid gloves.

"Found anything yet, Tom?" The DI asked one of the forensic team as they walked down the corridor that opened up into a small clerk's office.

"Ash, on one chair in this office and the same on the chair in the office right down the hall."

"Smoking at work, tut-tut." Atkinson quipped.

Milner gave him a sardonic glare, his lips yearning for a cigarette himself. It had only been two months since he quit, and it was doing nothing for his waistline or sense of humor.

"But it's the amount of ash and no scorch-marks on the seats or surrounding desks or carpet. I have an uneasy feeling that these two people were smoking literally. This is all that is left of them."

"You telling me, these guys spontaneously combusted? You're having a laugh aren't you?"

Now, the DI was really getting into the moody swing of a new shitty day.

"It's only a possibility at this moment. Once we test the ash, we will know for sure."

"Right then, let's see the other office with the ash." DI Milner stomped off down the corridor and entered the open empty office.

Another pile of ash lay on the leather chair and the carpets below.

"Maybe they were burning papers, covering their tracks for some reason and run off to where ever dodgy lawyers go?" DS

Atkinson suggested.

"What like the House of Commons," DI Milner gruffly replied.

* * * *

"These guys must have been in business for a long time, passed on from family member to family member?" DS Atkinson stated to the Tom Salisbury, the SOCS officer, as they stood in the other office used to store boxes of clutter and files.

"Why's that?" Tom asked, rising from a box of records he was leafing through.

DS Atkinson turned away from a portrait he was looking at and showed Salisbury a brochure for the lawyers he was holding. It had been done two years ago and showed Candlestick and Vaine working at their desks, all pompous and full of wordy PR.

"He looks like a happy bastard." Tom pointed at the picture of the unsmiling Mr. Candlestick at work, pouring over papers on his desk.

"Yeah, real life and soul of the office party, he'd be," Atkinson began then turned and pointed at the portrait on the wall, "now take a look at these guys."

In the painting, cast in hues of mahogany and ochre stood two stiff-necked and collared Victorian gentlemen, holding their lapels with their heads held high.

"They look the spitting image of the men in that brochure, uncanny, like you say must be distant relatives."

"Messers Rardin and Keene, eighteen eighty-nine," DS Atkinson read from a cut out strip in the thick cream border of the portrait.

* * * *

Extract from the *Dungarven Chronicle* Newspaper Ireland 21st March...

'Speaking for the first time about the English country mansion left to Donal Dunne, by a wealthy American heiress and author of cookery books via her New York lawyers Douglas, May & Hume, he said yesterday.

'I thought it was someone having a bit of a crack at my expense. The only connection to England is my love for Jack Charlton and that my grandmother Agnes Cromity was born in Liverpool.'

Miss Adams the former owner of the house was unavailable

for comment...

* * * *

Eighteen months passed since that fateful day in December, when her lover and fiancé were murdered. With a look out of her window at the fading sunshine above the mountains, Jennifer saw the dark shape of a figure mounted on a horse riding toward her heavily air-conditioned ranch way out in the boondocks of Arizona.

Purdy barked and leaped up from the rug she loved to sleep on at night, before she followed Jen to the double set of doors, one to keep out humans and one to keep out the flies.

She pushed open both and rubbed at the line of healed self-harming scars on her bare left forearm and walked across the porch and stood dead in her tracks. Purdy barking wildly sat down next to her, her wagging tail thumping on the dusty boards.

The rider in a cowboy hat and blue jean shirt checked back his mount just a few yards from the steps down from the porch.

"How's the leg?"

"Bearing up, Miss Jennifer," the English-accented cowboy replied, as he slowly dismounted the horse, with a pat of his old hand on the mare's neck.

"I've got something interesting to show you, Henry," Jen stated and pulled a few sheets of paper, with an article printed out from the internet.

"What's that then?" Henry asked as Tori, one of the girls that helped out in the stables came and took his horse away for him.

"An extract from the Sun newspaper about Donal Dunne and his family. They've packed up and left Adams House and returned to Ireland, vowing never to return."

"That don't sound good?"

Jennifer raised the pages next to the lamp on the side of the porch entrance, swatting away flies at first.

"Mr. Dunne told this reporter by phone that the ghost of old lady in white haunted the place. She would write messages on the walls of their children's bedroom in what looked like blood. The messages would tell them in no uncertain terms, 'Get out of my house.'"

Jen handed the pages over to Henry, who scanned through the story with his aged eyes.

"Told you your Great Aunt Gwen was one of a kind."

Jen put her arm into Henry's and led him back inside to have dinner that she had prepared from her latest cookbook. Purdy followed.

About The Author

P. M. May was born in Walton on Thames Surrey England way back in 1968 and still lives nearby in a place you've never heard of called Hersham. *Inheritance* is the third novel by the author who has had short stories published in genre Canadian & US magazines and in a UK anthology of horror.

P. M. May also co-founded http://www.Novelblog.com with his American friend, Dan Boucher and Canadian Chief Reviewer, Rachelle Gagne. P.M. has interviewed two of his heroes Simon Clark and Peter Straub for author of the month interviews.

Official Website
http://darkside6869.webs.com/

Also from Eternal Press

The Woman in Crimson
by Kathryn Meyer Griffith

eBook ISBN: 9781615721979
Print ISBN: 9781615721986

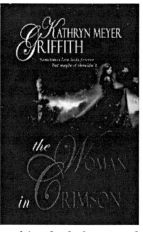

Genre: Romance
Sub Genre: Horror
Novel of 96,494 words

Sometimes love lasts forever...but maybe it shouldn't. Willowwind, a beautiful Civil War era bed and breakfast, is run by a loving couple, Adrian and Caroline Stone, but it's also haunted by a long-dead Civil War era vampiress, Lilith, who believes the man, Adrian, is her reincarnated soldier/lover and will do anything to have him, body-heart-and soul, for her own again, no matter how many she must kill. But Adrian's wife, Caroline, along with the help of the ghost of her dead father, will do anything to make sure that doesn't happen.

Also from Eternal Press

Unholy Alliance
by Tom Olbert

eBook ISBN: 9781770650343
Print ISBN: 9781770650428

Genre: Paranormal
Sub Genre: Horror
Novel of 31,000 words

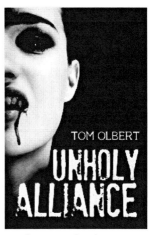

The story of Chris, a young vampire hunter who has known only hatred, battle and killing. His life changes dramatically when he falls in love with Sara, a female vampire. Their love is an impossible one, and the alliance of necessity that forms between them equally so. They find themselves pitted against dark forces that would exploit or destroy the innocent. The odds are against them, but Chris's greatest battle is within his own soul. He must choose between his love for Sara, and his faith in a greater good...

Eternal Press

Official Website:
www.eternalpress.biz

Blog:
http://eternalpressauthors.blogspot.com/

Reader Chat Group:
http://groups.yahoo.com/group/EternalPressReaders

MySpace:
http://www.myspace.com/eternalpress

Twitter:
http://twitter.com/EternalPress

Facebook:
http://www.facebook.com/profile.php?id=1364272754

Good Reads:
http://www.goodreads.com/profile/EternalPress

Shelfari:
http://www.shelfari.com/eternalpress

Library Thing:
http://www.librarything.com/catalog/EternalPress

We invite you to drop in, visit with our authors and stay in touch for the latest news, releases and more!

Breinigsville, PA USA
29 December 2010
252385BV00001B/17/P